Death by Contract

by Shirley Presberg

Cover design and illustration: Julia Rae Bell

ISBN 1-888745-01-0
Library of Congress Catalog Card No. 96-61732

Printed in the United States of America

To Harry,
who makes me smile.

Shirley Presberg
March 1997

Acknowledgements

Special thanks to all who contributed to making this book as realistic and technically accurate as possible. In alphabetical order:
Eve Blachman, Gloria Brown, Dr. Alan Cohn, Lynn Deas, Allan Falk, Lorraine Fink, Doug Grove, Alan Hecht, Joan Hess, Danny Kadish, Lt. Richard Saunders, Dorothy Truscott, and Judi Tull.

Foreword

The late Terence Reese, a world champion involved in a 1963 cheating scandal that haunted him until his death in 1995, once commented that "the world of top flight bridge harbors maggots that no self-respecting stone would shelter." Shirley Presberg has perfectly captured the zany denizens of this demimonde and brought them to life in a book destined to become a classic of the genre.

Not since Richard Powell's *Tickets to the Devil* has a writer with a gift for witty and penetrating dialogue and an eye for the foibles and eccentricities of the human condition addressed this intellectual battlefield in a novel. Tournament bridge is a game played, not for something as sensible as money prizes, nor from patriotic motives for the honor of one's homeland and Olympic glory. No, bridge tournaments are contested mainly for fiscally useless masterpoints, coin of the realm only in the Land of Giant Egos—*terra cognita* for serious players.

To fully appreciate the economic contrariness of bridge players, it should seem unremarkable that, when some very clever people wrote a bridge musical and performed it for free at a North American Bridge Championship, only a few hundred of the several thousand people in attendance took advantage of the opportunity to form an audience. True to form, the majority either played in a game starting at midnight, or retired to the bar or lobby of the host hotel to rehash the day's interesting deals until the wee hours.

Shirley Presberg gives the reader an expertly guided and entertaining tour of this strange culture, where a "geek" who can "turn the dummy" gets more dates as a bridge partner than the "hunk" who can't follow suit, and where an alcoholic who works magic with the cards, is more highly esteemed than the CEO with an eight figure income who just put a "cold game on the floor." So curl up with this mystery, and enjoy the ride.

Allan Falk, Publisher

Cast of Characters
(in alphabetical order)

Ron Albright	Hotel security officer
Gary Alexander	Lawyer, expert bridge player
Jennifer Brandon	Director (umpire) for bridge games
Cliff Bryce	CEO of a computer company, expert bridge player
Charles Canning	Executive with Century Bridge Supplies
Nadine Davis	Linda Mason's boss
Nancy Dunbar	Ralph Dunbar's mother
Ralph Dunbar	Teacher, expert bridge player, Jeffrey Howard's lover
Vivian Greene	Virginia Beach PD detective
Jeffrey Howard	College professor, expert bridge player, Ralph Dunbar's lover
David Jasper	Assistant to Jennifer Brandon
Kathy Jensen	Wealthy bridge player
Dr. Arthur Kingsley	Plastic surgeon, amateur bridge player
Herb Kramer	Private investigator
Eva Kaplan	Widow, bridge player, Sharon Price's sister
Linda Mason	Bank employee, addicted gambler, bridge player
Jonathan Meltzer	Professional bridge player
Alan and Sybil Nestor	The Battling Bickersons of bridge
Sharon Price	Widow, Bridge Player, Eva Kaplan's sister
Robert Rollins	Experienced police officer
Ruth Simmons	Assistant to Jennifer Brandon
Tom Stanhope	Amoral professional bridge player
Orin Staples	Charles Canning's boss
Lou Turner	Struggling professional bridge player

CHAPTER 1

Eva was bored. She sat in her den with her feet tucked under her, halfheartedly reading about bridge in the December issue of *The Bulletin.*

One of the ads in the back of the magazine caught her eye. She skimmed through it once, then read it more closely. Excitedly, she threw the magazine down and rushed out of her eighth-floor condo. She tapped her foot impatiently on the plush carpet while she waited for the elevator. At last, the doors opened and she rode to her sister's condo on the fourteenth floor.

"Have you seen the advertisement for the money bridge game in this month's *Bulletin?*" she called out as she unlocked Sharon's door.

Her only answer was the sound of a television blaring from the master bedroom. Following the noise, she found Sharon pedaling fiercely on her stationary bicycle while watching a video tape of *Jeopardy!* Eva motioned to her to turn the volume down, then repeated her question.

Sharon, slightly out of breath, pressed the stop button on her remote control. Then she slowed her pedaling down for a couple of minutes and pulled the towel off the handlebars to wipe the sweat from her face. "I haven't had a chance to read my copy yet," she finally answered, resigning herself to the interruption. "What's so interesting that you couldn't let me finish exercising?"

"Century Bridge Supplies is sponsoring a two-day bridge competition in Virginia Beach right after the North American Championships."

"So what? You've always said you weren't interested in playing in a money tournament."

"I know. But the prizes in this one are unbelievable." She pulled Sharon's copy of *The Bulletin* from the pile of books and magazines scattered on the nightstand and quickly found the advertisement. "This is what changed my mind," she said, pointing to the ad. "They're giving away *one hundred thousand dollars for first place*. I think we ought to enter."

"Let me see that." Sharon jumped off her bike, grabbed the magazine away from Eva, and scanned the page. "I knew there'd be a catch. The entry fee is two thousand dollars each! Forget it."

She tossed the magazine back to her sister and climbed back on the bike, stretching her five-foot-three-inch frame in order to reach the handlebars and pedals.

Eva wasn't deterred. "So what if the fee is steep? I think we should enter anyway. We'd have a good chance to win at least one of the prizes. Maybe we wouldn't come in first, but even if we were tenth, we'd get five thousand dollars. That would more than pay for our entry."

"It's tempting," Sharon admitted, "but what happens if we don't do well the first day? I'd hate to think I'd blown my money all at once. What are they offering to the losers?"

Eva looked at the ad again. "It says there'll be a consolation game on the second day for those who don't make the cut. The first place payoff for the consolation game is thirty-five thousand dollars. I could live with that."

"That is impressive," Sharon conceded. Then she frowned. "But the best players in the country will compete when they see how big the prizes are. I doubt if we'd have a chance. Even our sisterly ESP goes just so far."

"My ESP is telling me we should try," Eva persisted.

"Well," Sharon said with a sigh, "I know what I'd do with my share. I always wanted to fly on the Concorde and have lunch in Paris."

While Sharon continued to bicycle, Eva looked around her sister's bedroom. The bed was still unmade, clothes were strewn around the room, the closet doors were half open, and a bathrobe lay draped across the computer. She wondered how anyone could be so disorganized. Sometimes she couldn't believe they were sisters.

Eva and Sharon, who were highly competitive against others at the bridge table, were only mildly competitive with each other away from bridge. The two longtime residents of Norfolk, Virginia were financially comfortable widows in their fifties. Their petite physiques and strong family resemblance made them look almost like twins. When anyone asked who was older, each sister would always promptly point to the other.

"I still need to jog today," Eva said enviously when Sharon finally finished bicycling. "I gained two pounds last week. I'm up to one-fifteen. I was going to run this morning, but I wanted to come here first to see what you thought about the money game."

"Let me think about it for a while," Sharon said. She slipped off her bike and headed toward the kitchen. She was still in her warmups and needed to shower, but the exercising had made her hungry. "Want some juice and oatmeal?"

"Just a little juice. I'd better not eat anything before I jog."

Sharon ignored Eva's look of disapproval at the dirty dishes stacked in the sink. She put a bowl of oatmeal into the microwave, rinsed out a couple of glasses, and poured juice for both of them. After shoving aside the mail that had accumulated on her small kitchen table, she and Eva sat down.

"That'll be twelve full days of bridge, if we stay to play in the money game," Sharon said after she swallowed a mouthful of oatmeal. "Will you be able to get enough time off from your volunteer work?"

"I've already arranged to work extra hours in the hospital during the next couple of months. Alice's daughter is due any day now, and she'll want some time off as soon as the baby's born. I'll work for her then, and she'll pay me back when I play in the tournament. That's the easy part. The hardest part for me is getting attached to the sick babies and then leaving them."

"It must be hard. But it never takes you long to get involved with the new patients when you go back."

Eva hungrily watched Sharon put each spoonful of oatmeal into her mouth. "What about you?" she asked. "Will you be able to get enough restaurant reviews done ahead of time?"

"I guess I'll just have to eat out an extra night each week until the tournament starts."

"I hope you'll be able to fit into your clothes after eating all those desserts," Eva told her. She got up from the table, looked around the kitchen, and found some bagels. Slicing one, she dropped it in the toaster.

Sharon gave her a malicious grin. "If mine don't fit, I'll borrow yours."

* * * * *

Ralph Dunbar sat at his secondhand oak desk in the bedroom of the faculty apartment and stared unseeingly at the Chagall posters on the wall. On the desk in front of him were twenty-five tenth-grade history tests—two corrected, twenty-three untouched.

Instead of focusing on his work, all Ralph could think about was the impending loss of Jeffrey's affections. He had recently watched his young friend flirting with his own contemporaries at faculty parties. He knew it was going to be harder and harder to compete with younger men who returned Jeffrey's interest. He picked up another exam, but instead of correcting it, he sat there worrying about how old he looked. It was unbelievable how much he'd aged since turning forty-five last year. His black hair seemed to turn grayer daily. It would be easy enough to color, he supposed, but there wasn't much he could do about the receding hairline. He didn't even want to think about the jowls that had appeared over the past year or the new lines around his eyes.

Convinced that he needed to do something drastic to keep Jeffrey's attention, he'd consulted a plastic surgeon. They had discussed a lipectomy for the neck and surgery to remove the wrinkles around his eyes. The procedures would cost over seven thousand dollars—a sum he couldn't possibly afford on his academic salary. He had dismissed the whole idea.

But now, with the possibility of winning cash in the bridge game, he began to think about it again. He and Jeffrey had recently had a string of regional wins, and they had placed high in several national events. He thought they would have a good chance.

Convincing Jeffrey to stay in Virginia Beach for a couple of extra days would be a problem. Jeffrey was a stickler about not missing classes. Ralph had tenure, but Jeffrey hadn't been teaching long enough yet. He wasn't prepared to risk losing his job over a bridge game.

Over the last several days, Ralph had practiced many arguments in his head to persuade Jeffrey to enter the contest. The deadline for registration was only two weeks away. Deciding that he couldn't put it off any longer, Ralph threw his marking pen down on the desk and went to look for Jeffrey.

He found him in the den, preparing a lecture for his anthropology class. Ralph sat down in one of the comfortable armchairs, but Jeffrey ignored him—not a good sign. He cleared his throat and began with a tentative, "Jeffrey."

"What?" Frowning at the interruption, Jeffrey lifted his head up from his books and glared at Ralph. Even when Jeffrey was in a bad mood, Ralph found him attractive.

Although Jeffrey's front teeth were slightly too large, in Ralph's mind that defect only added to his blond friend's surfer good looks.

"As long as we're going to be in Virginia Beach for the Spring Championships, how would you like to stay for two more days and play in the money game?"

"I saw the ad, and I wondered how long it would take you to ask," Jeffrey said. "I don't understand how you can even consider playing in a game with such a huge entry fee." But when Jeffrey stood up and began pacing the room instead of going back to his work, Ralph knew he wasn't totally disinterested. "Even if we could afford it, it wouldn't matter. We'd have to be back that Monday to teach."

"I know that, but I think we'd have a good chance to win one of the prizes. Whatever we won would more than cover the extra expenses. And we both have lots of sick leave coming. We could use some of that."

Jeffrey looked exasperated. "How can we call in Sunday night and say we're going to be sick on Monday and Tuesday? In case you didn't know, private academies frown on that."

"We can call Sunday night and tell them we missed our plane back to Boston. Then we'll think of some other excuse to explain our absence for two more days."

"How will you explain it if we win one of the big prizes?"

Ralph had already anticipated the various objections Jeffrey would offer. "We'll tell them that as long as we couldn't get back, we decided to play in the money game. They won't fire us for missing a couple of days. Besides, if we won, think of the prestige it would bring to the school."

"Oh, sure. I can see the reaction of the parents who are paying a bundle in tuition. They'd be real proud of their teachers for winning a bridge game when they should've been here teaching their kids."

Ralph sighed. "Okay, you come up with a good reason for missing classes."

Jeffrey paused to think. "Well . . . we could tell them the CIA detained us because they thought we were hired by a foreign power to spy on the naval base in Norfolk. They wanted to stop us before we could make the penetration."

Ralph grinned. "I, for one, wouldn't mind that penetration."

* * * * *

That weekend, Ralph's mother, Nancy Dunbar, slim and much younger looking than her sixty-five years, came in from Washington to visit. Nancy accepted Ralph's lifestyle and got along well with Jeffrey. Jeffrey's parents, destroyed by his sexual preference, wouldn't speak to him. Jeffrey was grateful for Nancy's support and was fond of her.

Jeffrey was still working out in the gym when Nancy arrived Friday afternoon. As soon as she appeared, Ralph hustled her into the kitchen for coffee and donuts, and quickly told her about his dilemma. He wanted to hear her opinion before Jeffrey came home.

"I've been thinking about getting a facelift," Ralph said, unconsciously pulling the skin under his chin up toward his ears, "but I don't want Jeffrey to know about it. I thought I might have it done this summer, when Jeffrey goes to visit his sister in California. I'd like to look decent by the time he comes back. How long did it take for yours to heal?"

"I was black and blue here for nearly two weeks," Nancy said, placing her fingers below her eyes. "But I went out to a movie five days after the surgery. I covered the scars and the discolored areas with makeup. You could hardly tell they were there. I saw a real improvement in a couple of weeks, but it took months for all the swelling to go down. Why don't you make it easy on yourself and just tell Jeffrey that you're having it done?"

Ralph stiffened. "Absolutely not! I don't want him to realize how much I've aged recently. Right now, he's used to the way I look and he doesn't really notice."

Nancy was skeptical. "Don't you think he'll see the difference? After all, he'll see you when he gets back from his trip. You'll still be black and blue and swollen. And what'll you do if he decides not to go to California this year?"

"I've made some inquiries about having the surgery done out of town. If he doesn't go, I'll tell him I'm visiting you. Right now, though, he's planning on making the trip. His sister is the only one in the family who speaks to him, and it's important for him to see her."

Nancy reached for another donut. "Would you like to come to Washington and stay with me for a few days while you're healing?"

Ralph nodded and smiled at his mother. "That would be a big help. If Jeffrey notices the difference when I come back, I'll just have to tell him the truth."

"I think it would be better to tell him now, but it's up to you."

"I'll think about it," Ralph said. "But that's not the only problem. The fee for the surgery is over seven thousand dollars. There's a possibility that I can have it done without having to pay the money ahead of time, but I don't know if that'll work out. In case it doesn't, I'd like to try to win something in the money game after the Spring Championships in Virginia Beach. I think Jeffrey and I have a good chance to win. I've been trying to convince him to enter, but he's afraid to take the extra time off."

"You can't blame him. He does need his job. Do you want me to talk to him?"

"Please!" He offered Nancy the last donut. When she declined, he polished it off.

Nancy and Ralph were still sitting in the kitchen when Jeffrey arrived. He gave Nancy a big hug before he went to the freezer and took out a carton of nonfat raspberry yogurt. He scooped out a medium-sized portion, frowned at the empty box of donuts, then turned to Nancy. "What's new?"

"Same old stuff," she said with a shrug. "Hollywood wants me to double for Madonna, and the Metropolitan Opera wants me to sing Carmen. I told them I couldn't, because I've accepted an offer to go on the space shuttle as a biochemist next week. How about you?"

Jeffrey grinned at her. "Nothing quite that exotic in my life. The only thing new here is that Ralph's been bugging me to stay in Virginia Beach after the tournament in March and play in some money game."

"Sounds like a good idea to me. Why not?"

"For one thing, the entry fee is outrageous. Besides, I don't want to miss classes. I haven't been here as long as Ralph, and I'm afraid they won't renew my contract if I stay away for something that the board might consider frivolous. In case you haven't heard, playing bridge isn't everyone's idea of a serious way to spend time. Especially during teaching hours."

"I don't know why people are so stuffy," Nancy said. "If you win something, why not donate twenty percent to the school library fund? Since that's the dean's pet project, he'd probably forgive you for playing hookey."

Jeffrey nodded thoughtfully. "Not a bad idea. But what if we don't win anything?"

"Then you'd better start polishing up your résumés."

* * * * *

"Another new dress, Linda?" Nadine Davis teased. "You've been coming to work in a different designer dress every week, lately. And we've all noticed your new BMW. Did you inherit a fortune? Or are you hiding some rich lover from us?"

Linda Mason, a white-haired spinster in her sixties, smiled enigmatically at her boss. "Don't I wish! But it's nothing like that. I just decided that it's time to do something nice for myself."

"Well, whatever's happening, I think it's terrific. I've never seen you look better," Nadine told her. Smiling, she walked past Linda's desk and went into her office.

When the door closed behind Nadine, Linda shuddered. The auditors would soon be doing their routine check at the bank, and it wouldn't take them long to discover that over $30,000 was missing.

Linda had never considered stealing money until a few months ago, when she systematically began transferring customers' money to fake accounts and changing the computerized bank records. She'd been working at the bank for years, and she knew all the tricks. It had been easy for her to move money from one account to another and then into her own.

But the audit would surely reveal her embezzlement, and she knew that she didn't have any explanations that would satisfy anyone sitting in judgment. Donna Karan dresses, a vacation in the Caribbean, and a down payment on a new car would hardly provoke a sympathetic reaction from either a judge or a jury.

Soon after she had started her job at the bank in Norfolk over thirty years ago, she'd had an affair with one of the bank directors. But after his wife became suspicious, her lover had asked to be transferred to a branch in Virginia Beach. The affair ended, but Linda had never found anyone else—and no one else had found Linda.

She'd gained a pound a year and lived a lonely, solitary life. There were acquaintances from bridge and from church, but no close friends. At first, she'd envied her high school friends who had married and had children. But as she watched those marriages disintegrate and saw the problems that developed between the parents and their children, she felt more lucky than envious.

Linda realized that people would wonder why, after working all those years, she hadn't saved enough of her own money to pay for the few luxuries she'd recently bought. As far as anyone knew, she had been extravagant only once. Last year, she'd hired Tom Stanhope, a bridge professional, to play with her in a regional tournament. Even though she knew that he often humiliated his clients, she'd picked him because of his reputation for winning. Linda, who desperately wanted to win, thought she would be able to ignore any of Tom's sneering comments.

Although they had come in third overall in a tough event, playing with him had been one of the worst experiences in her life. Tom had belittled her bridge skills at every opportunity. What had unnerved her most was his habit of sticking his tongue out and licking his upper lip exactly three times immediately before he criticized her. She dreaded seeing that snake-like gesture. His constant berating had caused her to misplay an easy hand toward the end of the tournament, costing them first place.

After the game, Tom, drunk and surly, had told her that he expected her to give him a $500 bonus for coming in third. Outraged, she'd screamed at him in front of everyone. Tom had pulled her into the hallway and, in a chilling voice, promised her that she would be sorry for her outburst. No one humiliated him without paying for it. Terrified of his anger, Linda had fled the tournament two days early.

Now she had far more than a vengeful Tom Stanhope to worry about. Hiring a bridge pro had not been her only extravagance. If she were caught for embezzling, she would have to admit that she had lost all her extra cash at the blackjack and roulette tables. When the casinos opened in Atlantic City a few years ago, Linda had started driving up there once a month to gamble and see the shows. Since she had to account to no one, she could spend her time as she pleased. And what pleased her was gambling.

She'd take the $200 or $300 that she'd managed to save from her salary and head for the ten-dollar blackjack tables. Whenever she was lucky enough to be up $100, she'd switch to roulette. When she inevitably was reduced to her last twenty-five dollars, she'd play the quarter slot machines until the money was gone. Occasionally she would hit a jackpot and then would start the cycle all over again at the blackjack tables.

The lure of winning and the excitement of having this secret life soon tempted her into going to the casinos twice a month. When she occasionally won big, she'd use her winnings to buy fancy clothes or some other luxury.

After her gambling weekends, she would return to her mundane life on Monday morning. But as soon as she saved any extra cash, she'd embark on the cycle again.

She didn't regret one minute of her secret sprees. Her social security and her pension fund would provide for her retirement. There was nothing wrong with spending her extra money frivolously.

Except, suddenly, the extra money that she was spending wasn't hers. Somehow the excitement of gambling had transferred itself to the temptation of embezzling.

At first she felt terribly guilty, but her conscience bothered her a little less each time she manipulated the accounts. The whole process began to seem routine. Thinking about it now, she was appalled. She had always considered herself to be honest; she didn't like what she had become.

If she confessed and offered to pay the money back from her retirement fund, she would certainly lose her job. That would leave her with no income and no retirement fund. Even worse, there was always the possibility that she would end up in prison.

Winning one of the prizes in the money bridge tournament was the only way that she could think of to get her hands on some cash quickly. If she could win enough, she'd be able to cover her theft before the audit.

Her gambling instincts persuaded her that capturing one of the prizes wasn't quite the long shot it seemed. She was fiercely competitive at the bridge table—not the sweet little old lady she appeared to be. She believed that she had a chance.

Convincing her regular partner, Kathy Jensen, to part with the $2,000 for the entry fee would be harder than winning first prize. Kathy had inherited a fortune when her parents died several years ago, and she still had most of it.

She'd even made both her children take out loans to go to college, even though she could easily have paid all their expenses. Kathy parted with some of her money for the one thing that was important to her—a good divorce lawyer. She had recently hired the best one in town to thwart her husband's attempt to get part of her fortune in any inevitable settlement.

Kathy had been playing a lot of bridge lately to keep her mind off the impending divorce. Convincing her to play would be easy; getting her to part with the money for the entry fee would not. Linda knew she would have to appeal to Kathy's greediness.

She picked up the phone and dialed Kathy's number.

"Kathy," she began when her partner answered, "how would you like to win up to one hundred thousand dollars and have a wonderful time doing it?"

Kathy laughed. "How will I do that? Buy a winning lottery ticket?"

"I'm serious, Kathy. Did you see the ad for the money tournament in The Bulletin?"

"Of course I saw it. I was appalled. Can you imagine anyone spending that kind of money on a bridge game?"

"Think about it for a minute. Where else can you invest four thousand dollars and have a chance to win one hundred thousand in two days? Since the contest will be held right here, we wouldn't even have to spend money on a hotel room—or pay plane fare. I think we'd be crazy not to try."

During the silence, Linda imagined the dollar signs lighting up in her friend's eyes, just like in a Bugs Bunny cartoon. But then Kathy's innate stinginess took over.

"What if we invest four thousand and don't win anything? Besides, what chance do we have against the kinds of competitors who'll enter? We'd have to compete with professional players and international experts. Forget it."

"Kathy, listen! A hundred thousand in two days! Even if we don't win the grand prize, we certainly have a chance to be in the top ten. And you know how great you feel every time we get good results from expert players. On a good day, we can beat every one of them."

"Besides, they've limited the field to twenty-eight tables of contestants. That means fifty-six pairs, and we only have to beat fifty-five of them for first prize. If our game is on, we can surely beat fifty-five pairs. How can you turn down such good odds?"

The thought of winning all that money was more than Kathy could resist. As soon as she agreed to give it a try, Linda quickly hung up the phone. She wasn't going to give Kathy a chance to change her mind.

Then Linda began to worry again. She had a partner now, but she knew that she had to win a lot to pay the money back.

As she embezzled her half of the entry fee, she found herself wondering how well they play bridge in Leavenworth.

* * * * *

"Herb, would you hand me a towel?" Jennifer Brandon shouted from the shower stall.

"At your service," Herb said. He grabbed a towel and stepped into the shower stall, fully dressed.

"Herb! You're getting soaked!"

"Yes, but it's going to be worth it," Herb said with an exaggerated leer. "Just pretend I'm Cary Grant and you're Audrey Hepburn."

"He didn't get into the shower with Audrey Hepburn," she pointed out.

"What did *he* know?"

Many minutes later, Jennifer grinned as she got out of the shower. She still had to find a dry towel, but she didn't mind. It *was* worth it.

As she dried her red, curly hair, she looked at her distorted reflection in the steamed-up mirror. Not bad, she thought, for a thirty-eight year old.

Her divorce had become final last month, and she was relieved. She'd been married to an architect for over twelve years. The first few years had been incredibly good. Jennifer had worked as a librarian and had taught bridge classes one night a week. Steven had worked for three years in a firm with eighteen other architects. Not liking the anonymity that came with such a large group, he resigned and successfully opened his own firm.

Jennifer and Steven had enjoyed each other immensely. They amused each other, savored each other's bodies, liked the same people, movies, foods. The romantic glow lingered for a long time, but finally they both became restless. Jennifer learned how to run bridge games, and soon was directing several nights a week. She sold entries, seeded the players according to ability, handled whatever problems arose, calculated the scores and determined the winners.

Steven began to work late at his office, seldom returning home before midnight. Even so, Jennifer was shocked when Steven told her he was in love with a young architect who had recently joined his firm.

When Steven asked for a divorce, Jennifer decided to open her own bridge studio, as much for the therapy as for the desire to have her own business. Steven, feeling guilty, helped her purchase the building and buy supplies. Jennifer had devoted all her hours for the past two years toward making the bridge studio successful, and now all the bridge games in the Norfolk-Virginia Beach area were held there. By giving lessons at the studio and at the local colleges, she had tripled the attendance at her games.

She didn't know how serious her affair with Herb would become, but she was definitely enjoying it. She liked the calmness of this thirty-three-year-old private investigator. His Karl Malden nose and unkempt brown hair kept him from being handsome, but the very imperfection of his looks appealed to her.

Jennifer admired Herb's intelligence and determination. Recently, despite threats and attempted

15

cover-ups, his investigative work had led to an indictment of a state senator for drug dealing. Herb brought intense curiosity to whatever he tackled. Last year, when he had decided to learn how to play bridge, he quickly became intrigued with the game and the players. He used all his analytical skills to find out as much as he could about this new interest by taking lessons, reading bridge books, and asking countless questions.

When the first set of lessons ended, he'd invited Jennifer to go for a drink after class. One thing had led to another, and now they were here in his apartment on a Tuesday morning, both getting ready to go to work.

Jennifer sat down on the bed and pulled her pantyhose up over her feet and calves. "I'm beginning to feel a little better about directing the money game," she said. She stood and pulled the pantyhose the rest of the way up.

Herb gave her a puzzled look. "I never understood why you were so reluctant to accept Canning's offer. I thought it was a great opportunity. What took you so long to agree?"

"C'mon, Herb. You've played the game long enough to know how nasty some of the bridge players can be under normal circumstances. A money game is bound to make those players even more obnoxious." She buttoned her blue silk blouse and slipped on her skirt.

"You still don't sound very happy about directing it. If you feel that way, why do it?"

"The huge salary for two days' work, the suite at the hotel, the free meals, the prestige ... lots of reasons." She sat down on the bed and slipped on her heels. "And the publicity will be great for my reputation as a director—if nothing goes wrong."

"What do you expect to go wrong?" Herb asked, buckling his belt and slipping his wallet into his pocket.

"With bridge players' egos and all that money involved, it could be anything from cheating to murder."

"Herb, the Mighty Private Investigator, will come to your rescue."

She grinned at him. "Like you do with towels?"

CHAPTER 2

"We've done worse in this tournament than any other we've ever played in," Eva complained on the last day of the Spring Championships. She and Sharon had just finished the afternoon session and had returned to her hotel room. Eva took one of her suitcases out of her closet, pulled a bottle of merlot from it, and poured a large amount into each of the two wine glasses they had liberated from the hotel dining room. "We've hardly won anything. Even the beginners walked all over us. I'm glad tonight's session is the last one. I'm tired of having everybody beat up on us."

"Maybe we're saving all our luck for the money tournament tomorrow," Sharon said. She propped a pillow from one of the double beds against the headboard and sprawled out on the bed.

"I hope so. If we don't play any better or have any more luck than we've had all week, we won't win anything in that, either. Right now, I'm beginning to think we wasted our money. I'm sorry we entered."

Sharon took a big swallow from her glass of wine. "That's a terrible attitude, Eva. If you think like that, we won't stand a chance. As long as you're in such a rotten mood, let's go bug the registration clerk again. With all the checkouts today, maybe we can finally get connecting rooms. I don't like having to get dressed if I want to come into your room and have a cup of coffee with you in the morning."

"They've heard our complaints so many times this week, I doubt if they'll listen to us anymore," Eva said.

"It's the best time to go. I'm sure they'll give us what we want now, just to get rid of us."

Eva finished her wine, rinsed her glass, and marched out. Sharon filled up her glass again and took it with her.

Although Eva and Sharon lived in Norfolk, they preferred staying at the hotel hosting the tournament. They liked being able to go back to their rooms to rest after the afternoon sessions, and they especially liked having their rooms available at night instead of facing the long drive back to Norfolk after midnight.

The rooms they had occupied during the Spring Championships hadn't met their requirements, but the hotel had been too full for them to move. They always tried to get connecting rooms. They liked their privacy—and also wanted the option of having separate rooms in case they wanted to entertain. Now, with so many people checking out, they decided to try again to see if they could get exactly what they wanted.

At the registration desk, they began their usual hassle.

"Now that you have empty rooms again, we'd like to change ours," Sharon told the woman behind the desk. "I'd like a quiet room at the end of a corridor and away from other guests, and Eva wants a room with the morning sun. Please make sure we get connecting rooms. We'd also like to be away from the sounds of elevators and ice machines. And this time, please see if you can find rooms on the concierge floor -- preferably overlooking the ocean. It's silly to stay at the beach without an ocean view."

The registration clerk, tired of coping with bridge players' demands all week, pretended to listen sympathetically. Then she turned around, rolled her eyes, and made a face at the manager who was standing nearby. They'd heard all this before. Sighing, she turned back to her computer, and after a short search, found two rooms that looked like they might fit the sisters' requirements.

"Would you mind if we took the keys and looked at the rooms?" Sharon asked. "I don't want to pack all my stuff and get to a new room that I don't like."

"I'll have to send a bellman up with you," the clerk told her. "We can't give out keys to unoccupied rooms."

They went with the bellman to make their inspection. When they arrived, they found the connecting door between the rooms still locked. The bellman had neglected to bring the master key with him, and had to call down to have one sent up.

"I hope that's the *only* thing wrong with these rooms," Eva muttered.

They tested the showers, looked in the drawers to see if they were clean, and listened to the noises in and out of the rooms. Finally, they pronounced themselves satisfied.

It was a lucky day for the registration clerk. People who knew Eva and Sharon's reputation would never stand in a hotel registration line behind them if they could avoid it. At tournaments in the past, the sisters had been known to spend thirty minutes at the desk, go to their assigned rooms, and then come back and ask for two others. The people who had waited behind them were always undone and, because of their frustration, at a disadvantage for any event of the tournament that started that day. The sisters knocked off some of their competition without ever picking up a card.

Eva, hanging her conservative black and gray suits neatly in her closet, called to Sharon. "Did you hear the rumors about the Vanderbilt when we were in the lobby?"

Since this was the last day of the Spring Championships, the final session for the Vanderbilt Championship, a straight elimination event for teams, was scheduled for tonight. Several events at the three yearly national championship tournaments were contested by teams of four, five, or six players in head-to-head competition. The Spingold in the summer, the Vanderbilt in the spring, and the Reisinger in the fall were the three most prestigious events played at North American

Championship tournaments. The winners of these events would receive favorable seeding in the elimination event to determine who would represent North America in international competition.

Sharon, who had just finished tossing all her cosmetics onto the bathroom counter, heard Eva's voice, but didn't pay attention. Instead, she looked in the mirror and wondered if it were time to color all those silver strands in her black hair. She dismissed the thought with a shake of her head. She didn't want to go through the procedure every six weeks like Eva did. Besides, Eva was now a blond, and Sharon didn't know if she were ready for such a drastic change of color. With her pale skin, though, she might look good as a redhead ...

Maybe next year.

Suddenly aware that Eva was waiting for her to answer, she shouted into the other room, "What did you say?"

"I asked if you'd heard anything this afternoon about the Vanderbilt."

"No, I didn't," Sharon answered. "I was too busy trying to get us moved. What happened?"

"The rumor is that Gary Alexander's team accused two members on Tom Stanhope's team of cheating, but I don't know the details. All I know is that the Alexander team is contesting this afternoon's results."

Sharon stopped fiddling with her hair and walked into Eva's room. "That's awful. Are they going to play the last session tonight, or wait for a ruling?"

"I heard that they're going to play. They have to have a winner, no matter what happens. If the cheating accusation is dismissed, they'll just use the final score from tonight's game. If the committee decides that anyone on Tom's team cheated, they'll have to disqualify the whole team. I feel sorry for the other team members."

"I wonder what'll happen if they can't come to a decision tonight," Sharon said. "Would that mean they'd all stick around here and enter the money game while they waited for a ruling? That wouldn't be too helpful for us. They're all experts. I don't want to compete against every one of them tomorrow."

"We wouldn't have to. At least, not against any more than those who originally signed up. It's too late for new entries. If we're lucky, the committee will throw out all the hands for the afternoon session and call for a play-off tomorrow. Then we won't have to compete against any of them."

Sharon shook her head. "I don't see how they could do that. Either a team cheated or it didn't. If it didn't, then there's a winner—unless the game ends in a tie tonight."

"Now that would be a break for us. Then they would need to have a playoff. I wonder what'll happen if they find any of the players guilty of cheating. Would the guilty ones have the nerve to stay and play in the money game?"

"Maybe—if they're still allowed to play," Sharon said. "I hate to see anyone cheat in bridge, but I wouldn't mind having the whole bunch of them barred. It sure would improve our chances." She readjusted her black and pink flowered sweater over her black leather pants. "Let's go have dinner. It looks like we won't be the overall winners in today's event with our rotten afternoon score, but let's try to top our section tonight. Then we can get to bed early and be well-rested for tomorrow's game."

* * * * *

Ralph and Jeffrey were jubilant by the end of the Virginia Beach Spring Championships. They had come in first in a national event—an impressive victory for them. Below the national events were the regional events, and they had earned a second place in one of those. Besides winning a large number of masterpoints these past ten days, they had solidified their bridge reputation.

"We haven't had an ounce of alcohol all week," Jeffrey said to Ralph when they found out they had just come in fourth overall in the last pair game of the tournament. "It's time to go to the bar and celebrate our victories."

Ralph grinned. "My thoughts exactly." He was glad to see Jeffrey out of one of his interminable petulant moods. Lately, Jeffrey had been criticizing Ralph's bridge with more and more rancor. Since they had done so well this past week, Jeffrey had reverted to the charm of their earlier days together.

Ralph remembered how terrific their relationship had been in the beginning. He and Jeffrey had met at a party given by the dean for new faculty members. Jeffrey had come up to Ralph at the party and, without hesitation, launched into a determined flirtation. He'd invited Ralph to his apartment the following evening and cooked one of the finest gourmet dinners Ralph had ever eaten. Ralph later wondered where Jeffrey found the money to pay for the expensive wines and the truffles in the sauce, but he didn't want to spoil the enchantment of the night by asking.

Two days after the dinner, Jeffrey had moved in with Ralph. Now, three years later, they were big winners in a national tournament. Ralph hoped that the win would lead to an improvement in their deteriorating relationship.

They went into the bar off the lobby and sat at one of the few unoccupied tables. The Alexander team members were conferring around a larger table next to them.

"They don't look happy," Ralph observed in a low voice.

Gary Alexander, a lawyer, usually played with Jonathan Meltzer, a professional bridge player. Less experienced players often hired pros to play with them in tournaments, feeling that they would have a better chance of winning an event with an expert player sitting across the table. Some clients were already excellent competitors, but they enjoyed having the best players in the world for their partners.

Ralph and Jeffrey, along with most of the other bridge players, had heard rumors about the cheating, but they didn't know the details yet. They eavesdropped as Gary and Jonathan talked to the other members of their Vanderbilt team. Although Jonathan tried to keep his voice low, he sounded furious.

"I don't care what Tom or Cliff claims," Jonathan said angrily. "I'm sure they cheated. There's no way they could've reached the right contract time after time on some of those hands. It's statistically impossible using any bidding system to bid the slams they bid and to stay out of the ones that wouldn't make. I'm positive they had a look at those hands ahead of time."

"But how can we prove it?" Gary asked. "I don't know how anyone could see copies of the specific hands that we're scheduled to play. There are a million safeguards around the computers that devise and store them. I don't think there's anything else we can do right now. The committee has our written accusations. We'll just have to wait for a ruling."

They discussed the problem for a while longer and then left the bar.

"What an awful dilemma for them," Ralph said after they'd gone. "I'm sure the committee members are remembering all the lawsuits that've been filed in the past by players who felt they'd been wrongfully accused of cheating. It's going to be hard for the committee to make a ruling against the Stanhope team—especially if they don't have solid proof."

"But that shouldn't stop the losing team from trying to protect itself," Jeffrey said. "I'd be furious if I thought I lost the Vanderbilt to a team that cheated."

"Furious?" replied Ralph. "Just think of missing both the prestige of winning and the chance to represent the United States in international competition. Not to mention being set up for life to play as a pro." Then he paused. "Still, I'd almost *kill* for a Vanderbilt win, let alone *cheat*."

"Would you kill to win a hundred thousand dollars in a money game?"

"Ask me if we get to the finals."

"You mean *when* we get to the finals!"

CHAPTER 3

Jennifer Brandon checked into the hotel at 9:00 on the Monday morning of the money game. The desk clerk gave her a room key and a special elevator key that allowed her access to the concierge level. She followed the bellman to an elegantly furnished suite with a bedroom, living room, two bathrooms, a fully stocked mini-bar, and an ocean view on two sides. Century had certainly come through with their promise of luxurious accommodations for the chief director of the money game. Jennifer was pleased.

She handed the bellman his tip and quickly unpacked. Too bad she'd be spending so much time directing. What a waste of a great suite. Luckily, Herb would be joining her to share the perks. At least she'd be able to take advantage of the free breakfasts in the lounge and the cocktails and hors d'oeuvres served after five o'clock. Scoring the game would keep her working late after the afternoon sessions, but she would be able to go to the lounge for some food if she didn't have time to go out for dinner.

When she finished unpacking, she took the elevator down to the lobby and went into the ballroom to make sure the tables and supplies were there. Everything looked in order. After she told the workmen how to arrange the room for the game, there was nothing left for her to do. She looked at her watch. Only 10:30. Time enough for her to go to her suite, exercise, and take a shower.

Back in her living room, she put on a sweat suit and started her warmup exercises. While doing her sit-ups, she thought about Century's commitment to the money game and wondered if they had accurately crunched the numbers before agreeing to sponsor the event. It must be costing them a fortune. They would receive the income from the entry fees—which was considerable—but they would still have to sell a lot of products to recoup all the money they were giving away for prizes. It would take a tremendous amount of publicity and work to sell enough cards, books, and other bridge supplies to make the expense worthwhile.

When she reached her seventy-sixth sit-up, she heard someone knocking on the door. Damn! She hated having her routine interrupted. Reluctantly, she got up from the floor, straightened out her sweat suit, and opened the door.

Charles Canning, the manager of Century Bridge Supplies, stood there looking anxious. The head atop the large, gangly frame of the former basketball player nearly reached the lintel of the door frame. When he held out his hand for Jennifer to shake, she noticed an inch of wrist showing from the long sleeves of his casual sports shirt. The matching striped pants somehow managed to reach all the way down to his shoes. She wondered if he had to special order his clothes. If so, he should get someone to measure his arms more accurately.

"Please come in, Charles," Jennifer told him with as polite a voice as she could muster. She walked ahead of him into the living room and motioned for him to take a seat on the sofa.

"I hope I didn't disturb you, Jennifer. I had to do some fast talking at the desk to get them to let me come to the Concierge floor," Charles said sheepishly. "I convinced them that it was my company that was promoting the game you're directing. They still wouldn't give me a key to the elevator, but they sent someone up with me. When he saw that you knew me, he took off."

"You should have had them call my room. I would have told them it was okay."

"I never thought of it."

"Well, *they* should have," she said. "What can I do for you?"

"I just came up to see if you needed any help or if there were any last minute glitches."

"Everything seems okay so far," Jennifer said. She went over to her desk, picked up her briefcase, and took out the notes she'd made for the money game. She sat down on a chair opposite Charles. "Let's review these quickly. As far as I know, everything we arranged is still in place. David Jasper and Ruth Simmons from Washington agreed to stay in town to help me direct. They were happy to pick up the extra cash. I've also hired some of the local bridge players to caddy."

"I hope the caddies aren't too hypnotized by the experts to pay attention to their work," Charles fretted.

"Don't worry. I've drummed the rules into them. They know that all the scores after each round must be recorded on scorecards by the North-South pairs and that the East-West pairs have to sign the scorecards showing they agree with what's written there. I promise you, the caddies that I hired have all played duplicate bridge for years. They'll be careful.

"I also kept some of the restaurant guides and information about tourist attractions that were left over from the Nationals—although I don't think the contestants will have much time for anything but bridge. Most of them are tired out from playing the last ten days. They'll probably want to sleep late."

Charles, reassured by Jennifer's efficiency, relaxed a little. "I'm glad to see that you have things under control. To tell you the truth, I think I'm in over my head. Doesn't it worry you that only fifty percent of the players will qualify for the finals? Everyone will be trying to get one of those spots. I wouldn't be surprised if some of them turned vicious—especially during the session tonight."

Jennifer frowned. "It does worry me," she admitted, "but we'll be able to handle it. The contestants will just have to accept whatever scores they earn—and the good thing is that the losers will know they'll still have a chance to win a substantial amount in the consolation game. Have we had any changes on the standby list?"

"We have two pairs on standby," Charles said. "They kept pestering me all last week to play in the game, and I kept telling them that we had already filled all the slots by the time we received their applications. Since the standbys aren't guaranteed an entry, I told them we'd let them pay one thousand instead of the two thousand if they're accepted at the last minute. It'll at least give them some compensation for waiting. We had five extra pairs originally, but three of them didn't want to hang around any longer. They withdrew, and we returned their deposit."

"I heard there was an accusation of cheating in the Vanderbilt final," Jennifer reported. "According to our list of contestants, three pairs from the Vanderbilt finalists are registered to play in our game. What if there's a play-off and they have to withdraw? From what you just told me, we're down to only two standby pairs."

"That's terrible." Charles used a crumpled tissue to wipe perspiration from his face. "Let's pray that the Vanderbilt players will be able to play in our game," he said. "If not, we'll have to scrounge around and find another pair quickly. Maybe some of those who withdrew will still be around. Otherwise, you'll have to get some of the local players to fill in. I hope it doesn't come to that. Sometimes I wish I'd never thought of involving Century in a money game."

"I'm sure everything will work out," Jennifer said, distressed about having to constantly reassure him. "I just hope the committee will make a decision about the cheating quickly. I'd be more comfortable if I knew who's playing in our game as soon as possible. Let's see . . . there was something else I wanted to ask you. Oh, I remember—are we going to allow kibitzers?"

"I don't know. What do you think?"

"I don't see why not. If anyone objects, we can ask the kibitzers to go watch at another table. Sometimes it makes players nervous to have people watching all their plays.

They don't like to have others see their mistakes. The contestants are paying a lot to play in this game, so we should try to make them as comfortable as possible."

"Then let's allow kibitzers on that basis," Charles said.

"I'm glad to see that so many pros and top bridge players have signed up. That'll be great for the publicity."

"I hope so," Charles said anxiously. "Anything else?"

"Hmm . . . yes. Where are the bid boxes? I didn't see them when I went down earlier to watch them set up the room for our game."

Charles paled. "Bid boxes? I never thought about them. Why do we need them?"

"To help prevent cheating," Jennifer said. "Pulling out a card from the bid box instead of voicing a bid helps eliminate a lot of potential cheating and misunderstandings. There's no chance for a bid to be misheard or overheard, and there aren't any voice inflections for a partnership to take advantage of. And there's no need to review the bidding, since all the cards are left on the table until after the bidding is over. We really do need them."

"I don't know how I could have overlooked ordering them. Can't we borrow some from the ACBL's supplies? They had hundreds of them here for the Spring Championships."

She shook her head. "It's too late. They've packed up all their supplies and sent them back to Memphis."

"Can't we get along without them?"

"Not in a game with such high stakes."

Charles leaned forward and slapped the side of his forehead with his palm. "Damn! I knew I'd forget something important. I'll make sure we have them for tomorrow's game. I'll call Century as soon as I leave here and have them express ship them to us. I knew I'd goof up on something. Could you possibly borrow some from the local club to use today?"

"They've already started today's game," Jennifer said, looking at her watch. "I know we don't have enough extra ones at the Club for all the tables in the money game. We'll have to get by today without them, but this is really a major foul-up."

"I'm really sorry, Jennifer. It's all my fault. I'll leave right now and make sure you have them by tomorrow." He leaped off the sofa and scuttled out the door.

* * * * *

Charles walked slowly back to the elevator. He couldn't help but worry about how thoroughly he had committed Century to this venture. He feared that this project was beyond his capabilities. His six-foot-four-inch frame had made him a basketball star at Syracuse University ten years ago, and although he had majored in business, the basketball fame—not his business skills—had brought him his jobs.

Century had hired him to become their manager a few months ago. Orin Staples, a member of Century's board of directors, had been a student at Syracuse with Charles. He remembered the charisma that Charles had exhibited as a basketball star. Although Charles had had a mediocre record at his previous jobs, Orin convinced the board that he was the right person to manage Century. Luckily for Charles, there were no other outstanding candidates at the time.

Charles had initiated the idea of having Century sponsor the money game. He'd convinced the board of directors that the name Century would become familiar to thousands of bridge players from all the publicity that the game would generate. Whenever they needed bridge supplies, they would automatically call the Century 800 number and place an order. He was amazed that the board had listened to him—and more amazed that they'd believed him.

Back in his room, he took off his shoes and lay down on the bed. It was hard for him to get comfortable with his feet and ankles extending over the end of the mattress, but he didn't pay much attention to that now. How could he have forgotten those bid boxes? He knew he should call and get them shipped out right away, but he was reluctant to tell anyone that he'd forgotten such an important item.

While he lay there wondering how to word his problem so he wouldn't sound like an idiot, the telephone rang. He grabbed it off the nightstand. "Charles Canning speaking."

"Hello, Charles. This is Orin. I thought you might be feeling nervous about your big venture right now. I just called to reassure you and to see how things were going."

"Thanks, Orin," Charles said. "I was just about to call you. This is one of those days when I wish I had become a basketball coach instead of an executive. I hate to admit it, but I forgot to arrange to have bid boxes here. It's too late for today's game, but we really need them for tomorrow's."

"I'll send them out as soon as we finish talking. It's too bad you didn't remember to order them, but it's not a catastrophe. As long as they have them for the finals, it should be okay. As far as I can see, you haven't forgotten anything else."

Charles suddenly realized that it was just as important to Orin as it was to himself that the money game succeed. He *had* been hired on Orin's recommendation. It wouldn't look good for Orin if his protege botched things up.

"We've been reviewing the work you've done over the past few months for this contest, and it looks like you've been very thorough," Orin continued. "We were pleased to see the advertisements and articles about the money game that appeared in the last two issues of *The Bulletin* and *Bridge World.* And having reporters from those magazines right there to cover the event will generate a lot of publicity. Have you made sure that the columnist from *The New York Times* will be there?"

"Of course. During the past week, I've talked to all the representatives of the magazines and newspapers who might cover the game," Charles said. "They promised me they'd write a full report." It was a relief to realize he'd done something right.

"What about television? Have you been able to create any interest there?"

"I called the local television stations, and two of them sent reporters over to interview me during the Spring Championships. They were intrigued with the idea of a money game, and promised me they'd do feature stories on their evening news programs. All that free advertising from the press and television coverage will be invaluable to Century, especially if the story gets picked up nationally. I also called CNN and they sounded interested. They didn't promise anything, but I wouldn't be surprised if they sent someone here to see what it's all about."

"That's great," Orin said. "Since you left for Virginia Beach, we haven't had any notification of anyone pulling out of the game. As far as we know, you still have enough contestants—and several standbys. We have the required five hundred dollar per person deposit from all the applicants, and no one has asked for a refund. The forty-eight hour deadline for withdrawal with a full refund has passed, so we're assuming they all plan to play."

"No one has come up to me yet, either, so I don't expect anyone to withdraw. It was a relief to get such a good response. There is another problem, though." Charles told him about the Vanderbilt cheating accusation.

"Does that mean we might lose some of the pros who signed up to play?"

"Afraid so."

"That's not good. We were counting on them to make the game more newsworthy. But that's not your fault, Charles," he added hastily. "You've done everything you could. It'll all work out. You can use your standbys, if you need to."

Charles didn't tell him they were now one pair short.

Knowing about Charles' lack of confidence, Orin complimented him one more time. "I'm sure the publicity from this game will make people associate bridge products with the name of Century Bridge Supplies for a long time. The company will have a lot to thank you for. Well, good luck!"

"Thanks, Orin," Charles said with heartfelt gratitude.

He hung up the phone, relieved. He'd gotten over the bid box hurdle. Orin would be sure to get them here in time for the next day's game.

Now he only had to worry about the thousands and thousands of dollars he'd committed Century to spend. It amazed him that they had so much faith in an idea of which he was so unsure. He'd tossed the idea out at a meeting when he'd wanted nothing more than to let the Board know that he was in the room. Who would have thought they'd take his far-fetched proposal so seriously, or adopt it so enthusiastically?

He leaned over the bed and threw up into the wastebasket.

CHAPTER 4

Jennifer, refreshed from her exercises and shower, returned to the ballroom ready to go to work. She entered through the large glass double doors and looked around, pleased to see that the room was set up as exactly as she'd requested. The long mahogany directors' table stood in front of the gold velvet curtains at the end of a wide center aisle. Contestants could walk down the aisle to the table, buy their entries, and go to their assigned places.

Both Section A and Section B, on either side of the aisle, contained fourteen bridge tables which were spaced comfortably apart in the huge ballroom. The directors, sitting at their table at the end of the aisle between the two sections, would be in a position to monitor all the proceedings. The arrangement made it easy for them to get to the tables in either section whenever necessary.

Jennifer noticed Charles walking around Section A making sure that the guide cards were placed correctly on each table. The contestants would match the numbers on their entries to the numbers on the guide cards to find out where they'd be seated for the first round. Jennifer waved to Charles, and then went over to the directors' table where David and Ruth had collected the remainder of the entry fees from early arrivals.

"Have you heard if the Vanderbilt mess has been settled?" she asked them. "We have less than an hour till game time. It certainly would help if we knew how many contestants we have."

"We haven't heard anything," Ruth answered. "Charles was over here a few minutes ago talking about it, but he didn't have any news. He seemed a bit frantic. According to him, three of the pairs registered to play in this game may have to withdraw if there's a play-off for the Vanderbilt. We still have only two pairs on standby."

"We talked about the problem this morning," Jennifer said. "I'll go see if anyone knows what's happening. Keep selling the entries to the ones who've reserved places. We'll figure out what to do later if we need to find more players." She went to find Charles to see if he'd had an update.

* * * * *

Eva and Sharon had won a section top on the last night of the Nationals—to their great relief. They'd both been feeling low after their poor performances in the Spring Championships, but the win had helped restore their confidence.

Eva, dressed in high heels and a brown suit flecked with gold, barely glanced at the other contestants when she entered the ballroom. The substantial number of expert players in the room didn't intimidate her. Sharon was even more relaxed. She figured that she and Eva stood as good a chance to win as anyone. She strode into the ballroom in her sneakers and warmup suit, waving at the people she knew.

After they socialized with a few of their friends, Eva went to find a diet cola. Sharon decided it was time to pick up their entry, but when she approached the directors' desk, she couldn't get through. The standbys, trying to find out if they would be able to play, blocked the way.

"I'm sorry, but there's no news yet," Jennifer told them. She'd just returned from her talk with Canning. "We're as anxious as you are to find out who'll be playing, but the committee's still meeting."

The disgruntled standbys complained to her and to each other, but there wasn't anything Jennifer could do for them. She finally asked them, politely, to step aside so the other contestants could get their entries.

"Hi, Jennifer," Sharon said when she was able to get to the table. "Please give me a lucky seating assignment. I don't want any number twos or eights. I never win with them. And, if possible, let us have an East-West entry so we can move this afternoon and then sit North-South tonight. I like to be one of the stationary pairs after cocktail hour and dinner."

Jennifer, who knew the sisters well, made a halfhearted attempt to lecture her. "This is a serious and expensive game, Sharon. Why don't you save your drinking until after the evening session?"

Sharon sighed. "I wish I could, but it's hard. When George was alive, he was always after me to lose ten pounds, but I liked chocolate too much. I got used to drinking a glass or two of wine at five o'clock to hide the smell of chocolate. Now I'm hooked on both."

"I notice you lost the ten pounds."

"What's a widow to do?" Sharon asked with a slight shrug. "I was getting so heavy, I considered starting a line of clothes and calling it 'Petite Chubettes.'"

"From what I hear, you do okay." Jennifer lifted an inquisitive eyebrow. "What was that rumor about you and the pro from Pittsburgh in the glass elevator at the Dallas tournament?"

Sharon flicked a hand in dismissal. "I don't know how these rumors get started. It wasn't glass."

Jennifer laughed as she shook her head and handed Sharon her entry. "You and Eva can sit East-West at table seven in Section A. You'll be pair seven North-South in Section B tonight. I hope you qualify for the finals."

Sharon thanked her, stuck the entry in her pocketbook, and scanned the ballroom looking for Eva. She frowned when she noticed the Nestors coming into the room. They were a husband and wife pair who constantly fought at the bridge table. Even though she liked them personally, she didn't enjoy playing bridge against them, because their constant bickering made her lose her own concentration. More often, though, they'd be so upset with each other that they'd play poorly and give her good results. The trick was to be their opponent at the right time.

As she looked for Eva, she surveyed the room to see if there were any prospects for after the game. No one here looked interesting, but Gary Alexander, one of the Vanderbilt finalists, had always intrigued her. With his short stature and gray hair, he reminded her of Stuart of the old *L.A. Law* show. She wondered if he liked chocolate.

* * * * *

A few minutes later, Linda Mason entered the ballroom. Since she couldn't afford to stay in the hotel, and Kathy wouldn't spend the money to stay there, they were both commuting from their respective homes. No designer dresses for Linda today; she wore one of her old dresses. In her opinion, it was psychologically better not to look too sharp to the better players.

Linda sat down at one of the empty bridge tables, dropped her purse and sweater on it, and waited for Kathy to arrive. When Kathy didn't appear after ten minutes, Linda began to worry. It would be just like Kathy to decide she couldn't afford to play. Linda snorted in disgust at her partner's frugality. Finally she got up and went out to the hallway to look for her. She stopped to talk to another player for a few minutes, but still saw no sign of her partner. Shrugging her shoulders, she went back to the ballroom to wait.

As Linda approached the table where she'd left her purse and sweater, she suddenly froze. Tom Stanhope, the bridge pro she'd hired and with whom she had fought, was sitting with her pocketbook open in front of him. He held her checkbook in both hands and appeared to be studying the register with great interest.

"What do you think you're doing?" she asked angrily. "You have no right to look at my checkbook! Give it to me."

"I saw a purse sitting on the table when I came into the ballroom," Tom said, ignoring her demand. "I thought it was careless of someone to leave it around where anyone could steal it. It's a good thing I came along and found it first. Naturally, I had to look inside to see whose it was so I could return it to its owner. Imagine my surprise when it turned out to be yours."

"That's right! It is mine!" Linda snapped. "Now give it to me!" She tried to grab the checkbook away from him, but Tom held it tightly. He pushed her away and slowly leafed through the register.

"Some interesting entries in here," he said. "I found it to be fascinating reading while I waited for you to come claim your purse."

"How *dare* you go through my checkbook? My finances are none of your business."

"They are now." Tom's tongue darted out to his upper lip, and Linda knew something awful was coming. "You've been making some large deposits every two weeks for the last several months. I remember you tried to get me to reduce my rates when you hired me. You claimed that you couldn't afford my regular rates. Now, where would someone with such a limited budget suddenly find all this money?"

"I had a perfectly legitimate reason to make those deposits, and I don't owe you an explanation. Now please give it back to me." She lunged toward him, but Tom pulled it farther away.

"It seems to me that there's an obvious pattern here for anyone who might be looking for some missing funds. I would think that someone with your experience with money would be more discreet. It wasn't very bright of you to deposit your sudden wealth into your own account—and even more stupid of you to carry the evidence around."

Linda was livid. "Give that back to me right now," she repeated, as quietly as possible. She looked worriedly around the room, hoping that no one had heard any of this conversation.

"In a minute. I'll bet it never occurred to you that anyone would study your checkbook—or notice anything suspicious in it even if you lost your purse. You just didn't count on my being the person to get his hands on it. Now what do you think would happen if your boss got wind of those strange deposits? I imagine an investigation would follow pretty quickly. I doubt if you'd like that." He put the checkbook back in her pocketbook. "Catch," he said suddenly, and he tossed the purse to her. "I've seen all I need to see."

"You can tell my boss anything you want," Linda said. "I have nothing to hide."

"In that case, you don't have anything to worry about," Tom said. "But everyone knows you're not rich. Even your stingy friend Kathy was surprised that you could afford to hire me. I bet you're playing in this game to win some extra money for reasons I'm sure you'd rather not have made public. We'll talk about this later, after you've had time to think about it." He gave her a mock bow and left the ballroom, nearly bumping into Kathy on his way out.

Kathy, who could have worn a new outfit every day of her life, appeared in an outdated flowered dress. She wasn't going to waste money on fancy clothes for a bridge game. Oblivious to Linda's distress, she began talking as soon as she approached her. "We must be crazy," she griped. "Look around at the competition. Some of the best players in the world are here. We don't stand a chance. I don't know why I let you talk me into playing."

"Of course we have a chance," Linda replied as calmly as she could. She didn't want Kathy to realize how upset she was. "Don't think so negatively. All we have to do is play our usual steady game. And we may have a better chance to win than you think. When I walked through the lobby, I heard that the Vanderbilt teams might be involved in a playoff. If we're lucky, they'll have to withdraw from the money game. That would improve our chances enormously. And don't forget, if we place anywhere, we could win a *lot* of money."

Kathy didn't look convinced, but she couldn't bear the thought of losing her deposit. She took Linda's check and went over to the directors' desk to pay the rest of their entry fee.

* * * * *

Ralph and Jeffrey wandered into the playing area at 12:30. Earlier, when they were in the lobby, they had talked to some of the other contestants about the cheating scandal. They'd learned that it centered around the suspicious number of slams that Tom Stanhope and Cliff Bryce had either managed to bid—or to accurately refrain from bidding—during the last afternoon session of the Vanderbilt. Gary Alexander and Jonathan Meltzer, members of the losing team, were sure that Tom and Cliff had cheated. They'd written up their accusations and sent them to a committee. Now everyone was waiting for the ruling.

"What do you think?" Ralph asked when they were out of hearing range of the others.

"I wouldn't be at all surprised if Tom had figured out some way to cheat. My guess is that he and Cliff did something unethical, but the Alexander team couldn't pinpoint *how* it was done. You'll notice that no one's talking about specifics. If the committee doesn't have anything concrete, Stanhope's team will win."

"There must be *some* proof. You can't just make a wild accusation about cheating," Ralph said.

"They may not have any more proof than the statistical improbability of having such a perfect round. I heard that they violated several of their own bidding agreements in order to arrive at the right contracts. I'm glad I'm not on that committee. What a nightmare."

"I don't understand all the talk about a playoff," Ralph said. "If Cliff's team cheated, they'll be disqualified and Gary's team will be declared the winners. There won't be any need for a playoff."

"But what happens if the committee doesn't feel it has enough proof, but still feels something was wrong? They might throw out the results of the last session and make them play a whole new set of boards."

"I don't think that'll happen. They'll either declare them guilty or let them off the hook."

Jeffrey looked at the directors' table. "I guess this is a good time to pick up our entry. There's nobody there right now. Why don't you go get it, and I'll go back out to the lobby and see if there's any news."

* * * * *

Jennifer congratulated Ralph on the successes he and Jeffrey had enjoyed during the past week. "Nice going, Ralph," she said. "All those victories, plus your recent regional wins, put you in a good position for this event. I've assigned you to one of the secondary seeds. You and Jeffrey will start out at table six in Section B this afternoon. Good luck."

"Thanks, Jennifer. It sure feels good to achieve some recognition." He picked up the entry and joined Jeffrey, who had come back into the ballroom.

"I'm not sure how smart we were to try this," Jeffrey said, suddenly feeling outclassed. "I've been watching the contestants as they've come in. Out of the fifty-six pairs, at least forty have national reputations. And I'm sure that the ones I don't recognize are better than average. No one without a lot of bridge expertise would pay these prices to play in such a strong field. I wish we'd stopped while we were on a roll."

"It's too late to back out now," Ralph told him. "Besides, the other contestants must be at least as scared of us as we are of them, after our solid performance last week! Don't be discouraged. Remember, even the pros make mistakes. Some of their bids and plays that get reported in *Bridge World* and *The Bulletin* are worse than anything we ever do. If we're lucky, they'll make those same kinds of mistakes when they're playing against us."

Jeffrey looked doubtful. He was afraid an error of *his* would be reported in the next issue of one of the bridge magazines. He hoped they wouldn't use his name. Calling him the "East" or the "South" player would be more than enough publicity. Naming him would be humiliating.

He would prefer to have an article written about a brilliant play of his against a pro. In that case, he wouldn't mind having his name and the pro's name appear. It didn't occur to him that the pro might be humiliated by such an article.

* * * * *

"Where's the checkbook?" Alan Nestor demanded.

"What do you mean, 'Where's the checkbook?' You always pay our entry fees with cash. *I* don't have the checkbook," Sybil snapped at him.

"I know I usually pay cash, but we've never had to pay a four thousand dollar entry fee. You can't expect me to carry that much money in my wallet."

"It's not four thousand—it's three thousand," Sybil said. "We've already given them a five hundred dollar deposit for each of us. You'd better be able to add and subtract better than that at the bridge table. And you know I don't take the checkbook with me to tournaments. I have enough other stuff cluttering up my pocketbook."

"Well, what do you suggest we do?" Alan demanded. "They're not going to let us play on credit."

Sybil glared at him. "Maybe I still have a blank check left in my wallet," she said, exasperated. "I used one a couple of days ago when I went shopping, but I might have an extra one somewhere." She pulled her wallet out of her purse and rummaged through all the compartments. Alan hovered over her while she searched, causing her to drop several bills and credit cards on the floor. She finally found a blank check in with her change. "Here's one that's pretty beat up," she said, handing it to him.

"This check is awful," Alan complained. "It looks like you've been carrying it around for two years. I doubt if anyone will cash it."

"Well, it's all we have, so you'd better try. Jennifer knows us. I'm sure she'll take it."

Alan picked up the check by the corner and took it to the directors' desk.

"Sorry about this," he mumbled to Jennifer, "but it's the only check we have with us."

Jennifer had heard them fighting from across the room, and was appalled that they'd begun already. Usually they waited until the game started. But she wasn't about to exclude a pair over anything so trifling as a messy check—especially with the threat of losing the Vanderbilt group.

"It'll be okay," she told Alan. "I'm sure Century will be able to cash it. If there's any trouble, you can write them a replacement check later."

While Alan paid the balance of their fee, Sybil came over and asked how the seeding was done for the money game.

"Last week, Charles Canning gave me a list of the contestants," Jennifer explained. "I took the names of all the professional and top expert players who'd entered as pairs and gave them the top seeds. Then I gave the remaining seeds to the partnerships who did exceptionally well in the Spring Championships, like Ralph and Jeffrey. The rest of the players will be seated randomly. If anyone has a preference, we try to accommodate them. Would you prefer any particular number or direction this afternoon?"

They looked at the places that were left, but couldn't make up their minds. Finally Alan said, "Just turn all the entry slips over and pick one. It doesn't matter which one we get. Sybil can mess up a contract in any seat."

"Why are you picking on me already?" Sybil asked, dismayed. "We haven't even begun to play. How do you expect me to play well if you criticize me all the time?"

"I don't," Alan muttered, but low enough so that she couldn't hear.

Jennifer drew an East-West entry in Section A for them. Sybil, ready to explode at Alan, grabbed the entry and ran out of the room with it.

"See what I mean?" Alan asked Jennifer. "I can't rely on her for anything. She didn't even tell me where to sit."

"Don't worry," Jennifer soothed. "I'm sure when she comes back she'll tell you exactly where to go."

CHAPTER 5

Jennifer glanced up at the large crystal clock over the entrance to the ballroom. Only fifteen minutes left until game time. If the players from the Vanderbilt teams were going to withdraw from the money game in order to continue their match, someone had better let her know soon.

Charles, looking panic-stricken, rushed over to talk to her about it. They decided they'd better look for an extra pair to fill in. Just as Jennifer approached the doorway to phone some of the local players, the six entrants from the Vanderbilt teams came into the room.

"What's happening?" she asked Jonathan Meltzer, the first one through the door. "Have they made a decision?"

"Not yet," he said, shaking his bald head. "Apparently there are some legal problems. If the committee members decide Tom's team cheated, they'll have to be damn sure that they have overwhelming proof. They remember all those times the American Contract Bridge League was sued over its mishandling of cheating scandals, and they don't want a repeat of that. Since they haven't yet concluded their deliberations, they told us to play in this event. If there's going to be a playoff, we'll have to wait until Wednesday."

Relieved, Jennifer headed back to the directors' table, followed by the rest of the Vanderbilt players. She took Jonathan's check first and handed him his entry. "Can everyone stay here past tomorrow if it's necessary to have a playoff?" she asked him.

"None of us likes the idea, but for a Vanderbilt win, you change your plans if you have to," Jonathan answered. After he took his entry from Jennifer, he turned around and glared through his black, horn-rimmed glasses at the accused pair. He raised his voice deliberately and said, "What I don't understand is why Tom Stanhope and Cliff Bryce would even want to play in this game. If I had a cheating accusation hanging over my head, I would at least wait until my name was cleared before I played in any other bridge game."

All other conversation in the room abruptly stopped. Tom, looking tired and disheveled in his brown tweed suit, responded to Jonathan angrily. "If you're going to make a public accusation against us before a decision is made," he said, shaking a finger in Jonathan's face, "I'll bring you before an ethics committee. Otherwise, shut up."

Gary grabbed Jonathan's arm and pulled him away. "Are you crazy?" he asked when he got him over in a corner away from the others. "You can't go around accusing people of cheating. If you keep this up, you could be barred from the game. And wouldn't that be ironic. Even if they were found guilty and we were declared the winners, you wouldn't be able to play. Listen to me. The ACBL has a longstanding and rigid policy. Accusations of cheating must be presented in strict confidence to an Ethics Committee. Just mentioning a pending charge is grounds for disciplinary action."

"Well, I resent having to play against them. I *do* think they're cheaters," Jonathan growled, but this time, grudgingly, he spoke more softly.

"You've made your point. Now let it go. All we can do is wait until the committee rules. Right now, the only thing you should concentrate on is beating them in the money game."

"I will," Jonathan said. "But if they make any plays that even slightly resemble anything unethical, I'm not sure I'll be able to control my temper."

"You'd better," Gary said in a disgusted tone. "It's bad enough to have a cheating scandal tainting one team without having a violent outburst from a member of the other team. The world is really going to be impressed with this year's Vanderbilt winners—whoever they are."

Jonathan scowled at him, but sat down in the top seeded number three position in Section A. Gary noticed with relief that Tom and Cliff were starting at table three in Section B. They wouldn't have to play against each other until tonight. Maybe Jonathan would be a little calmer by then.

* * * * *

Tom and his partner, Cliff, were usually relaxed before the start of a bridge session, but now they were feeling the pressure of the accusation. Instead of talking quietly and clearing their minds, as they ordinarily did before a game, they began to argue angrily over one of the hands that Tom had played last week.

"I know I didn't make my contract, but your analysis of how to play it is dead wrong," Tom said. "I'm sure I played it correctly. I went with the percentages, and I was unlucky."

Cliff, in his impeccably tailored suit, sat stiffly upright in his chair. With his short white hair and striking baritone voice, he bore a startling resemblance to one of the top anchors of a national television news show. "And I say you didn't play it right," he told Tom angrily. "If a similar situation comes up today, play it the way I suggested or you're liable to go down in an unbeatable contract again. After dinner, I'll retrieve the percentage tables from the bridge files in my portable computer and prove to you that you played it wrong."

"I already *know* the percentages for that play," Tom insisted, "and I bet your computer program will back me up. Until you can convince me that I'm wrong, I'm going to play the cards exactly the same way under the same circumstances."

"You'd better hope it doesn't come up today, or you'll be looking for another partner."

They glared at each other across the table. It was a terrible way to start a game, but neither of them was willing to back down.

CHAPTER 6

The bridge players checked their seating assignments for the first session and went to their respective tables. Alan and Sybil called a truce—temporarily—and chatted amiably with their opponents. Gary and Jonathan quietly reviewed parts of their bidding system. Sharon pulled her legs up under her and sat on them in a yoga position. She was comfortable and ready to begin.

When Jennifer could see that all the contestants were at their assigned tables, she announced, "We will allow kibitzers to watch the players of their choice—if no one at the table objects. If any of you finds it unsettling to have another person at the table watching you play, you have the option of barring kibitzers from that table."

She looked with interest to see which experts the local people would pick. She was not surprised to see two of the best players from the community go over to Gary and Jonathan and ask permission to kibitz. After Jonathan told them they would be welcome, he got up and brought chairs over to the table for them.

Two other players were interested in kibitzing Jeffrey and Ralph. Dr. Kingsley, who had been one of the people on standby, went to their table and introduced himself.

"I tried to play in this event, but I sent my application in too late," he said. "I didn't expect to win any of the prizes, but I thought I might learn something just playing against so many pros. I was really annoyed at myself for not sending in my application as soon as the contest was announced."

"We'll be glad to have you kibitz us," Ralph told him. "I don't know if you'll learn anything or if we'll win, but you're welcome to watch."

Marylou Simson, always looking for a new liaison, sidled up to Jeffrey and asked in her little girl voice if she could please watch the expert play. Jeffrey told her he would be flattered. As she went to find a chair to place next to his, he grinned at Ralph and lifted his shoulders in a shrug.

* * * * *

When everyone settled down again, David and Ruth passed out the hand records. These were sheets of paper with diagrams of bridge hands that were randomly dealt by a computer program. Each player would arrange the cards according to the hand records and then insert the cards in the North, South, East, and West slots in the rectangular plastic boards that were on the tables. Eventually, all the other North, South, East, and West players would play the same cards as every other person sitting in the same direction, allowing direct comparisons of the score achieved by each pair on each deal.

David placed the computer-generated hand records for Boards 13 and 14 on Eva and Sharon's table. The North player was responsible for making sure that the North hand on the printed sheet was pointed in the same direction as the plastic board used to hold the hands. Then all the players, having previously sorted the cards into suits in preparation for the exercise, pulled one suit each from the slots in the board in front of them and distributed the cards to match the hand records.

When the players finished duplicating the hands, Jennifer announced that it was time to begin. "All North players pick up your boards and pass them to the next lower numbered table. Good luck, everyone!"

Sharon surveyed the room before she looked at her first hand. "I see they've seeded the pros at tables three, six, and nine," she said. "We'll have to play against all of them, but I'm looking forward to it. Even if we don't beat them, it's exciting playing against the best bridge players in the world."

Eva stared at her. "Don't be silly. The fun is in beating them," she said disgustedly.

They picked up their cards and proceeded to play the first round. It was a decent start for the sisters, with an average score on the first hand and close to a top on the second.

"I'm glad we went back to our simpler bidding system," Eva commented while they waited for Jennifer to call the next round. "The system I made you try a couple of years ago was much too complicated. At the time, I thought it would help our game."

"Yeah, but it did just the opposite," Sharon said. "I was so furious at you, I wanted to end our partnership. I could never remember all those obscure bids you insisted we use."

It was the only time in all the years they'd played together that they had lost their tempers at each other over bridge.

"I thought if the Courtney brothers could win so often using that system, we could do the same. I should have known that it wasn't so great when hardly anyone else used it. And I've noticed even the Courtneys aren't winning that much lately."

After Eva and Sharon had gone back to their old system, they had started to win again. Since then, if they had any bidding disasters, they would ask one of the experts how the hand *should* have been bid. If the answer involved a new convention, they would try it out a few times. If it improved their game, they continued to use it. But if it caused more disasters than successes, they would discard it. They were willing to try anything that might help, as long as it fit in with their general bidding style—and wasn't too hard to remember.

They began the next round against two strangers who smoothly bid a slam on the first hand. It needed two finesses to work, but the cards were right. Sharon looked at Eva and made a face. Eva nodded in agreement at their certain zero. The following hand wasn't much better. They'd played only four boards so far tonight, and they already had two scores that were below average.

Sharon stuck her finger down her throat, doing a Joan Rivers vomit imitation. "This is awful. We need to do something drastic, or we won't even qualify."

"Any suggestions?"

"Looks like we'll have to beat the best pairs if we can't get good boards from the worst. We're playing against Lou and Jake next—our first seeded competition tonight. Let's get 'em."

* * * * *

"Hi, Lou. Hello, Jake," Sharon said to her new opponents. After they acknowledged her greeting, she turned toward Lou. "I'm surprised to see you here. What does May think about your being away for such a long time?" Lou had recently married a woman who didn't play bridge. Non-bridge players usually don't understand the devotion of serious players to the game.

Lou looked sheepish. "I'm wondering what I'm doing here myself. I should be home with my bride. After the way I played the last hand, I'm afraid my partner is beginning to think so, too. I figure the only way I'm going to get May to forgive me is if I win this tournament and give her all the money."

"And if you don't win?"

Lou sank down lower in his chair. "I don't even want to think about it."

On the first hand, Sharon bid a shaky game. She realized that she and Eva didn't have enough points to bid it, but she also knew that they needed some tops to get back into contention. And it was psychologically a good time. Lou was obviously still upset from the last round and not playing his best.

She played the hand carefully and, when Lou faltered on the defense, she made her contract.

"I guess I should have switched to spades when I got the lead," Lou apologized to his partner.

"The heart continuation wasn't your best play," Jake responded, clearly annoyed.

Trying to compensate for that bad result, Lou bid a questionable slam on the second board. When Jake put the dummy down, Lou studied it carefully. It was going to take a lot of work and not a little luck to bring this one in.

He folded his cards and put them down on the table while he considered his options. Sharon had interfered with a preemptive three club bid, giving Lou a clue about the distribution of the cards. He pointed his thumb and nodded toward her while he unconsciously moved his lips, trying to count out the hand. Then he nodded toward Eva and went through the same movements. After that, he put his elbows on the table and rested his forehead on his hands. He sat in that position and thought about the hand for several more minutes.

When Sharon looked at the large timer near the directors' desk and saw that there were only three minutes left out of the fifteen allotted for each round, she began to fidget. Although Lou usually played fast once he worked out his strategy, she was worried about being late for the next round. She doodled on her scorecard, then looked pointedly at the clock and back at Lou.

"Sorry," Lou apologized. "I know I'm taking a long time." He studied the situation for another thirty seconds. Finally, he called for the first card to be played from the dummy, and then played the rest of the hand quickly.

When it was over, Sharon and Eva were back in contention. Sharon had preempted her three club bid on a six-card suit instead of seven, causing Lou to misjudge the distribution.

Lou shook his head in despair. "Well, at least you got your share of the good boards I've been giving away this afternoon," he said to the sisters.

"Yeah, I'd hate to see you lose out on our generosity," Jake said bitterly.

Eva and Sharon tactfully did not comment.

* * * * *

While the sisters were making their successful foray around the room, Tom Stanhope was making enemies. After being rude to all the North-South players he had played against so far, he outdid himself when he came to Jeffrey and Ralph's table.

He sat down and sneered. "Well, here we are, playing against Jessie and Rita. And how are the sweet boys doing today? I understand you had a gay old time when you won your national event."

Ralph was furious, but Jeffrey was unperturbed. "You could at least be more subtle, Tom," he said calmly. "You embarrass yourself more than anyone else with those asinine remarks."

"Wrong," his partner Cliff said. "He embarrasses *me* even more. If you're done with your juvenile insults, let's get on with the game." He was still angry at Tom over their earlier argument.

Jeffrey, in his unflappable manner, decided to make a psychic bid on the first hand. Ordinarily he would pass with the cards he held, but since Tom had been so insulting, Jeffrey decided it was a good time to confuse him and Cliff as much as possible. Such a tactical maneuver would usually be rejected by a good player, because it tends to leave everything to chance instead of skill.

The auction was short and simple. Ralph put his dummy on the table, and Jeffrey proceeded to play the hand. By the fifth trick, Tom and Cliff were exchanging frustrated glances. Then they glared at their opponents; they knew they'd been had:

North Deals

E-W Vul.

	Tom	Jeff	Cliff	Ralph
	West	**North**	**East**	**South**
		1♠	Pass	2♠
	Pass	Pass	Pass	

```
              ♠J8
              ♡532
              ◇J97
              ♣K10543
♠K1042                    ♠A953
♡AJ4        N             ♡K107
◇A865     W   E           ◇Q102
♣J8         S             ♣A76
              ♠Q76
              ♡Q986
              ◇K43
              ♣Q92
```

It was clear that Jeffrey's psychic bid had kept *them* from bidding and making a game in spades. Instead of scoring their own vulnerable game in spades, 620 points, they were defeating Jeffrey's non-vulnerable 2♠ contract seven tricks, for 350 points.

Never one to gloat, Jeffrey quietly put his cards back in the board when the hand was over. Ralph, pleased with Jeffrey's maneuver, couldn't keep a small grin from escaping.

"A cute bid from a cute little boy," jeered Tom. "You may think you're clever, but over the long run you'll lose. And just to make sure you don't pull that kind of stunt during the rest of the tournament, I'm calling the director to put it on record that you psyched. Director!"

Jennifer came to the table with her director's rule book in her hand. "What's the problem?" she asked.

"Jeffrey just psyched against us. I want it recorded."

"So noted. Jeffrey, now that you've made a psychic bid in this tournament and it's been recorded, be careful about doing it again. If you make any more psychics and Ralph figures out what you're doing each time, then it's no longer considered a psychic bid. You'll keep any bad result, and I as the director, or an appeals committee, will probably cancel any good one."

"I don't intend to psyche again; that was my psyche for the decade. It just seemed right for that hand," Jeffrey replied.

Tom and Cliff earned what looked like a better than average score on the second hand, but they weren't mollified. When the round was over, Tom said to Jeffrey, "Just let me play rubber bridge for high stakes for a whole evening against you, Pretty Boy. You wouldn't have a dime left."

Jeffrey gave him his most charming smile and winked. "Any time. I'll send a cab for you."

* * * * *

"Why don't you ever return my leads?" Alan Nestor screamed at Sybil. "I've told you and told you. Why don't you ever listen?"

"You've also told the whole room again," Sybil said, close to tears.

"Well, then, why can't you learn? Every time you stubbornly refuse to return the suit I lead, we get a bad result. You'd think after thirty-two years of this, you'd know what to do. You act like you don't want to win." Alan shoved his cards into the board. "Explain to me what you were thinking. Why did you shift to the spade when that couldn't possibly be right? Let me hear your reasoning ... if you have any."

"Poor Sybil," sympathized Sharon, who was sitting nearby. "It's interesting that Alan keeps asking why Sybil can't learn. You'd think *he'd* have learned by now that yelling at her destroys her game. I don't know why husbands and wives insist on playing together. Those partnerships almost always end up in a fight."

"Well, that's one way to eliminate a pair from the finals," Eva replied. "Now Sybil will be so upset, she'll blow the next three boards."

"Suits me. I wish we could get rid of the rest of the competition that easily."

"Maybe we should establish a Bridge Abuse Anonymous group," Eva mused. "BAA is even the appropriate acronym."

"I think we should give offenders three warnings and then, if they continue to be obnoxious, bar them from playing for six months," Eva said.

"We might not have enough people left to play. Looks like they're ready for us at the next table. I'm glad it's the last round coming up. I'm ready for a glass of wine and some food."

CHAPTER 7

As soon as they finished playing their last hand, Eva and Sharon went back to their rooms to get ready for dinner.

"How do you think we did this afternoon?" Eva yelled from her room.

"I'm pretty sure we were above average, even after that horrendous start. If we play as well tonight, we won't have any trouble qualifying for the finals." Sharon pulled off her warmup suit and flipped through the clothes in the closet. She put on her green wool pantsuit, but didn't like the way it fit. Those extra desserts *had* made a difference. She took it off and tossed it on the chair. After rummaging through her closet again, she finally settled on her black pantsuit. Thank God for slimming black.

Eva, in the next room, touched up her eye shadow. "Do you want to stop and see our score before we leave for dinner?" she asked. "It should be posted by now." Hurrying to get ready, she smudged her mascara and had to start all over again.

"No . . . I'd rather be surprised. If we didn't do well, I don't want to find out 'til after dinner. We'd better hurry if we're going to Salvatore's. I recommended it to several people. We need to get there before it gets too crowded with bridge players. Are you going to wear a coat?"

"No. I called the weather number. It's still in the seventies. I can't believe it's March. I'm sure my suit jacket will be warm enough. Are you almost ready? I'll go ahead and get the elevator. Hurry up."

"Be right there." Sharon looked around her room for her pocketbook, found it on the chair under her sweat suit, and ran down the hall to catch up with Eva before the elevator arrived.

* * * * *

When they entered Salvatore's, they weren't surprised to see that many of the other players had taken their advice. The sisters had a knack for finding the best restaurants when they traveled to bridge tournaments in other towns. People who knew them trusted their recommendations.

"Eva! Sharon!" Antonio Salvatore met the sisters at the door and gave each of them a hug. "I might have known you'd appear tonight when people came in and began arguing over bridge hands. A lot of the bridge players ate here during the Spring Championships, and I learned to recognize their special 'you hold' language. But I thought the tournament was over."

"There's a special two-day money game going on now, Tony," Eva told him. "When our friends asked us where to eat, we told them your restaurant was the best."

"No wonder you're my favorite patrons," Tony beamed. "Your first glass of wine is on me. And be sure to order the veal or lamb. It came in fresh today. Stay away from the beef."

"Thanks for the advice—and the wine," Eva said graciously. "We accept your offer, but we'd have told our friends about your place anyway."

After they were seated, Eva looked around to see who was there. Sybil and Alan were sitting two tables away under an imitation Tiffany lamp. The decor at Salvatore's was "uniquely Tony"—imported linen tablecloths on wobbly tables, K-Mart silverware with exquisite china, thick red carpeting that clashed with the disastrous silver foil wallpaper. The patrons didn't seem to mind; in fact, they were rather fond of the hodgepodge. As long as the food pleased their palates, no one cared how Tony decorated the place.

"I'm glad Sybil's still speaking to Alan after his outburst this afternoon," Sharon said. "She asked me where to eat. I'm surprised they didn't eat here last week during the tournament. I gave it a top rating on the restaurant list I put together." She paused. "Oh no ... Here come Tom and Cliff. Too bad I couldn't have hidden my list from them."

"I don't understand how Cliff can socialize with Tom," Eva said. "Being in his company all day at the bridge table would be more than enough for me. Cliff never struck me as either a martyr or a masochist."

"Did it ever occur to you he could simply be a nice person?"

Eva thought about if for a minute, then shook her head. "Nah."

As the hostess led Tom and Cliff toward their table, they passed the Nestors. "Well, if it isn't the happy couple," Tom said with a sneer. "I don't know why you play with her, Alan. Can't you find someone who can follow suit?"

Everyone in the room could hear Tom's insults.

"He really has a talent," Eva said. "He managed to humiliate both of them in twenty seconds. I'm sure no one will shed any tears if he's found guilty of cheating."

"It'll be tough on the other team members, though."

"And unlucky. What a way to lose the Vanderbilt."

* * * * *

Tom and Cliff had had many successful games in regional and national events, but Tom was irritating Cliff more and more. As soon as they had sat down, they began to argue. "Why do you take such perverse pleasure in offending everyone you talk to?" Cliff asked. "Can't you simply say 'hello' to people without insulting them?"

"Don't play 'holier than thou' with me, Cliff, just because I tell people the truth. After all," he said, lowering his voice, "you're the one who figured out how to cheat in the Vanderbilt."

Cliff, who'd been studying the menu, snapped his head up. "What do you mean? We played well and we won. That's all there is to it."

"Not so," Tom said. "I happen to know that you had information about those hands before we played them. And I can prove it."

Cliff stiffened. "Don't you *ever* say that in public or even mention it to me again. Remember, you can't expose me without putting your own reputation on the line."

"I realize that. I just want you to know I can produce enough evidence to prove you cheated. And you have a lot more to lose than I do. I'm just a bridge pro, but you're the CEO of your computer company. Knowing their CEO cheated probably wouldn't sit too well with your board of directors or your stockholders."

"Why are you threatening me like this? What do you hope to accomplish? I can't imagine you'd jeopardize your own chances to play in international competition."

"Of course not," Tom replied. "And I think your plan was ingenious. I just want you to be aware that you're not necessarily getting a free ride with our somewhat tainted victory."

"And you'd better bear in mind," Cliff retorted angrily, "if you decide to suddenly bare your soul, instead of absolution you'll no longer be able to get a job as a pro or even be able to play bridge. In your own world, you have as much to lose as I do, so don't threaten me." He picked up his menu and tried to find something that appealed to him, but his fury at Tom and his fear of exposure had ruined his appetite. The only thing he wanted to do was shove the menu down his partner's throat.

* * * * *

When the waiter came over to take the sisters' dinner order, Sharon said, "We've both decided to have another glass of red wine. I want the veal chop, medium rare, and Eva would like the lamb special. And by the way, don't worry about giving the men over there good service." She pointed to Tom and Cliff. "They never leave a tip."

* * * * *

After dinner, everyone returned to the hotel and gathered around the computer printouts to see their afternoon scores.

"Look at this," Sharon said when she was able to move through the crowd to see the results that were posted on the wall. "We did better than I thought. We were second in our section." She wasn't surprised to see that the Nestors had the lowest East-West score. And poor Lou was in last place North-South.

"Which pairs have the top scores in our section?" Eva asked.

"I don't recognize the names of the pair that beat us for the East-West top," Sharon said. "But look . . . Linda and Kathy beat Gary Alexander and Jonathan Meltzer for first place North-South. They must be thrilled, upsetting the top seeded pair. Let's go see how the people in the other section did."

They went to the other side of the room. Eva stretched up on her toes, trying to see over the players in front of her. Finally someone moved out of her way.

"Cliff and Tom won first place East-West in Section B," she told Sharon. "No surprise there. Ralph and Jeffrey won first place North-South. I don't envy them. It must get pretty boring to have win after win."

"Things won't be boring for anybody tonight. All the below-average pairs are going to do a lot of scrambling to make the cut. And we're going to scramble just as hard. I want to play in the finals."

"Wouldn't you rather win the thirty-five thousand first place in the consolation than nothing in the finals?" Eva asked.

For once in her life, Sharon didn't have a snappy retort. Finally she said, "That's not how I look at it."

Before Eva could ask what she meant, Kathy and Linda came into the ballroom. "Have you seen your score yet?" Sharon asked them.

"No. We just got back from dinner. Did you see how we did?"

"I didn't notice," Sharon said, not wanting to spoil their surprise. "Go look."

Linda's gleeful shriek said it all.

CHAPTER 8

At exactly eight o'clock, Ruth and David distributed the hand records for the evening session. While the contestants arranged their hands, the chairman of the committee hearing the Vanderbilt cheating allegations came into the room and found Jennifer. He stood with his back to the players while he talked to her, preventing them from either overhearing or lipreading his news. As soon as the contestants finished duplicating the hands, they looked at Jennifer expectantly.

Appreciating their mostly morbid curiosity, she quickly made her announcement. "Before you pass the boards to begin tonight's session, I want to let you know about the Vanderbilt Committee's decision. The results stand; the Stanhope team wins."

For once, the announcement of winners brought no cheers or congratulations. The roomful of players clearly favored the Alexander team, and most of them believed that some form of cheating had taken place.

At table three, where Tom and Cliff were playing against Jonathan and Gary, Tom couldn't hide his glee. "That'll teach you to accuse us of cheating," he gloated. "If I didn't feel so generous because of our win, I'd be talking to a lawyer about a slander suit. I don't like people trying to ruin our reputations with a frivolous complaint. In fact, I may still do just that."

Gary and Jonathan were too furious to answer, and not a little concerned about their legal exposure. Feeling more disappointed than surprised at the decision, even they recognized that the circumstantial evidence was too meager to convince a committee that cheating had occurred. All they could do at the moment to salvage any pride was to try to beat Tom and Cliff in this event.

They had a chance for a good result on the first board, but it was difficult to bid it to the optimum contract.

Jon	Tom	Gary	Cliff
West	**North**	**East**	**South**
1♠	Pass	2♠	Pass
Pass	Pass		

West Deals
N-S Vul.

♠9
♡AJ543
◇1074
♣KJ63

♠AJ5432   ♠Q1076
♡876   ♡2
◇A2   ◇K853
♣A7   ♣8542

N
W E
S

♠K8
♡KQ109
◇QJ96
♣Q109

When the dummy came down, Jonathan was sick. He could see that Gary had a "perfecto," and they simply hadn't bid enough. Their somewhat old fashioned methods, and Gary's conservative single raise, had kept them from even sniffing the potential of their combined holdings.

Although they had only seventeen points between them, they were cold for game, with an overtrick if the spade king was onside. What a miserable contract. Bidding two—making five. And against Tom and Cliff! It was exasperating. He'd rather beat them than qualify for the finals. He particularly hated giving them a tie for top. With the popularity of modern methods, he could hardly hope that many other contestants would have any difficulty bidding this hand to game.

The second hand didn't turn out any better for them. Gary over-thought the defense and ended up giving away an extra trick. When they left the table, Tom said scornfully, "I don't know how you two earned your reputations. A pair of novices would bid game on that first hand. Someone with your so-called skills should be able to investigate slam with those cards. It's a joke that you two are considered top players in this country."

Jonathan made a fist and swung his arm back, but Gary pulled him away. "Can't you see that's exactly what he wants you to do? Despite the Committee's verdict, he's under a cloud of suspicion—unless you do something to prove you're a hothead who might make a wild accusation! If you hit him, he'll get just what he wants."

"You're right," grumbled Jonathan through clenched teeth. He snapped his pencil in half. "I'd like to stop him from playing any way I can. He's the last person who should be representing the ACBL in international competition. It's an embarrassment."

"He'll probably be on his best behavior if his team makes it to international competition, assuming the WBF allows him to play." Gary said. "Besides, it's done. They're the winners, and there's nothing we can do about it."

"We'll see," muttered Jonathan.

* * * * *

A few rounds later, Linda and Kathy sat down to play against Tom and Cliff. Linda looked uncomfortable, but Kathy thought it was because playing against them intimidated her.

Linda really *was* scared, but not for the reason Kathy assumed. She was thinking about the conversation she'd had with Tom before the evening session started . . .

"Linda, would you please come over here?" Tom had asked after she examined her afternoon score. "I want to talk to you." He was standing near a window at the far end of the room.

Linda, still elated at her section top, bounced over to him and then suddenly stopped. He stood there with his arms folded, his tongue working furiously. He waited for a couple of minutes, enjoying her discomfort.

Finally he said, "When you sit down to play against us tonight, Cliff and I will get two tops. You had a good game this afternoon, and if you play as well tonight, you should be able to play in the finals tomorrow. You'll still have a chance to win enough to get yourself out of whatever mischief you're involved in. A couple of bad scores won't hurt you that much, considering you never had a chance at the jackpot anyway."

"You're crazy if you think I'm going to do that," she hissed, her face red with anger. "I haven't done anything wrong, so your blackmail won't work."

"It's your choice. If I'm not satisfied with our round against you, I'll be calling your bank in the morning. If you've done nothing illegal, there'll be nothing to worry about."

Linda was appalled. Not only did she owe the money that she'd stolen, now she would have to throw boards to Tom to keep from being exposed. And he might decide to report her anyway. She had to find a way to stop him ...

The animation Linda had shown after seeing her afternoon score had disappeared completely. With shoulders slumped, she refused to make eye contact with her partner or anyone else at the table. She detested the thought of giving Tom good boards, but was afraid not to give in to his demands. How was she going to let him get good results without it looking obvious? The only illegal activity she'd had any experience with so far involved embezzlement, and she didn't seem to be doing too well with that.

The players each pulled their hands for the first deal out of the plastic boards. As dealer, Linda made the obvious 1♡ opening bid, and Kathy gave her a limit raise. With minimum high cards but a singleton and prime values, Linda mulled over her problem for some time. Finally, she passed instead of bidding game.

West Deals
E-W Vul.

	Linda	Tom	Kathy	Cliff
	West	**North**	**East**	**South**
	1♡	Pass	3♡	Pass
	Pass	Pass		

♠K72
♡86
◇K752
♣KJ32

♠A63   ♠QJ5
♡K10975   **N**   ♡QJ32
◇AJ83 **W E** ◇1094
♣7   **S**   ♣A108

♠10984
♡A4
◇Q6
♣Q9654

As she fully expected, game was cold. At the end of the play, she apologized with apparent sincerity to her partner. "Sorry, it seemed right not to jeopardize our sure plus score. In a team event I'd have bid game like a shot. If you have any club honors other than the ace, game has no play."

Linda took some pleasure in this ruse. After such a plausible explanation, no one but Tom suspected a thing.

Defending on the next hand, Linda had a choice of reasonable leads between two suits. Her selection allowed Tom to make two extra tricks, but Kathy couldn't very well complain. Linda felt relieved that she had made the "right" lead.

As they got up to go play at the next table, Tom stared at Linda. He smirked, then said, "Must you leave so soon?"

Linda's fury neared its breaking point, but she kept her voice under tight control. "Don't be so smug, Tom. Eventually, I get even."

* * * * *

Eva and Sharon were not doing well that evening. Sharon had overbid on the first hand, and Eva on the second. The next few rounds were equally dismal.

"If we're going to qualify to play in the finals tomorrow, we'd better improve—and fast," Sharon said.

"It looks to me like we'll be in the consolation no matter what we do," Eva griped. "This game's going like all our games went last week. It's so damn discouraging. I thought we were over our bad luck streak. We need to do well on all the rest of the boards, but most of the East-West pairs coming up are strong players. Ralph and Jeffrey are next. Not much chance of getting tops from them."

"Don't you dare give up. Stand up and get a glass of water. Walk around until you change your frame of mind."

Realizing her sister was right, Eva walked across the room to the water cooler and brought back a glass of cold water for each of them. Maybe uprooting herself from her seat would help.

* * * * *

Since the sisters were usually cordial to their opponents, their perfunctory greetings to Ralph and Jeffrey slightly unnerved the men. They knew that if Eva and Sharon needed good results, they were likely to take outrageous chances with their bids.

They had reason to be wary, but they didn't realize yet how they'd be harmed. On the first hand, Sharon did exactly opposite of what they feared. Usually an aggressive bidder, Sharon chose to stay out of an odds-on slam, and she was right. The trumps broke badly and they could only make game. This time they would get a good result for being conservative.

"Congratulations on your section top this afternoon," Eva said to them, brightening up. "How's tonight's game going?"

"It was fine until we sat down at your table," Ralph grumbled good-naturedly.

"Well then, I imagine you can afford a bad board or two and still qualify. We need every point we can get tonight." Eva knew that she and Sharon had been lucky, not brilliant.

On the second hand, Eva and Sharon got another top, but this one was skillfully bid and played.

"Nicely done," Jeffrey said. "At least it's a little more palatable getting a zero by being outplayed."

"Thank you," Eva said, pleased. The praise had a remarkable effect. Her concentration improved, and their game rallied considerably.

* * * * *

Lou, one of the top pros in the country, was having one of the worst games of his career. He knew he had to do something extreme to stay in the main event. He decided to make his move when he and Jake arrived at Tom and Cliff's table.

"Evening, gentlemen," Lou said as he sat down.

As usual, Tom couldn't resist a chance to needle. "How come the big pro came in last in the section this afternoon? I must be wrong, thinking you know how to play this game."

"I've been saving up to get my good boards from you," Lou told him.

"After seeing your afternoon score, I'm not too worried."

Cliff couldn't stomach any more. "Tom, it's your bid."

			Tom	Lou	Cliff	Jake
West Deals			**West**	**North**	**East**	**South**
N-S Vul.	♠Q107		Pass	Pass	1♡	Pass
	♡4		2♣	Pass	2♢	Pass
	♢K542		2♡	Pass	Pass	Pass
	♣K9543					

♠KJ6   **N**   ♠A95
♡A976   **W E**   ♡KJ853
♢A109   **S**   ♢QJ76
♣J107   ♣Q

♠8432
♡Q102
♢83
♣A862

Cliff alerted the 2♣ bid as "Reverse Drury", showing a passed hand worth a limit raise in hearts; the 2◊ bid suggested a minimum opening bid but still some chance for game. Tom's 2♡ rebid denied serious game interest.

When Tom's hand, which was dummy, hit the table, everyone immediately saw that Tom had originally passed a full opening bid. Cliff, who held a mediocre but full opening bid himself, with careful play but every suit lying poorly, took just nine tricks. His opponents immediately smelled a rat.

Lou was livid. "No one passes a full opening bid unless he knows something about the hand ahead of time," he said angrily. "You must've heard someone discussing this hand or seen the results on a scorecard before the caddie picked it up. Otherwise, you never would've passed. Director!"

Jennifer came to the table. "What's wrong?"

Lou explained the situation to her. She looked at Tom's hand and asked why he'd passed.

"I simply chose not to open it," Tom said. "There's nothing in the rules that says you have to open every thirteen-point hand. I decided I didn't have a good rebid if I opened this particular hand, so I passed. And with my flat distribution I thought game would need some luck opposite a minimum opener."

"That doesn't fit your usual style," Jennifer told him. "I kibitzed when you were playing in the Vanderbilt, and I noticed that you didn't even pass any twelve-point hands. Your bidding style has always been aggressive. I've never seen you pass a hand like this."

"If you want these lessons, you all really ought to pay me for them. This is not a team event like the Vanderbilt, and bidding chancy games is bad strategy," Tom replied, annoyed. "And I resent the cheating insinuations."

Jennifer strongly suspected that he'd overheard something about the hand ahead of time, but she didn't know how she could prove it, a common problem when suspicious incidents have to be officially considered in isolation. "Enter the score. In the absence of evidence to suggest Tom or Cliff had unauthorized information, the result stands, but I'm going to make a record of what happened. Don't forget, Tom, you yourself made a big deal this afternoon when someone psyched against you, and the rules apply equally to psychic underbids and overbids. Lou and Jake are within their rights to request a committee if they view the internal evidence differently."

"I may do that," Lou said. "I don't see why we should let Tom get away with this kind of stuff. No wonder he wins so often."

"If you call a committee," Tom said, "you'd better be able to produce some evidence proving that I had information about that hand before we played it. I've had enough of everyone's accusations. I'm certainly entitled to pass when I want to."

Lou was fuming when he left the table. Jennifer came over and asked if he and Jake would like to protest her ruling. She rather hoped they would.

"I'm not going to call a committee," Lou finally decided. "How can I prove he knew about that board ahead of time? I'm really getting tired of the uncanny luck that attends his blatantly unorthodox actions. His smug answers annoy me, and I'm tired of seeing him get away with it. But I guess I'll have to hope the Recorder can do something about it."

CHAPTER 9

At the end of the evening session, most of the players knew whether or not they were going to make the cut. Lou, Jake, and the Nestors didn't even bother to wait for their scores. They, along with several other pairs, left the ballroom as soon as the game was over. The best they could hope for was to win the consolation.

While Sharon waited with Eva to get the final scores, she thought about Gary Alexander. She knew that he had a reputation for superb manners at the bridge table and that he was separated from his wife. She decided to find out how his manners were away from the table. She found him sitting alone reading a paperback mystery while he waited for the day's results.

"How was your game with Jonathan?" she asked. *Yuck...some opening line*, she thought. *He'll probably walk away in disgust.*

But Gary looked at her and smiled. "Sharon Price, isn't it? We had a decent game. I imagine we qualified. How about you?"

"We were hopeless when we started tonight, but our luck changed after we amazed Jeffrey and Ralph with our bidding and playing skills," Sharon said. "I like them, and I hope we didn't ruin their game, but we were desperate. We did well on the rest of the hands after we played them, so I'm pretty sure we qualified."

"Would you like to go to the bar and have a drink while we wait for the results?" Gary asked.

"Yes, I'd like that." *Bingo!* "Let me find Eva and tell her I'm leaving."

When Sharon told her sister where she'd be, Eva felt a momentary flash of jealousy. She wished she were the one anticipating an evening of fun, but she was also pleased to see Sharon looking so happy.

"After the scores are up, I'll come look for you in the bar and tell you how we did," Eva told her. "Enjoy yourself."

* * * * *

The bar, tastefully decorated with cherry panelling and discrete lighting, was nearly empty. Gary and Sharon sat down near a window with their backs to David Letterman and his guest. When the waitress arrived at their table, Sharon decided on a glass of pinot noir, and Gary asked for a Jack Daniels.

"I'm glad I'm finally getting a chance to talk to you," Gary said after the waitress had left. "I've seen you at several tournaments, but we've never had a chance to meet. Tell me about yourself."

"The usual get-acquainted stuff, or the real stuff?" Sharon asked.

Gary smiled. "Some of each—with more emphasis on the real stuff, please."

"Okay. I'll start with the routine part. No yawning! I'm a widow, like my sister Eva. Both of us have children who are grown up and married, so we're free to go to bridge tournaments whenever we please. When we're home, I write restaurant reviews. I don't dare show my face anymore in some of the restaurants I've reviewed, but since I wouldn't want to eat in them again anyway, I don't care. Eva spends her free time doing volunteer work for the Children's Hospital. She's nicer than I am—she's doing something for humanity."

"But look at all the people you save from eating bad food," Gary pointed out. "And you help keep the good restaurants in business."

The waitress was back. She put the whiskey in front of Sharon, and the wine in front of Gary. They politely

73

waited until she left, and then, grinning at each other, switched the drinks. After they lifted their glasses in a silent toast and took a drink, Gary asked, "Where do your children live?"

"My daughter lives in San Francisco, and my son's in Chicago. I'm always looking for tournaments in one of those cities so I can visit them. Well, that's all of this kind of chitchat that I can manage. I can never get past the 'chit-' part. Your turn."

Gary smiled at her. "You're a funny woman. Okay, I'll take care of the chat. I'm a fifty-six-year-old lawyer working for an indulgent law firm. They know I'll be away from my practice playing bridge fairly often but, happily for me, they keep me on their payroll. My wife and I separated three years ago. Neither of us has gotten around to getting a divorce yet, but we will eventually. I've been playing on the bridge circuit for a long while now, and the marriage couldn't survive all my absences. I have two sons and three grandchildren scattered around the country. The end."

"A very succinct autobiography," Sharon said. "Now that we know each other's intimate secrets, we can have a real conversation. I'm glad you asked me to join you tonight. I've seen you many times at tournaments, but Eva and I seldom play in the high-level events that you do—although we like tough competition."

"You should try playing in the Vanderbilt some time. I bet you'd acquit yourselves nicely."

"Maybe we'll get a team together and take you guys on next year."

"I look forward to it. Now, there's something else I've been wondering about. You two have quite a reputation for changing hotel rooms. There's a rumor that you moved four times when you arrived at the Summer Championships in Las Vegas, and never settled down till four-thirty in the morning."

"How did you hear about that?" Sharon asked, surprised.

"When Jonathan checked in the next morning, one of the bellmen was muttering about crazy bridge players. He said he moved luggage for two woman half the night. The person standing behind Jonathan had seen your act before. She said it could only have been you and Eva. Why on earth did you change so many times? What was wrong with all those rooms?"

"The first one was too close to the elevators."

"What's wrong with being close to the elevators?"

"They ding."

"'Ding'?"

"Yeah, 'ding'. Every time an elevator in a hotel stops to let someone on or off, there's a loud 'ding'. Sometimes you can hear the ding three rooms away. We like to sleep late in the morning when we're at tournaments, and we don't want any noisy elevators waking us up. Besides, people tend to talk while they're waiting for elevators. That wakes us up, too."

"Okay. You turned those rooms down. What was wrong with the next ones?"

"The air conditioner in Eva's room sounded like an airplane reversing engines after landing. Even the bellman had to agree with us. When we walked into that room and he heard the noise, he didn't even bother to unload the luggage. He was a fast learner. He just led us back to the registration desk."

"The desk clerk must have been happy to see your faces again."

"You're just as much of a quick study as the bellhop. When the woman who'd checked us in saw us coming, she suddenly found something urgent to do. So we had to explain the noise problem to a new person. He listened politely and then sent us to the two rooms farthest away from the elevators on another floor."

"I assume the air conditioning was quiet in the new rooms. Why didn't you keep them?"

"They were adjoining rooms, but not connecting. We were getting pretty tired by then—it was nearly four o'clock—so we called the front desk instead of walking back down there, and went through the whole rigmarole again. The hotel finally wised up and gave us what we asked for in the first place."

"Why didn't they just do that when you checked in?"

Sharon shook her head. "Beats me. I always feel like we're in the 'Twilight Zone' when we check into a hotel. Nobody ever *listens.* They give away all their connecting rooms for people who don't want them or need them—even when they receive special requests like ours months ahead. It really pisses me off."

"I think I'll call on you the next time I have trouble checking in. You seem to get what you want."

"Occasionally we're lucky. Someone reads our reservation forms and gives us what we ask for. Otherwise, it's just a matter of stamina. One more appearance at the registration desk defeats either them or us."

After they'd had a few more sips of their drinks, Eva and Jonathan came into the bar.

"I'm glad to see you're both smiling," Gary said. "It looks like we're going to be fighting each other for the hundred grand tomorrow. I hate to ask, but did Tom and Cliff qualify, too?"

"Unfortunately," Jonathan answered, frowning. "It's going to be one tough game tomorrow. High stakes and big egos. A lethal combination."

"Who's leading?" Sharon asked.

"Ralph and Jeffrey had the highest overall score for the day. They've been playing very well lately."

"Yeah, I've noticed," Gary said. "We should watch them. They might make a good addition to our team. Would you two like to celebrate our qualifying and join us for a drink?"

"No, thanks," Jonathan replied. "I didn't get much sleep last night. I'm going to rest up for tomorrow."

"Same for me," Eva said to her sister. "Don't stay up too late, Sharon."

When they were alone again, Gary said, "Now that we know each other so well, tell me something really *bad* about Sharon Price."

She thought for a moment, then said, "I have ordinary clavicles."

"Oh no! I've never admitted this to anybody, but at the top of my list of fetishes is an irresistible urge to gape at ordinary clavicles."

She grinned. "I might give you a peek if you tell me something bad about Gary Alexander."

"I'd gladly kill Tom Stanhope for stealing the Vanderbilt," he said promptly. "I'm sure he cheated."

She nodded slowly. "That's earned you a lengthy inspection."

CHAPTER 10

Kathy and Linda stopped Jeffrey and Ralph as they left the ballroom after the evening session to ask them a question about one of the hands they'd just played. Jeffrey launched into a long explanation about which line of play was technically better. When he finished, he turned to see if his partner agreed with his analysis, but Ralph had disappeared.

Jeffrey quickly said goodnight to the women. Then he looked in the bar and all around the lobby, but he couldn't find Ralph. He finally went up to their room—still no Ralph.

Jeffrey was puzzled; Ralph had never done anything like this before. He turned on the television set, absentmindedly switching channels. A half hour later, when Ralph still hadn't shown up, Jeffrey became annoyed. He desperately wanted to know where his friend was, but he didn't want to appear too eager to find him. It seemed to him that Ralph had been acting worried about their relationship lately. How could he have the nerve to pull a stunt like this?

Jeffrey waited another thirty minutes, then decided to go search for Ralph. He took the elevator to the lobby and skulked around the bar and playing area. He really didn't want Ralph to know how upset he was, but couldn't stop himself from looking for him. Finally, disgusted and angry, he returned to their room. It was still empty.

* * * * *

By the time Jennifer finished tabulating all the scores and putting the supplies away, she was exhausted. She waved goodnight to Ruth and David and wearily headed toward her suite. Gary and Sharon entered one of the elevators just ahead of her, but the door closed before she could get them to hold it for her. She sighed. It was nearly 1:30. Herb had a key to the suite, but she almost hoped he wouldn't be there. All she wanted to do was sleep.

She pushed the up button for the elevator and leaned tiredly against the wall, idly wondering if the woman entering the ladies' room was Kathy. Kathy should have left the hotel nearly an hour ago. Maybe she'd stayed around to have a drink with someone—providing he paid the bill.

The elevator finally arrived, and Jennifer gratefully put her key in the slot for the concierge floor. When she reached her suite, she quietly opened the door and went through the living room to the bedroom. Herb was sitting up in bed. Scattered all over the bedspread were papers from his latest investigation into the burning of abortion clinics. He looked so pleased to see her that she felt guilty about the mixed feelings she'd had on the way to the room.

"How'd it go?" he asked.

"Surprisingly well. There were the usual hassles, and one upsetting episode with Tom tonight. Lou was pretty sure that Tom knew something about one of the hands before he bid it. I think Lou was right, but it's hard to prove something like that. Tom's always just clever enough to avoid anything that's clearly illegal."

He grinned at her. "It's time for us to do something illegal."

Jennifer, who was sitting on her side of the bed, leaned over and hugged Herb. "I'll shower while you clear the bed." She got up and began discarding her clothes on the way to the bathroom.

Herb leaped out of bed and stopped her. "Shower in the morning."

"What about all your papers on the bed?"

"Don't worry about them."

He never did find three of those pages.

* * * * *

Just before 3:00 a.m., Eva awakened to a strange sound.

"Damn," she muttered when she realized it was the fire alarm. This was the third time a fire alarm had gone off and disturbed her sleep at tournaments over the past two years. Probably false like the others, but she was afraid to ignore it.

"Sharon," she called through the connecting door.

"Yes," came the muffled reply. "I'll be with you in a minute."

Eva was amazed to get an answer. "You're back?" She was so surprised, she momentarily forgot about the fire alarm.

"I thought I'd better get some sleep so we'd have a chance in tomorrow's game," came the reply through the door. "I was just getting ready to put my nightgown on. The only good thing about the alarm going off now is that I'm still dressed."

"If you're not going out in your nightgown, I'm not either. Wait for me while I get dressed."

"Eva! It's a fire alarm. You don't have to look your best. We have to get out of here. Fancy clothes won't count if we burn to death. Move!"

"Well, at least let me put on some lipstick."

* * * * *

"You might know we'd be on the twelfth floor," Eva grumbled as they made their way down the staircase. "From now on I'm going to ask for rooms on one of the lower floors. Wait for me, Sharon. I can't see."

"Where are your glasses?"

"You kept hurrying me, and I didn't have time to put my contact lenses back on. It's bad enough I have to go out in my nightgown and bathrobe, but I'm certainly not going to be seen in my glasses. I wasn't all dressed up at three in the morning like some people."

"Not my fault," Sharon said. "You just didn't bother to find anyone interesting. What was wrong with Jonathan?"

"Too old. Too stuffy. And mostly too uninterested in me. When we left the bar, he made it clear that he wanted to go to sleep alone. So I went up to my room and read. I was just falling asleep when I heard the alarm. Hey! What was that? I'm getting wet. And there are puddles on these steps."

"The sprinkler system must have turned on," Sharon said. "Damn! My clothes and shoes are getting soaked."

Eva looked at Sharon. "I'm sure glad I'm in my bathrobe and slippers."

When they finally made it down all the flights and walked outside through a back door, they found themselves in the large parking lot behind the hotel, surrounded by bridge players. There were also a few tourists and businessmen milling around.

"I don't see any smoke or flames coming out of the hotel," Sharon said. "The hottest thing I see are Jennifer and Herb. They sure look like they dressed in a hurry. Jennifer's bathrobe is inside out."

"They're walking over to us," Eva said. "I don't know if it would be kinder to point that out or not."

"Not."

"I'm glad to see you escaped the big conflagration," Herb said when they reached the sisters. Everyone looked back at the hotel, but there wasn't even one wisp of smoke.

"I'm really tired of these false alarms in the middle of the night," Eva complained, running her fingers through her wet hair. "Next time an alarm rings, I'm staying in the room."

"What if it's a real fire next time?" Herb asked.

"I'll take my chances. Right now, I'd rather burn than go through this again." She squeezed the water out of her slippers, then tried to get her feet back into them. The slippers felt soggy and tight. She gave up in disgust.

"Congratulations on your qualification," Herb said, trying to take Eva's mind off her misery. "The locals are proud of you."

"Thanks," she responded rather curtly. She was in no mood for polite conversation. She looked around to see if there were any items worthy of her attention. "I wonder who that is sleeping against the wall of the grocery store next door," she said to Sharon. "The light is dim, but doesn't that look like Tom? Why would anyone choose to go over there alone and settle down next to a smelly dumpster? If I didn't know him so well, I could almost feel sorry for him."

"But you do know him well," Sharon said, unsympathetically. "He's probably drunk too much again. It's a good place for him. The only better place for him would be *in* the dumpster. I hope he stays there until we go back in the hotel. I'm too tired to put up with more of his sarcasm tonight."

Eva continued to look around for something to interest her. "Look over there," she said, pointing to the row of cars in the farthest end of the parking lot. "Isn't that Linda Mason driving away in her BMW? What on earth is she doing at the hotel at this hour? And there're the Nestors standing next to that blue Cadillac holding hands. I guess she doesn't hold a grudge. I wouldn't talk to him for three weeks if he yelled at me that way."

"Neither would I," Sharon agreed. "But their marriage has lasted all these years, and they seem happy enough away from the bridge table, so maybe she knows what she's doing. Or maybe it's none of our business."

Eva gave her a sharp look. "That doesn't sound like you, Sharon. Since when don't you want to know what's going on everywhere?"

Before Sharon could answer, Gary and Jonathan joined the group. Eva saw the glow on Sharon's face when Gary came over, and understood her sister's distraction. She wondered if she ought to remind Sharon that Gary was still married.

Over on the other side of the parking lot, Ralph and Jeffrey were arguing.

"Where were you?" an infuriated Jeffrey asked. "I looked all over for you after the game. I finally fell asleep. I didn't even hear you come in."

"I had something to take care of," Ralph told him.

"What do you mean you 'had something to take care of'? What kind of answer is that? You disappear for several hours, and that's all you're going to say? That's it?"

"Yes," said Ralph, and changed the subject. "Eva and Sharon are over there. Let's go talk to them."

Jeffrey wanted to know more, but feared to ask. He'd already sounded too curious. This was not how their relationship was supposed to work. He didn't like it at all. Putting his hands in his bathrobe pockets, he stomped off after Ralph.

"Anyone have any cards?" Ralph asked when they joined the other players in the parking lot. "We could get a couple more people and play a team game right here. Cliff and Lou could join us. And if we're real quiet, maybe we won't attract Tom's attention. It looks like he fell asleep over there by the dumpster."

"You want to play cards at 3:30 a.m.?" Herb asked.

The bridge players stopped their conversations and looked at Herb as if he were crazy. Jennifer laughed.

"You should realize by now that bridge players will play anywhere, anytime," she told Herb. "Why is this night different from any other night?"

Eva yawned. "I'm tired and damp and uncomfortable. If they keep us out here much longer, we really *will* be playing tomorrow's game in the parking lot. I need to sleep."

A few minutes later, a hotel functionary gave the all-clear signal. A second voice announced that someone had tossed a cigarette into a wastepaper basket, causing a small fire that activated the sprinklers. The fire was out, and they could all return to their rooms.

No one bothered to attempt to wake Tom.

CHAPTER 11

The next afternoon, the contestants slowly dragged themselves into the game. Everyone looked exhausted.

"At least no one has the advantage of getting much sleep," Sharon said. "Except for Kathy and Linda, everyone else is staying here at the hotel, so the fire alarm kept all of us up. What an equalizer! And since, for some unknown reason, Linda was here last night too, that just leaves Kathy as the only one of us who got any rest."

"I wouldn't worry about Kathy," Eva said. "She was probably up half the night counting her money."

* * * * *

Jennifer had arranged for the consolation and the finals to be played on opposite sides of the ballroom. The contestants would play the same hands, but the tables in each event would be far away from each other, substantially reducing the chances for—accidentally or deliberately— passing unauthorized information. It was impossible to stop all the conversation about the hands, but at least the bid boxes had arrived.

Jennifer was relieved to see them. If Charles had had them here yesterday, as he should have, Tom might not have produced that very questionable pass in first seat the previous evening. She was sure he'd overheard someone discussing that hand.

* * * * *

"I'm glad to see they finally got the bid boxes," Eva said as she watched the caddies place them on the tables. "Now, at least some people won't have the advantage of voice inflections. I'm tired of coping with people who pass information when they bid aloud."

"There are always ways to cheat—even with the bid boxes," Sharon replied. "Haven't you seen some players slap their bidding cards down for special emphasis? Still, the boxes are a great improvement."

Eva yawned. "I've never seen so many people look so zonked. It's too bad we have to play for such high stakes when we're exhausted. I don't know how I'm going to concentrate."

"Me neither," Sharon said. "At least you got some rest before the fire alarm went off."

Eva glared at her sister. "Thanks for reminding me that *I* didn't have anything better to do."

Sharon got a sheepish look on her face. "Whoops. I guess that wasn't too tactful. I only meant that at least one of us got a chance to rest. Sorry."

"Forget it," Eva said, relenting. "Let's find our table and sit down. I don't want to argue with you. I need to conserve what little energy I have."

* * * * *

By 1:00, all the contestants except Tom were sitting in their places. Cliff went out to the hallway several times to look for his partner, but there was no sign of him. He dialed Tom's room twice from the house phones, but no one answered.

Finally, Jennifer walked over to Cliff's table. "I'm sorry," she said, "but we have to start the game on time. If Tom isn't here after everyone finishes duplicating the boards, I'll have to penalize you. The rules for the money game state that a partnership will lose one quarter of a board for every five minutes someone's late after the game starts."

"I can't imagine where he is," Cliff fretted.

"Well, it'll be about ten minutes before the boards are ready. You do his share of duplication, and maybe he'll show up by then." Jennifer went out in the hall to look for Tom, but the hall was empty.

* * * * *

While the contestants duplicated the boards, a man wearing a blazer with the hotel crest on the breast pocket and a slender woman in a smart navy blue suit came through the double doors of the ballroom. They spotted Jennifer at the directors' desk and went over to speak to her.

The man made the introductions as Jennifer stood up to greet them. "I'm Ron Albright, the hotel security agent, and this is Detective Vivian Greene. She's with the Virginia Beach Police Department. We're looking for Jennifer Brandon."

When Jennifer confirmed that they had found the right person, Vivian flashed her badge with her left hand and stuck her right arm out sharply for a firm, quick handshake. Jennifer guessed that Vivian was in her late thirties or early forties. There was very little gray showing in her shiny brown hair, and few wrinkles to be seen behind her designer glasses.

"I understand you're the person in charge of this game," Vivian said in a clipped voice when the introductions were completed.

"Yes, I am," Jennifer replied. "What's wrong?" She had a dreadful feeling that she knew exactly what was coming.

"There's no easy way to say this," Vivian said, "so please forgive me for being blunt. One of your contestants has been found dead."

Although she suspected that she would hear something like that, Jennifer felt queasy. "It must be Tom Stanhope.

He's the only one who didn't show up for the game. What happened to him?"

"When the owner of the grocery store next door took out some garbage early this morning," Ron said, "he found Stanhope near the dumpster. He thought the man might be sleeping off a drunk, so he shouted at him to get out of there. When he got no response, he called the Virginia Beach Police. As soon as the police arrived, they confirmed that Stanhope was not only dead but had been murdered."

"Murdered?" Jennifer felt her heart rate kick up a notch.

Vivian said, "The patrol officer who was first on the scene saw a bullet hole in the front of his shirt. The officer called Homicide, and I caught the case."

Jennifer felt shaky. She sat down and took a couple of deep breaths.

"Are you all right?" Vivian asked.

"I'll be okay. I just need a few minutes to absorb all this. It seems so unreal."

When Jennifer had regained some of her color, Vivian said, "Mr. Albright mentioned that the fire alarm had gone off last night. I wonder if you could tell me what happened."

Jennifer nodded. "As soon as the alarm rang, everyone evacuated the hotel. Tom was propped against the wall at the grocery store by the time I got to the hotel parking lot. We all saw him there, but everyone assumed he was drunk, which would not be out of character for him. Do you suppose he was already dead?"

"I have no way of knowing that yet," Vivian answered, "but I wouldn't be surprised. We'll have more information about the exact time he died after the coroner examines the body. Our technicians are out in the parking lot now. They've blocked off the area and are searching the grounds. Are you sure it was Tom Stanhope you saw against the wall?"

"I can't be positive, but it looked like him. There were only a couple of dim lights over there, but the person sitting there had on a bright yellow shirt like the one Tom wore yesterday. As far as I know, no one went over to talk to him."

"Why didn't someone wake him up to go back to his room after the all-clear announcement? I would think his partner would at least have checked to make sure he was all right."

"Detective, you're going to find out soon enough everyone was happy to let that sleeping dog lie. I think we were all afraid that if he were awake he'd be harassing somebody," Jennifer said. "He wasn't too popular with the bridge group."

"I'll need to hear more later about why he was disliked in the bridge world. Right now, we're trying to determine if anyone besides a bridge player might have killed Tom. His wallet was still in his pocket—with the money in it—so I doubt it was a routine mugging. We're running his name and fingerprints through our computers to see if he had any connection with drug dealers or anyone else related to crime locally."

"If you can't find any connection between Tom and someone in town, what's your next step?"

"We'll have to interview all the bridge players in your game."

"It'll be a disaster if you interrupt the play," Jennifer said. "This is a special game. Usually bridge players play for masterpoints, but this time they're also playing for money. This is the final day of the competition, and there's a huge amount of cash at stake. I know you need answers, but please, can you work around our schedule?"

"We'll do our best, but it's going to be hard to keep the game from being interrupted. I understand some local reporters and photographers are already on their way over."

"How is that possible? How'd they find out about it so fast?"

"Police use radios and the media all have scanners," Vivian shrugged. "When news of a homicide comes over the air, they get on the story right away."

"I don't see how anyone will be able to concentrate on bridge if reporters are allowed to come into the playing area," Jennifer said. "Is there any way you can keep them from disturbing the game?"

"We can try. I'll ask the reporters and photographers to talk to the players and to take pictures outside the ballroom only. Ron can use his authority as hotel detective to keep them out of here for now. At least we have the backing of the city fathers. In the past, when there have been murders in the area, they've urged reporters to keep any adverse publicity to a minimum whenever possible. They don't want to lose any future conventions because people think it's unsafe to come here. We'll do our best, but we can't stop them from publishing the story."

"I realize that, and I appreciate whatever you can do to help us," Jennifer said. "What's next?"

"The hotel management is setting up a room where we can question the bridge players. I can start the questioning with those of you who aren't playing bridge. I'll come back here after we get situated and begin with you. Who else will I be able to question without interrupting the game?"

"You can talk to the other directors, and to Charles Canning. His company is sponsoring this event."

"That should keep me busy for awhile. How long will the afternoon session last?"

"It should be over between 4:30 and 5:00."

"Okay. We'll wait until the game breaks up before we do the rest of the interviews. Maybe by then we'll have a local suspect and we won't have to bother the players."

"I certainly hope so! And thanks for being considerate of our schedule. There's another problem you ought to know about. Very few of the contestants in this game are local players. Most of the people are planning to leave tomorrow. What if you haven't solved the murder by then?"

"We may have to ask some of them to stay longer," Vivian replied. "We'll worry about that later. For now, please let everyone know what's happened as soon as you can. And one more thing. The game of bridge stymies me.

Do you know of anyone who can sit in on the questioning and help me ask intelligent questions? It would also help if that person could give me a little background on the players."

"You might try Herb Kramer. He's a private investigator who knows a little about the game and has met several of the people here. He's a friend of mine, but I don't think that'll cause any problems or interfere with his judgment." She handed Vivian a card. "Here's his office number, if you want to call him."

"Thanks. I appreciate it. I'll get back to you as soon as I can. I'm off to see the hotel management to find out what they've arranged for us."

Jennifer briefly wondered if it were smart to introduce the attractive detective to the eligible investigator. She wished she'd noticed if Vivian wore a wedding ring on her left hand.

* * * * *

After Vivian left, Jennifer sat down at the directors' table and tried to figure out how to break the news of Tom's murder to the bridge players. She concluded that there was no subtle way to do it. Suddenly she noticed how quiet the room was; everyone was waiting for her to start the game. There was no time left to figure out clever phrases. She stood up and asked for their attention.

"Before we begin, I have an important announcement," she intoned. "Tom Stanhope was found dead this morning, and the police believe he was murdered. Assuming no suspect is caught this afternoon, the police department will question everyone here. A room is being set up nearby for that purpose. The questioning will take place between sessions and, if necessary, after the game is over tonight. The first interviews will take up most of the dinner hour, so we'll start the game at 8:30 tonight instead of 8 o'clock. That way, everyone will have a chance to eat.

"Since we obviously don't have any precedent for handling a situation like this, I guess I'll have to make up my own rules. It'll be a few minutes before we can start the game, because I'll have to find a substitute for Tom. If there are any kibitzers in the room who would like to play as Cliff's partner, please come and see me. If any of the original standbys are here and would still like to play, we'll consider you first. There'll be no entry fee for the substitute.

"There's one other thing. I understand that there are photographers and reporters in the hallway outside the ballroom. If you talk to them, you may be quoted in tomorrow's paper or be seen on television. If you prefer not to speak to them, you can tell them 'no comment.' It's your choice."

There were mixed reactions to Jennifer's announcement. Those who didn't know Tom well looked genuinely disturbed.

* * * * *

"Well, that puts us closer to the one hundred thousand," Kathy said. She didn't notice how frightened Linda Mason looked.

* * * * *

Jeffrey couldn't hide his satisfaction when he said to Ralph, "Imagine that! Someone hated him more than we did. Or at least someone else had more courage."

"It couldn't have taken much in the way of courage to exterminate that toad," Ralph said. "I wish I had done it."

"How do we know you didn't?" Jeffrey asked. "What will I tell them when they ask if you were with me last night? After all, you *did* disappear for a couple of hours."

"You know very well I didn't kill him. And I'm not going to tell you where I was." It suddenly occurred to Ralph that

Jeffrey might be jealous. The thought pleased him immensely.

* * * * *

"I wonder how Tom's death will affect the Vanderbilt results," Gary said to Jonathan.

"Can't do anything but improve them," Jonathan told him with a satisfied smile. "I guess the rest of Tom's team will still be considered the winners, but they'll have to find a replacement for him. I wonder if they'd consider adding both of us and making it a five-man team."

"I'm sure they know we're available," Gary said.

"Too bad someone didn't murder him before the Vanderbilt," Jonathan continued happily. "Or last year. Or ten years ago."

"Try not to sound so pleased. Someone may think you did it."

* * * * *

Lou looked around nervously. Everyone had heard how angry he was yesterday when Tom passed that opening bid. He'd even muttered some threats against Tom. Now he would have to suffer through a lot of questioning and possibly by skeptical detectives. May, his wife, was angry enough before this happened. If he were detained, she'd never forgive him.

* * * * *

"This is awful," Charles Canning said to Ruth and David. "This is *not* the kind of publicity Century expected. I know they're going to fire me."

* * * * *

"I'm glad to see that Tom finally made the Zen leap from pass to passing on," Sharon said.

* * * * *

While the contestants reacted to Tom's death in their various ways, Detective Vivian Greene sat by herself in the room that the hotel had provided as a temporary field headquarters, and stared at the phone. It was time to find out if anyone local had had any criminal connections with Tom, but she didn't relish having to speak to that pompous Captain Blake again.

She wondered why she felt so hurt. She'd never cared that much for Blake. But to get dumped for that non-entity Charlene in the records department was humiliating. Blake thought he could make up for it by putting her in charge of her first case. Some favor. He'd given her the dubious opportunity of coping with a card game she didn't understand, and the chance to solve a murder case in which all the suspects were getting ready to leave town!

To hell with him. She sat up straighter in her chair and dialed headquarters. After identifying herself, she waited to be put through to the Detective Division, hoping Blake wouldn't answer. After her initial interview with Jennifer, she'd already asked him for a consultation fee for Herb—which he reluctantly granted after she pointed out that none of the investigators in the department had any knowledge of bridge.

With relief, she heard Detective Donnelly's voice.

"Hi, Viv. How's it going? I wish I could spend my afternoons in a plush hotel."

"Right now, I'd be happy to trade places with you. I haven't the vaguest idea what the game of bridge is all about."

"I hear you conned Blake into paying someone to keep you informed."

"I didn't want to ask the favor, but there was no way I could get anywhere without an interpreter. Have you made any connection between Tom and anyone local?"

"Not a thing. There's no evidence that he was involved with any criminals or criminal activity in the area."

"I was afraid that would be the answer. I guess I'll have to look at his murder from the bridge perspective."

"Good luck."

"Thanks. I'm afraid I'll need it."

CHAPTER 12

Cliff, totally disoriented from the news of Tom's death, leaned against the directors' desk. His expert partner—with whom he shared over 100 pages of notes on bidding and defense, representing an investment of ten times as many hours of discussion and study—had been murdered, and now he was expected to find a replacement among these amateurs.

Four people had answered Jennifer's appeal for a substitute. Dr. Kingsley, who had been kibitzing Ralph and Jeffrey, was the only one of the original standby players still around. Cliff quickly agreed to play with him. He didn't care who sat across the table from him; he just wanted to get through this nightmare.

Dr. Kingsley was thrilled to get such an outstanding partner. He was also terrified.

* * * * *

Detective Vivian Greene returned to the ballroom an hour after the game began and found Jennifer.

"We'll be meeting in Room 111," she reported brusquely. "The hotel personnel are setting it up. I took your suggestion and called Herb. He's agreed to help me. I even persuaded Captain Blake to pay him a small consultant's fee."

"Great. I think you'll be pleased with Herb. He's a superb investigator. He pays attention to small details and is a good listener. Not much gets by him. What's next?"

"This would be a good time to question you, if you're not too busy. The reporters are out in the hall, and I'd rather not have them overhear us. Room 111 isn't ready yet, so let's grab a couple of extra chairs and go over by the windows. We can talk privately there."

"That's fine," Jennifer agreed. "This is a good time for me; everything's calm in here. I'm sure it won't be this peaceful much longer." She asked David and Ruth to take over for a few minutes.

They went over to the far end of the room and sat down. Vivian opened her notebook and looked at Jennifer. "What can you tell me about Tom Stanhope?" she asked in a low voice. "You implied before that he wasn't too popular. Did he have any enemies?"

"I'll say! You couldn't have a more ideal victim. If anything, you're going to have too many suspects. Tom insulted everyone he talked to—including several people at the national tournament last week. And he didn't let up at this game. Even Cliff Bryce, his partner, seemed to be losing patience with him."

"Do you spell Bryce with an 'i' or a 'y'?" Vivian interrupted as she looked up from her notes.

"With a 'y'. Tom and Cliff were on the team that won the Vanderbilt—a prestigious team game held last week—but some of the members of the losing team accused them of cheating. A committee met to consider the accusations, but concluded that there wasn't enough evidence to find them guilty. That left Tom's team the winner. That verdict wasn't popular—with the losers or anyone else."

"Are the losers playing in this game?"

"Some of them. Gary Alexander and Jonathan Meltzer are here. They looked angry when I announced the committee's decision yesterday—but that doesn't mean I think they killed him," she added quickly.

"Was there anyone else in the money game who was upset with Tom?"

"There are at least two others that I know about," Jennifer said. "One of the professional players, Lou Turner, had an argument with Tom at the table last night. Tom took a very unorthodox action that was suspiciously successful, and Lou was furious. He called me to the table for a ruling.

"When I looked at Tom's cards, I agreed with Lou that the bid wasn't consistent with Tom's style. He usually opens hands with a very light point count, but this time he passed a full opening bid. I realize you don't understand bridge, but that pass just didn't fit his bidding pattern. I couldn't rule against him, though; I had no proof that he'd cheated. I guarantee that if Tom had lived, his actions would have been monitored the next few times he played. He'd been involved in too many questionable incidents lately. But we needed actual proof of his cheating to bar him from playing, and we didn't have that."

"Then so far, it looks like Gary, Jonathan, and Lou were all upset with Tom over cheating. I don't know enough about bridge to know if losing to someone who cheated would be a strong enough motive for murder."

"It's certainly possible," Jennifer said. "Bridge players are the most competitive people I know; the dedicated ones have a passion for the game. Some of them give up their families, jobs, and friends to pursue the game. But so far, I've never heard of anyone murdering an opponent over cheating."

"Did Tom upset anyone else?"

"I didn't hear the conversation," Jennifer said, "but I saw him talking to Linda Mason before the evening session started. She's a local player who works in a bank. Even though I was across the room, it was obvious that she was upset about something. I wanted to go over to see if I could do anything for her, but it was too close to game time, and I was busy. You'll have to ask her what happened."

"What did you do last night?" Vivian asked.

Jennifer blushed at the thought of the true answer to that, and quickly gave something less than the whole truth to hide her embarrassment. "I stayed in the ballroom with

Ruth and David and helped them finish scoring the game. Then we seeded the qualifying players for the final."

"Did you see anyone?"

"Sharon Price and Gary Alexander had just gotten on the elevator, but the door closed before I could reach it. I saw someone going into the women's room off the lobby while I was waiting for the next elevator. She looked a little like Kathy Jensen, but I don't know why she'd still have been here at that hour. She lives in town and isn't staying at the hotel. Maybe it was just the flowered dress that the woman was wearing that made me think it was Kathy."

"Anything else?"

"There was one curious thing," Jennifer said. "Right after the fire alarm rang and we reached the parking lot, I saw Linda Mason driving away from the hotel. Linda's staying at her home, so I don't understand what she'd be doing here so late. A bunch of the bridge players gathered together in the parking lot and joked about setting up a bridge game. Then someone made the all-clear announcement, and we gratefully went to bed. That's really all that I can tell you."

"What time did you say the game will be over this afternoon?" Vivian asked.

"Somewhere between four-thirty and five o'clock."

"Okay. I'm going to go back to Room 111 now. I asked Herb to meet me there so we can get acquainted. And I want him to meet Officer Rollins, who'll be helping me."

"Then what?"

"I'd like to question Charles Canning next. After we interview him, we'll talk to Ruth and David, if you can spare them."

"That'll be fine—if you don't need to see them together. I can work with just one other director on the floor for a short time. Tell Charles to come back here after you're done with him, and I'll send Ruth in first. Anything else?"

"I'll need a list of all the players in the money game."

Jennifer nodded. "I'll prepare that right now and send it in with Ruth."

* * * * *

When Vivian returned to room 111, she found Herb waiting for her. She gave him her quick, efficient handshake and introduced him to Patrolman Rollins, a short, balding man whose face seemed to wear a permanently puzzled expression. More than one lawbreaker had unsuspectingly confided too much to the innocent-looking, veteran beat cop.

"I'm glad you agreed to help me," she told Herb, after the introductions. "The game of bridge totally baffles me."

Herb laughed. "I'm only one step ahead of you. I guess I do have the advantage, though, of Jennifer's familiarity with most of the players here. Apparently there's always tons of gossip in the bridge world, and Jennifer hears a lot of it. I feel like I know several of the players just from listening to her."

"Good. That should help."

"Before we start questioning the suspects," Herb said, "what can you tell me about the murder?"

"I'm waiting for the official report, but I can tell you what I *think* happened. I think Tom was shot with a twenty-two or twenty-five caliber handgun. It appears that the bullet went directly into the heart, killing him instantly. I don't know how many murder investigations you've done as a PI, but you probably know that when the heart stops pumping, the bleeding stops almost immediately."

"Whatever blood was produced simply spilled into the chest cavity. Since gravity causes the blood remaining in the veins and arteries to settle in the lowest part of the body, with the body propped up against the dumpster, very little would leak out around the wound. That's why there was very little blood around the body. It would have been difficult for the people in the parking lot to tell from a distance that he was dead last night. According to Jennifer, it was fairly dark over by the dumpster. Stanhope just looked like he was sleeping, or more likely drunk."

"That's what we all assumed. Do you know if that's where he was killed?"

"Not yet. The technicians are still examining the area. They'll let us know what they find as soon as they can."

"Where do you want me to sit during the questioning?" Herb asked.

They turned their attention to the room. The hotel management had furnished them with a beautiful redwood desk—and then had spoiled the effect with worn plastic green and yellow chairs.

"I wonder where they dug these up," Vivian muttered. "I think you should sit next to me behind the desk," she said to Herb. She picked up one of the chairs and placed it next to hers. "Ron Albright will escort the bridge players into and out of the room. Officer Rollins will sit behind me where he can quietly observe their expressions and gestures."

"Do you want me to do any of the questioning?" Herb asked.

"I'll ask the routine questions, but either of you should feel free to interrupt at any time. Now, unless there's anything else, I'm going to ask Ron Albright to send Charles Canning in."

* * * * *

Charles, ashen and shaking, stumbled into the room and immediately burst into a nervous dialogue. "I don't know what to do. I wanted publicity, but a murder is outrageous. I didn't want *that* kind of publicity." He placed his gangly frame down on one of the green chairs, completely covering it.

"I don't think you ought to be too worried about the publicity," Vivian said. "It should benefit your company."

"That depends," Charles replied anxiously. "If the public thinks about bridge products every time Century Bridge Supplies is mentioned on the news, it'll be great. But if they associate *murder* with Century, we're finished. No one will buy our products, and I'll be fired." He suddenly noticed how uncomfortable the chair was and squirmed around, trying to fit himself into it.

"I understand your concern, but I imagine that almost any publicity will be good for you. Now, we don't have a lot of time, so let's begin. How did you spend yesterday evening?"

"I came down from my room at the beginning of the session to see how the game was going. I stayed until about eight-thirty and then went to the hotel restaurant for dinner."

"Did anyone join you?" Vivian asked.

"No. I ate alone. Look, I have my dinner receipt," he said, pulling it from his pocket. He had obviously come prepared. "You can check with the waiter to confirm that I was there."

"I don't have any doubts," Vivian assured him. "What did you do when you finished your dinner?"

"I went back and checked on the game."

"What time was that?"

"A little after ten o'clock. Everything was running smoothly, and I was tired, so I went back to my room. I read for a little while, watched the eleven o'clock news, and then went to bed. I slept until I heard the fire alarm go off. I got out of the hotel as fast as I could."

"When you arrived in the parking lot, did you talk to anyone?"

"No. I saw most of the bridge players there, but I'm not too social at that hour of the morning. I went outside and stayed near the door. I nodded to several of the bridge players who walked out after me, but I didn't start any conversations. I'm sure lots of people will tell you they saw me. As soon as the all-clear announcement came, I went back to my room."

"Didn't you even ask anyone which pair was leading in the money game?" Vivian asked.

Charles looked embarrassed. "I'm afraid I didn't. I'm more interested in the success of the event than who wins it."

"I'm surprised you didn't kibitz the game, with so much riding on it for your firm and your career," Vivian said.

"Well, I would have, but I don't know how to play bridge."

* * * * *

"Century sure got a winner with him," Vivian said after Charles had gone. "He doesn't even know how to play the game they're sponsoring."

"Actually, he *may* be a winner," Herb replied. "The idea to sponsor a money game was probably brilliant. And there's no way he could have arranged for so much free publicity. Century stands to come out way ahead."

"As long as Canning didn't commit the murder."

"Even if he did, his company will get a lot of coverage in the news. They can't lose either way."

"Do you think he could have killed Tom Stanhope for the publicity?" Vivian asked.

"Not a chance," Herb said. "He's only capable of one brilliant idea."

CHAPTER 13

The players were subdued. The bid boxes reduced the ambient noise to a barely audible murmur, and the Stanhope murder made the ballroom eerily quiet. Even the Nestors weren't arguing.

"I've never played in a tournament with such a spooky atmosphere," Sharon whispered to Eva after the second round. "What happened to all the bragging and yelling and complaining? There's always *something* going on. But now —nothing. I don't like it."

"Anything that keeps the Nestors quiet can't be all bad," Eva replied. "I wonder how much the murder will affect the results. It certainly makes it harder to concentrate when you're wondering whether your next opponent is a killer, or who will be the next victim."

Sharon shivered. "I wish you hadn't said that. I was just trying to figure out who killed Tom. I hadn't thought about another murder. I hope nobody's after us."

"As long as we don't win the Vanderbilt, we're probably safe."

"That should guarantee us a long life."

* * * * *

After the players had distributed the cards in accordance with the computer diagrams, Jennifer gave the starting directions. The boards were duly passed and the players got down to business.

Eva, sitting North, picked up her cards to start the first round. She held:

♠AK53
♡3
◇107542
♣A87

She pulled the 1◇ card from the bid box and placed it on the table. The auction then proceeded:

West	North	East	South
	1◇	Pass	1♠
Pass	3♠	Pass	4♠
Pass	Pass	Pass	

Sharon, sitting South, held:
♠Q10642
♡8752
◇void
♣KJ103

When she saw the dummy, she was astonished. Eva had jumped the bidding with nothing more than a minimum hand. Few others would be in game on these cards. The points just didn't add up.

She set up a cross ruff and made her contract easily—much to the disgust of her opponents. After the round was over and the opponents left the table, Sharon confronted her sister. "Eva! Where on earth did you find that 3♠ bid?"

"I guess I did overbid a little," Eva acknowledged. "But after you bid one spade, I liked the texture of my hand. Besides, I don't want to miss any games."

"We're not playing in a team event where it's important not to miss any games. We're competing with the rest of the field in a *pairs* game. We don't want to be the only ones in the room to go minus on a hand and get a zero."

"Well, it worked, didn't it? How can you complain about a top?"

Sharon didn't have a good answer.

* * * * *

At 3:00, Jennifer interrupted the game to give the players an update on the murder investigation.

"The interviews will be held in Room 111 as soon as this session ends," she announced. "Turn left when you leave the ballroom; it's the first room on the right. Detective Vivian Greene will question everyone briefly. Then tonight, she'll ask anyone whom she wishes to see again to remain after the game. Any questions?"

Although she heard mutterings of "I didn't even know him," or "I don't know anything about it," nobody asked any questions or refused to be interviewed. The game continued, but the quiet spell was over. There was more buzzing about the murder than about the bridge. Considering all the money involved, that was remarkable.

The Nestors still weren't arguing.

* * * * *

Ron Albright, the hotel detective, entered the ballroom at 4:30 and waited impatiently for the afternoon session to end. By the time the last hands were completed, all the contestants were aware of his presence. He didn't even have to ask for quiet; the players were eager to find out what would happen next.

"We'll call you in alphabetical order," he told them. "We expect to speak to each of you briefly this time. Those of you who didn't know Mr. Stanhope will probably not be questioned for more than a couple of minutes. If your name is in the last half of the alphabet, I suggest you get your dinner now. Please be back as quickly as possible."

"That's just great," Sharon said to Eva. "We won't be able to eat together. Kaplan and Price are hardly together alphabetically. I'll go to the room now and order room service while you're waiting to be called. Tell me what you want, and I'll order yours before I come back down here."

"I'll have a chef's salad," Eva said. "That won't spoil or get cold in case I'm late. And it'll be great for my diet. Tell them to leave it in my room if I'm not back when they deliver yours. You can sign for it when your meal comes. Thanks, Sharon."

"No problem," Sharon said, hurrying toward the door.

"And order the triple-layer chocolate cake for dessert!" Eva shouted after her.

* * * * *

Gary Alexander, the first one called, walked calmly into the interrogation room.

Vivian stood up, briskly extended her arm to shake hands with Gary, and quickly made the introductions. "I'm Detective Vivian Greene." Then she nodded toward the man sitting in the chair next to him. "This is Herb Kramer, a local private investigator. He'll be sitting in on the interviews and asking questions from time to time." She purposely didn't introduce Officer Rollins. It was better for the suspects not to feel that they were being closely observed.

Gary acknowledged Herb, sat down, and waited for the first question.

"How well did you know Tom?" Vivian began.

"I play on a professional level like Tom did, and I've played against him for years. Most of the professional players compete against each other in regional and national tournaments around the country. Tom's teams and mine nearly always competed against each other in those tournaments."

"You mean like the Vanderbilt team game that was held here last week?" Vivian asked.

"Yes. The competition to win the Vanderbilt, the Reisinger, and the Spingold is fierce. The winners of each compete against each other to represent the United States in international competition. That's what we all aim for."

"How did you feel about Tom as a competitor?"

"He was formidable. I respected his game immensely."

"And how did you feel about him personally?"

"I didn't like him. He was overbearing and obnoxious."

"Do you think that was a common feeling about Tom?"

"Yes. I suspect you'll hear the same opinion from everyone else you interview."

"I understand your team lost to Stanhope's in the finals of the Vanderbilt," Vivian said, using the information Jennifer and Herb had given her. "I was also told that there was a question of cheating."

"That's correct," Gary said. "The committee ruled in favor of the Stanhope team. Our team didn't like the decision, but we had to accept it. It was a final ruling with no attractive further appeals available to us."

"You must have been pretty upset."

"I was. My whole team was. But not enough to murder anyone."

"It may not be entirely coincidental," Vivian replied. "that Stanhope was murdered shortly after it was confirmed that his team had won. Now, let's get to specifics. I need to know what you did last night."

Gary knew he'd be asked this, but he still didn't know what to say. He was stuck with his 1950's hang-ups about promiscuity, and felt that he needed to protect Sharon's reputation.

"I sat in the bar with Sharon Price until close to one-thirty, and then went to my room," he said, omitting the fact that she accompanied him. "I stayed there until I heard the fire alarm ring."

"Can you prove that?"

"If I have to," he said stiffly.

Vivian glanced at Herb, who made some kind of indecipherable signal to her.

She decided to discuss the matter with Herb later, and changed the subject. There was a printout of the first day's scores in front of her. "I see you did well yesterday. How'd you do this afternoon?"

"The scores weren't ready yet when I came in here, but I'm sure we had a good game," Gary said. "We have a chance to do very well overall, if we don't blow it tonight. It's hard to know what'll happen, though. The murder changes the equation. Some people play better under stress, while others go banzai. We can get tops or bottoms from them. It's too bad something other than bridge skill can affect the outcome of a game involving so much money. I just hope Jonathan and I will be able to concentrate on the game and not let the murder distract us too much."

"I hope so too," Vivian said. "I'll have more questions for you later, but that's all for now. Please tell Mr. Albright to send the next person in."

* * * * *

"Jennifer told me she saw Gary leave the bar with Sharon around one-thirty," Herb said after Gary left. "She assumed they both went to Gary's room—although she didn't really see them after they got on the elevator together."

Vivian was amused. "Imagine that. Chivalry still exists. I hope the two of them didn't do the murder together. They could give each other alibis that would be hard to disprove."

"According to Jennifer, this is a new romance. I suspect they were too busy to carry out any murders."

"Well, if they weren't murdering anybody, I hope they were enjoying themselves." She turned to Rollins. "What did you think?"

"He was obviously flustered about his fling with Sharon. I doubt if anyone who shows his feelings that easily would be able to lie without it being apparent."

"I agree. Who's next?"

"Tom's partner, Cliff Bryce."

* * * * *

Cliff, poised and assured, came into the room, swaggering slightly. Vivian introduced him to Herb and asked him to be seated.

"Well, Mr. Bryce, it looks like you have a lot on your plate," she began. "First you win the Vanderbilt, then you and your teammate are accused of cheating, and then your partner is murdered."

"I may look calm, but inside, I'm reeling," Cliff admitted, losing a little of his superior air. "It's been an emotional roller coaster—joy at winning, anger at the cheating charge, joy again when we were cleared, and now horror at the murder. It's hard to take it all in."

"I'm sure it must be," Vivian sympathized. "We've heard that Tom irritated a lot of people recently. Had he gotten worse lately?"

"Insulting others was always part of his personality, but yes, I think he was more offensive recently. He was nasty to almost everyone he encountered. I imagine plenty of people fantasized about killing him, but I have no idea who would actually carry it out."

"We know that the losing team accused you and Tom of cheating, but we don't know the details. Please tell us what it was all about."

For the first time, Cliff looked uncomfortable. He sat there for a few minutes, trying to figure out how to explain the situation to this non-bridge player. "There are extensive safeguards to prevent cheating in major events," he began. "Bid boxes and screens were on each table for the Vanderbilt. The screens were placed diagonally across the table to prevent partners from seeing each other. That way, no unauthorized information could be passed through looks or gestures.

"The accusation came from the afternoon session of the last day, when Tom and I gained a bundle of IMPs by making the right decisions on all the slam hands. The opponents became suspicious when we were consistently right."

"Wait a minute. What are IMPS?" Vivian asked.

"International Match Points, a form of scoring designed so that one big swing doesn't decide a long match. For example, if my team bids and makes a vulnerable small slam in spades, we get a total point score of fourteen hundred thirty," Cliff said. "If the opposing team bids the same slam but doesn't make it, their score is minus one hundred. We then score a net of fifteen hundred thirty points. The opponents would now need to manufacture an equal swing, or more than two regular game swings, to get back to even.

"But if you convert the scores to an IMP scale, where specific ranges of points convert to a specific number of IMPS, the fifteen hundred thirty translates to seventeen IMPS. And seventeen IMPS are a lot easier to make up than fifteen hundred thirty points. One game and one partscore swing just about equal seventeen IMPs, depending on vulnerability. A team can drop seventeen IMPs on one hand, but by playing well on the other hands, still have a good chance to win."

"I see," Vivian said, although her level of understanding was still somewhat on the hazy side. "Now let's go back to the actual game. So what if you didn't miss any slams or didn't bid the ones that went down? Why should that indicate that you cheated?"

"Statistically, that kind of bidding's supposed to be impossible," Cliff replied. "No one bids that well. But we did. And in a close match, if you bid and make just two slam hands that the opposing team doesn't bid, you'll have quite a cushion. If your other errors are minimal, you rate to win. By the same token, you'll have a similar advantage if you stay out of a slam or two that don't make."

"How are bridge hands constructed?" Vivian asked. Although she didn't understand how to play bridge, at least she'd learned enough from Herb to be able to differentiate between pairs games and team games and to comprehend what a bridge hand looked like. "Would it be theoretically possible to know what the hands looked like before you sat down to play them?"

"No way that I know of," Cliff said. "A computer program at the ACBL headquarters in Memphis creates random bridge hands. When it's time to use them in a tournament, they are printed onto hand records and put into sealed packages. The packages are sent to the tournament sites and opened just before game time. Since the committee couldn't find any way that we could have seen the hands ahead of time, they had no way to make the charges stick."

"How do you account for your perfect decisions?" Vivian asked.

Cliff shrugged. "I suppose the same way a detective who hasn't made an arrest all month suddenly picks up on clues that solve a bunch of pending cases. We played the best bridge we've ever played. I have no special explanation for the perfect judgment. I guess it's possible to have games like that after all. We certainly did."

"Tell us what kind of relationship you had with Tom."

"I didn't like him, but it isn't necessary to like your partner in bridge. Tom was an excellent player. He seldom made mistakes. He never lost his ability to concentrate, and that's very important for playing at the top level. He remembered what every bid meant in the various systems he played with different partners. And he had an amazing amount of stamina."

"This is the first I've heard so many good things said about Stanhope all at once," Vivian said. "It's a relief to know the poor man had some outstanding qualities."

"I think most people would admit that he was a fine bridge player," Cliff said. "But I don't believe you'll hear too much complimentary about him otherwise. And he was even more obnoxious when he drank too much."

"Did you socialize with Tom?" Herb asked.

"No. We're both from Rochester, New York, but I seldom saw him there. I'm busy running my computer company when I'm not at bridge tournaments. Since I'm away a lot, I spend all my time catching up with my work when I'm home. I divorced several years ago, and my only son lives in California, so I don't spend too much time with family. I occasionally date a woman in Tennessee, but other than that, I work when I'm not playing bridge."

"What did Tom do for a living?" Herb asked.

"He made his living playing as a pro and writing occasional articles. He played in about twice as many tournaments a year as I did. He didn't have any problem getting clients—only keeping them. Even then, he was able to keep more than you'd think because he'd win with a lot of them. He was really gifted."

"I understand that you and Tom had an argument in the restaurant last night," Herb said. The sisters had mentioned it to Jennifer, and she'd told Herb. "What was that all about?"

Cliff had anticipated being asked about their fight in the restaurant. He obviously couldn't tell them that Tom had discovered that he'd cheated in the Vanderbilt, so he told them about the quarrel they'd had earlier.

"It was just a continuation of an argument we'd had about how to play a certain hand," Cliff lied. "I told him I could prove that he'd taken the wrong line of play. I have the bridge statistics in my portable computer. I always travel with it in case I have to take care of any emergencies that come up with my company. I told Tom that I'd look up the information and show him he was wrong. But it was too late by the time we got back from dinner last night to go back to the room and retrieve the statistics from the computer."

"We understand the word 'cheating' was overheard at the restaurant," Herb persisted.

"After we finished talking about that hand, we discussed the cheating accusation," Cliff said. "We were still angry about it, and I guess our voices were loud."

Neither Vivian nor Herb totally believed Cliff's facile explanation, but they had no information that contradicted his story.

"Please tell us what you did after the game last night," Vivian said.

"There's not much to tell. I knew we had a good game. When I checked the preliminary scores after the twelfth round, I saw that we would easily qualify. I was tired, so I went right to bed without checking our final score."

"I assume you and Tom each had your own room."

"Definitely," replied Cliff. "I saw enough of him all day at the tournament without sharing a room with him. I needed to be far away from him after the game."

"Did you often argue about hands?" Vivian asked.

"No. It's odd, with Tom's personality, that we had very few arguments. We usually calmly discussed the hands after each session. We'd try to figure out the best way to handle the problem ones so we'd know what to do the next time a similar situation came up. Occasionally we'd ask other pros' opinions about specific hands. Surprisingly, Tom wasn't insistent that his way was best. He was open to suggestions and thoughtful about new possibilities for bidding or playing difficult hands. I was amazed that he was so insistent that he was right on the hand that we were having the disagreement over."

"Why do you suppose he didn't try to find the solution peacefully, as he normally did?" Vivian asked.

"I don't know. As I told you, he'd been particularly offensive to everyone he'd encountered at bridge all week. I have no idea if anything special was upsetting him lately, or if he was just getting more obnoxious. Even though we were winning, it was becoming difficult to play with him."

"What will happen to the Vanderbilt team now that Tom's dead?" Herb asked.

"I don't know. I'll have to see what my teammates want to do. I know that I'll have a tough time replacing Tom as a partner."

"One more question. Did you talk to Tom or anyone else after you left the game last night?"

Cliff shook his head. "I didn't see anyone else until the fire alarm rang and I went to the parking lot. I talked to several of the players there."

"Did you notice Tom over by the dumpster?"

"Of course," Cliff replied. "Several of us commented about it. I didn't particularly want to talk to him, so I made no effort to go over there. I think everyone was relieved that he wasn't joining us."

"Okay, Mr. Bryce. We'll talk to you again after the game."

* * * * *

"Well, that gave us a lesson in IMP scoring, but not much information about what Cliff Bryce did last night," Vivian said after he left.

"He's lying about something," Rollins said. "He gave his answers like he'd rehearsed them."

"True, but so far, we don't have any evidence to show that Cliff didn't do just what he said he did," Herb replied. "I wonder where Tom was killed. It would be useful to know if he was murdered in the hotel or near the dumpster."

"I'm still waiting for the report. But even if the murder took place outside, we'll still have to search the rooms of the suspects. We'll do that tonight while they're playing their final session. Since we can't get search warrants for all those rooms, I've asked the police department to send over some consent slips that'll give us permission to inspect each room."

"How can you possibly expect to do that in so short a time?" Herb asked.

"We'll have to do the best we can. I'd appreciate it if you would help me in case we run into some clues connected with bridge."

"What are we going to be looking for?"

"Too many things. So far we haven't found the murder weapon. We also need to see if there are bloodstains anywhere. We'll have a better idea where Tom was shot after we get the report from the investigating team, but my gut feeling is that he was shot at or near the dumpster. There'd be too big a chance of someone seeing the murderer carrying the body out of the hotel."

"But it *could* have been done in the hotel."

"I know." Vivian issued an uncharacteristic sigh. "It's complicated enough now without that. Imagine all the lab work and time it would take to look for bloodstains in the rooms of all the suspects."

"I've had experience searching homes for some of my investigations, but I haven't done any hotel room searches," Herb said. "Obviously, there'll be a limited amount of personal items in each room. And it doesn't seem likely whoever committed the murder would bring incriminating evidence and leave it in a hotel room."

"True," Vivian conceded, "but since no local connections with Tom have been found, other than those in the bridge world, we'd better play it safe and make the search. We'll be looking for *any* information that might implicate someone—something hidden in closets, drawers, anywhere. It's an enormous task to do in such a short amount of time."

"What if we don't find the murderer tonight?" Herb asked.

"Then we'll have to keep the suspects here," Vivian replied. "I don't even want to think about the outcry if we have to ask them to stay."

* * * * *

After Cliff's interview, Vivian and Herb held several brief conversations with people who didn't know Tom well. Then it was Ralph Dunbar's turn.

Vivian immediately thought Ralph had something to hide when he marched into the room with an overconfident air. He sat down before she could even introduce Herb. She decided the best way to handle him was to get right to the point.

"Tell us what you did last night after the game ended," she said.

"I can't."

She lifted a questioning eyebrow. "What do you mean you can't? This is a murder investigation. Whatever you did, it can't be as bad as murder—unless you are the murderer."

"I didn't go back to the room immediately because I had something private to take care of," Ralph said. "It has no bearing on the murder, and I'm not going to discuss it."

Vivian looked at Herb, who had no signal to give her this time. "We'll ignore what you were up to last night for now—but we *will* get back to it. Since you weren't in your room, you must have been wandering around somewhere in the hotel. Can you tell us if you saw anything unusual going on?"

"I can tell you what I saw, but I don't know if any of it has anything to do with the murder. I saw Tom Stanhope waiting for the scores right after the game ended, but I didn't pay any further attention to him. I also noticed that Cliff Bryce left in a hurry. He didn't even wait for the scores. I'm sure he knew his and Tom's score was high enough to qualify. It's possible that he came back later to check, but I have no way of knowing."

"What else?"

"I saw Gary Alexander and Sharon Price in the bar when I walked by. That's about it."

"Does Jeffrey know where you went when you disappeared?"

"No."

Frowning, Vivian said, "When you come back tonight, you'd better be prepared to tell us where you were and what you did last night. And that doesn't mean I'm giving you time to concoct a story. I want the truth."

"Not only does what I did last night have no bearing on the murder, I also had no motive to kill Tom. You'll just have to solve the case without knowing what I was doing. I'll be glad to cooperate about anything else."

Vivian wasn't at all pleased with Ralph's answer, but she reluctantly let him leave.

"Do you have any idea what that was all about?" she asked Herb after he'd gone.

"Nope. Jennifer never mentioned seeing him after the game. I wonder if he's found a new lover."

"He was pretty cool," Rollins noted. "He never even blinked when he said that what he did had nothing to do with the murder. He kept the same composure no matter what you asked him. Jeffrey Howard is next. It'll be interesting to hear what he has to say about Ralph's disappearance."

* * * * *

Jeffrey looked disconcerted when he entered the room. Herb noticed that he lacked the air of confidence that he'd had last week when he and Ralph won their events. He wondered if Jeffrey's demeanor had anything to do with Ralph's disappearance.

When Vivian asked Jeffrey to report on what he did after last night's game, he told her that he looked at the score, saw that he and Ralph had done well, and went to his room.

"Was Ralph with you?" Vivian asked.

"No."

"Where was he?"

"I don't know," Jeffrey replied. "He was right next to me when we checked our score, but when I stopped for a few minutes to talk to Linda and Kathy about one of the hands, he disappeared."

"Did you look for him?"

"I looked around the lobby and didn't see him. I finally decided that he must have gone back to our room. But when I went up, he wasn't there. I couldn't imagine what had happened to him. He's never disappeared like that before." He sounded both indignant and upset.

"Was Ralph back in the room by the time the fire alarm rang?" Herb asked.

"Yes. We left together. When we got to the parking lot, I asked him where he'd been earlier, but he refused to tell me."

"Where do you think he was?"

"I don't know," Jeffrey said. He looked even more dejected. It had occurred to him last night that maybe Ralph had found someone else. Jeffrey had always assumed he would be the one to end the affair, and the new prospect troubled him. He didn't like—or expect—the power shift.

"You already interviewed him. Where did he tell you he was?" Jeffrey asked.

"We can't give out that information."

"He probably didn't tell you. Otherwise you wouldn't have asked me if he went back to the room with me."

"We ask everyone where they were, whom they were with, and what they saw," Vivian said. "That's the only way we can confirm what people tell us. We'll see you again after the game." She stood up, indicating that the interview was over.

"He didn't like Ralph's disappearance one bit," Officer Rollins said after Jeffrey had closed the door behind him.

Vivian agreed. "So far, Ralph is our only possibility—and a remote one at that. He *did* disappear, but as far as I can tell, he doesn't have a motive. Or at least not one that we know about. Let's get on with it."

* * * * *

They quickly interviewed two more people, and then called Kathy Jensen. She flounced in as though she were doing them a favor, grabbed a chair, and sat down.

"I don't know anything about the murder," she announced before they could question her. "I hardly knew the man. All I know is that he got two good results from us last night, and I got the impression Linda was actually relieved at doing badly. I could have killed her. . . ." As her brain caught up to her mouth, Kathy quickly stopped in mid-sentence.

"Tell us about those hands, please," Vivian said.

"Well, both of the bad scores were just matters of judgment," Kathy conceded. Then her face got red and her words poured out angrily. "But on the first one, Linda rejected my game invitation holding the sort of hand with which she'd bid game seven days of the week. It cost us a lot of points. You can't afford to make mistakes like that, especially in a money game." She sat back in her chair and emphatically folded her arms.

"What did you do about it?" Vivian asked.

"There was nothing I *could* do about it, but you can be sure I let her know what I thought about it. It's a good thing we still qualified, or I would never have let her forget it."

"Do you have any reason to believe she did it on purpose?" Herb asked.

Kathy looked astounded. "That's preposterous! Why would she do that? She was the one who insisted on playing in this game. I told her we weren't good enough, but it seemed really important to her. We may have a good partnership, but we're not *that* good. The truth is, the competition in this event is too tough for us, even if we did have a section top. I tried to talk her out of it when she asked me, but she insisted on playing."

"Does she have any special need for money right now?" Herb asked.

"If she does, she didn't tell me. Nor do I want to know about it if she does. I'm certainly not about to loan her any."

"What was your relationship with Tom Stanhope? I understand you hired him several times to play with you," Vivian said, glad Herb had filled her in.

"That's true," Kathy said, glaring at Herb. Damn Jennifer. She must have suggested having Herb help with the investigation. Keeping secrets wasn't going to be easy. "The last time I hired him was several months ago. His manner was very annoying, and I decided not to hire him again."

"What did you do after the game? Jennifer thought she saw you going into the Ladies' Room after she left the Ballroom."

"That's impossible. It must have been someone else. I went straight home to bed. Do you have any more questions?"

"Not now," Vivian said. "We'll talk to you again later."

* * * * *

"I'll bet she let Linda know what she thought about that bad bid," Vivian said after Kathy had gone. "And no doubt she'll keep on letting her know. Poor Linda."

"Linda must have wanted some money pretty desperately to play with Kathy in a field this difficult," Herb said. "They're pretty good players, but Kathy's right. They're really not in the same league as most of the other contestants here. I think we need to find out why it was so important for Linda to get her hands on some money."

"Kathy's definitely hiding something—or at least not telling the whole truth," Rollins said. "Did you notice how she frowned at Herb when he asked about her relationship with Tom? I think there was more going on between them than she admitted."

* * * * *

When Kathy left the interrogation room, she thought about the last time she'd hired Tom ...

"It's time to end this sordid business," Tom had said as he climbed off Kathy, leaving her unsatisfied again. They'd been seeing each other at various tournaments for about six months and were currently in Kathy's room at the North American Bridge Championships in Miami. The relationship had started out purely as business, but had drifted into an unfulfilling affair.

"Why do you want to end it?" Kathy asked, surprised. After all, Tom earned a lot of money playing as a pro with her. Plus he had the extra benefit of their sexual liaison—such as it was.

"I found someone who is more generous financially, and better in bed," Tom replied cruelly. Before Kathy could respond to his insult, he continued. "There is just one final detail. I know you're filing for divorce soon and that you don't want to let your husband get his hands on any of your family money. I'm sure it wouldn't help your case if he were to find out that we've been playing at more than bridge. Even though it's been hard to get you to part with a penny, you did write checks to me when I played with you. And I have photocopies of them."

"So what?" Kathy asked. "I *hired* you to play with me. The checks were written to pay your pro fee."

"Your husband doesn't know that. All he knows is that you were always too cheap to hire a pro when you were living with him. He and his lawyer would be very happy to get their hands on those checks. Here you are, spending time with me in a hotel out of town, and suddenly, several canceled checks appear. And they're all made out to me. Who knows what the judge would think?"

"You bastard. Why would anyone believe you? If I'm so cheap, why would I pay you or anyone else to be my lover?"

"I made sure that several bridge players saw us enter the room together this week. It wouldn't be hard to get them to testify to that. Maybe the judge wouldn't believe you paid me to be your lover, but the checks and the witnesses would create some doubts. If you have money to pay a lover, it might be harder for you to get out of your marriage without having to part with some of your cash for your dear husband. I think a little spending money might convince me to rip up those copies."

"Not a chance," Kathy said. "At least when I pay you to play with me at the table, I get better results than I do with you in bed."

* * * * *

Shortly after Kathy left room 111, Eva Kaplan arrived. She walked in confidently. "Hi, Herb," she said. "I heard you were helping. I wonder if Ms. Greene realizes what a clever investigator she has assisting her. You can ferret out anything."

Herb laughed. "Well, not quite. I never did find all the senator's drug sources." He turned to Vivian. "Let's pray it wasn't Eva and her sister Sharon who planned the murder. If they did it, we're in trouble. They'll have concocted some outlandish scheme that we'll never figure out."

Vivian smiled. "In that case, I hope it was someone else too," she said. "Now, excuse me for getting down to business right away, but we don't have a lot of time and we still have several more interviews to do. Please tell us what you did after the game last night."

"I stayed in the playing area to see if we qualified. When I saw that we'd made the cut, I went to the bar with Jonathan to tell Sharon and Gary the good news. Then Jonathan and I left to go to bed. At least I went to bed," she added, sounding a little miffed. "I really don't know what Jonathan did."

"Did anything strike you as unusual when you went to the bar?" Herb asked.

"I saw Ralph Dunbar getting on an elevator with someone, but I couldn't tell who it was. I don't know if Ralph was with the other person or just taking the elevator with him."

"Was the elevator going up or down?" Herb asked.

Eva pressed her eyebrows together, trying to recreate the position of the elevator light in her mind.

"I believe it was going down. There's another small bar downstairs. Maybe that's where they were heading, although I don't know if it was open. Since most of the hotel guests left after the national tournament, I don't know if there was enough business to keep both bars open. Even the one on this floor where Sharon and Gary were was nearly empty."

"We'll check into it," Herb said. "What happened when you heard the alarm? Did you see if Sharon was in her room?"

"Of course! I wouldn't think of leaving after a fire alarm goes off without checking on her. She was there—and still dressed," she added, with a trace of jealousy. "I was in my nightgown, but Sharon insisted that I didn't have time to get dressed. We walked down the stairs together. When we arrived in the parking lot, several of the bridge players were already there."

"Did you see Tom Stanhope?" Herb asked.

"Yes. He looked like he was sleeping against the grocery store wall next door. It's unnerving to think he was dead while we were joking about how glad we were that he wasn't joining us."

"But didn't it seem strange to you that he would fall asleep so quickly after the alarm rang?"

"I guess I was so relieved that he wasn't around harassing us that I didn't think about it."

"Did you notice anything else?"

"I saw Linda Mason driving away, and wondered what she was doing there. I know she wasn't staying at the hotel. I hope I'm not getting her into trouble by mentioning that."

"Don't worry," Herb told her. "We've already heard that she was here. You just confirmed the report."

"How well did you know Tom?" Vivian asked.

"I knew him a little better than some of your suspects did," Eva said. "Right after my husband died, I was very lonely. For a while, I played more bridge than usual to keep my mind occupied. I hired a couple of pros, and Tom was one of them. I played with him once but didn't enjoy it, so I never hired him again. Soon after that, I was able to get my life back together, and I cut down on my bridge. In the last few years, I've played mostly with Sharon."

"Were you and Tom still friendly when you stopped playing?" Herb asked.

"Was *anyone* ever friendly with Tom?"

"It appears not, from what we're hearing," Vivian said. "If you've nothing to add, we'll see you after the game. Good luck tonight."

Vivian waited until Eva had gone, then turned to Herb. "Think there's anything there?"

"I never heard any rumors about Eva and Tom from Jennifer," Herb said. "Besides, I'm sure she has better taste."

"I didn't pick up any gestures or spot any nervousness to indicate that she wasn't telling the truth," Rollins added.

* * * * *

It was after 7:00 when Linda Mason arrived in room 111. Herb and Vivian glanced at each other as Linda slowly dragged into the room, keeping her eyes on the floor. Vivian said, "I believe you know Herb Kramer?"

Linda vaguely nodded in Herb's direction and then sat down, directing her eyes back to the floor. Since she was obviously uncomfortable, Vivian signalled Herb to do the questioning. Linda might be more relaxed with him.

Herb did his best to put her at ease. "Your section top yesterday afternoon was terrific," he began. "I'm glad to see you playing so well."

Linda nodded again, but remained silent.

"What made you decide to play in the money game?" he asked.

"I thought we should try to win a really tough game. We can play in the local games or in regular tournaments anytime. But a money game is something special. I guess I just wanted to do something different."

"How did Kathy feel about playing in it?"

Linda snorted. "You know Kathy and her love for every cent she owns. She didn't want to part with the entry fee, but she couldn't resist the chance to win a hundred thousand dollars. Even then, I had a hard time convincing her. Luckily, she's greedy. When she thought about how much she might win, she couldn't resist."

Now that Linda had become a little more animated, Herb decided it was time to get a little tougher. "I understand the temptation to play in an exciting event, but was there any special reason? After all, the entry fee was steep, and even though you two play well together, the odds of your winning in such a tough field couldn't be that high."

Linda expected this and had an answer prepared. "I've worked for years in the bank in Norfolk," she said. "I have a retirement pension coming in a couple of years, but I haven't saved much else. I thought if we won, I'd have some extra money to take a trip or to make some investments for my fast-arriving old age. Like I told you, it was no hardship to come up with the entry fee, and I thought it was the right time in my life to take some chances. Besides, I thought it would be fun."

"Has it been?"

"It was wonderful yesterday afternoon when we got our section top," she said, perking up for a minute. "But with Tom's death, it's turned into a nightmare."

"I think everybody would agree with that." He waited a minute and then said, "I have another question for you. We've been told by several people that you were seen leaving the hotel parking lot after the fire alarm went off. Can you tell us what you were doing here at that hour?"

Linda sat quietly for a minute, and then began to cry. Vivian handed her a tissue and she wiped her eyes. After she calmed down, she slowly began to talk. "I knew I'd be seen. When that fire alarm rang, I was terrified. I went home right after the game, but came back later to talk to Tom. He'd given me a hard time about something earlier, and I wanted to talk to him about it."

"What happened when you came back?"

"As soon as I got here, I called his room on the house phone, but he refused to talk with me. Tom said he was tired, and he hung up on me. I wandered around the hotel trying to decide what to do next."

"Did you talk to anyone?"

"No. I saw one couple left in the bar off the lobby, and two people talking in the downstairs bar, but I didn't speak to anyone."

"Did you recognize the people in the downstairs bar?" Vivian asked.

"One of them was Ralph Dunbar. The other one had his back to me, and I couldn't tell who it was."

Herb glanced at Vivian. "Was it a man or a woman?"

"A man."

"Was there anything familiar about him?"

"I really didn't pay much attention. All I wanted to do was talk to Tom."

Vivian wished that Kathy could have identified the other man in the bar. It would save them some precious time.

"What did you do after that?" Herb asked.

"By then it was very late, and I was getting frantic. I had overheard Tom telling Cliff his room number before the first session started yesterday, so I went up there and knocked on his door. I thought I heard voices when I arrived, but after I knocked, it was quiet. I waited for a few minutes, but no one came out."

"What time was that?"

"I don't know exactly. Somewhere around two o'clock. I went back downstairs and sat in the lobby, trying to figure out what to do. I couldn't understand why Tom wasn't answering the door. I knew someone was in there—unless it was just the television set. But I didn't think it was."

"Then what did you do?"

"I sat in the lobby a little while longer, wondering whether I should try again or go back home. Around two-thirty, I saw Ralph come into the lobby and get on an elevator. I don't think he noticed me."

"He came in from outside?"

"Yes."

"Was he alone?"

"Yes. I think I dozed off then, because the next thing I knew, I heard the fire alarm ringing. I raced outside to get into my car, but I couldn't get away before some of the others had reached the parking lot. I was afraid I would be recognized -- and apparently I was."

"Linda," Herb said gently, "we need to know why you came back so late to speak to Tom. Jennifer told me that you had hired him once. Did he do something then that made you angry?"

"Yes. But I was furious at him about something else last night. It's true that I was here, but I didn't kill him. I couldn't even find him!"

"You were seen talking to him before the evening session started and, according to our sources, you looked very upset. What was that conversation about?"

Linda started to cry again, but wouldn't give them a direct answer. "All I can tell you is that I didn't kill him," she repeated. She ran out of the room.

"What do you think she wanted to talk to Tom about?" Vivian asked.

"I haven't a clue," Herb said. "Tom must have really gotten to her if she came back at that hour of the night to see him."

"Any ideas?" Vivian asked Officer Rollins.

He shrugged. "It's hard to say she lied, because she didn't tell us anything except what she chose. Did you notice that she kept her eyes down except when she talked about her section top? That woman is very worried about something."

"What a frustrating case," Vivian said, shaking her head. "Ralph doesn't seem to have a motive for killing Tom, but he won't tell us what he was doing after the game. Linda may have a motive, but we don't have any idea what it is. And nobody liked the victim. I don't understand anything that's going on with these people. Who's next?"

"Jonathan Meltzer. He's Gary Alexander's partner."

* * * * *

Jonathan walked into the room and sat down without being asked. He took off his horn-rimmed glasses, cleaned them carefully with a blue handkerchief, and finally looked at his interviewers.

Vivian, annoyed at his behavior, didn't waste any time with preliminaries. "I understand your team lost the Vanderbilt to Tom Stanhope's team and that you thought they won by cheating."

"I'm sure they *did* cheat, but we couldn't prove it," Jonathan said bitterly. "The ACBL has to be really careful about convicting someone on flimsy evidence. They've been hit with too many lawsuits in the past. I thought they let Tom's team off the hook too easily, but there wasn't anything I could do about it."

"Couldn't you challenge the committee's decision?" Vivian asked.

"Theoretically we could go to the National Laws Commission. But as a practical matter, the original hearing was the ball game. I suspect Tom's teammates were embarrassed by the whole thing, but they surely weren't about to turn down a Vanderbilt win for which they played hard and fought cleanly."

"I understand that Tom belittled you at the table last night when you didn't bid to a game," Herb probed.

"He certainly did, and that was typical of him," Jonathan said indignantly. "He knew that the game we missed was difficult to bid in our methods. He is—was—an excellent player, and I doubt if he would have bid the game either. But that didn't matter. As soon as he found a chance to ridicule anyone, he jumped at it."

"Why do you think he bothered? After all, the round was over and you were going to be playing new people."

"Tom did anything he could to upset his opponents. He'd do whatever he could if he thought it would give him an advantage."

"Can you tell us what you did after the game last night?" Vivian asked.

"I waited till the scores were posted to make sure we qualified. Then I went to the bar with Eva Kaplan to look for Gary and Sharon. After we told them the good news, I left and went to bed."

"Did you see or hear anything else that might be connected to the murder?"

Jonathan thought for a moment, then shook his head. "I'm afraid not."

"Thank you," Vivian said, dismissing him. "We'll talk to you later."

* * * * *

"He was certainly angry at Tom," Herb said after Jonathan left.

"Yeah. Just like nearly everyone else we've interviewed. It would be refreshing to find someone who actually liked the guy. Who's next?"

Patrolman Rollins looked at his list. "The Nestors."

"Don't expect to hear anything flattering about Tom from them," Herb said. "I understand they weren't too fond of him, either."

* * * * *

Alan and Sybil Nestor walked into room 111 holding hands. Vivian made the introductions and asked them to be seated. She began with an attack. "I believe that you had a nasty exchange with Tom Stanhope at dinner last night."

"It wasn't exactly an exchange," Sybil protested. "The conversation was all on his side. He came over to our table and tried to humiliate us for no reason. He insulted me by asking why Alan played with me. Then he asked Alan why he couldn't find any good partners. Who our partners are was none of his business, but that didn't matter to him. He enjoyed putting us down."

"How did you feel about his sarcasm, Alan?"

"Pretty much as Sybil did—resentful. He was very nasty. And there wasn't any reason to pick on us. He didn't even know us that well."

"Perhaps he heard you arguing at tournaments," Herb offered.

Alan, looking a little sheepish, said, "Well, I admit, I do get upset with Sybil, and sometimes I give her some rather loud lessons at the table. But that's between us. It was none of Tom's business."

"It's not just between the two of you when the whole room can hear your comments," Herb pointed out. "Several others have also mentioned your fights. Do you control your temper better when you get upset with someone other than Sybil—like Tom?"

"Oh, he's wonderful when he isn't angry with me at the table," Sybil said quickly. "The only time he loses his temper is when he plays bridge. And then it's only at me, never the opponents."

"I understand that you yell back at him when he attacks you."

"Well, he's not always right. I don't like to be criticized publicly, but I can't convince him of that," Sybil said irritably.

They scowled at each other; then Alan diffused the tension. "Sybil is like me. We both get exasperated over bridge, but we don't carry the anger any farther. Away from the bridge table, Sybil is a kind, sweet person."

"And Alan is too," Sybil said, then muttered, "although he always starts the arguments."

Tired of the bickering, Vivian said, "Tell us what you did last night after the game."

"We didn't have to look at the final scores to know that we didn't qualify," Alan told her. "Not that we thought that we'd make the cut after we saw our afternoon results, but we always enter bridge events with great optimism. Since we knew we'd be playing in the consolation, we went right to our room as soon as the game ended. We read for a few minutes and then went to bed. We were both asleep when the fire alarm rang."

Vivian turned to Sybil. "Anything to add to that?"

"There is something that might interest you," Sybil said. "I woke up briefly when I thought I heard voices coming from the room next door, but the sounds suddenly stopped, and I fell asleep again."

"Do you know whose room that is?" Vivian asked.

Alan and Sybil looked at each other. "It was Tom Stanhope's room," Sybil said.

"Could you make out any of the words?" Vivian asked.

"No. I thought Tom might have come into his room and turned on the television set for a few minutes. I don't know if anyone was there with him or how long there had been sounds coming from the room before I woke up. Since the noise stopped pretty quickly, I thought it was probably from the TV. Lots of bridge players turn their sets on when they return to their rooms late at night."

"Do you have any idea what time you heard these voices?" Vivian asked.

"I glanced at the clock radio. It was close to two o'clock," Sybil replied.

"Did you hear anything?" Vivian asked Alan.

"No, I sleep through everything. Sybil had to wake me when the fire alarm rang."

"Okay, if that's all you can tell us, you can go now," Vivian told them. "We'll call you back later."

* * * * *

"What do you think?" Vivian asked.

"They've given us a little more information," Rollins said. "Sybil confirmed that someone was talking in Tom's room at around two o'clock. Remember, Linda heard voices at about the same time when she went to his room and knocked on his door. With voices loud enough to wake Sybil, it's possible there was a fight going on in there. Linda's knocking must have warned them to be quiet."

"What about the rest of the Nestors' story?"

Herb spoke up. "From what Jennifer told me about them, I'd say they were telling the truth about themselves. They *do* seem to have a good relationship away from the table. They may not be able to control themselves at the bridge table, but I doubt if they're murderers. How many more people do we need to interview before the game starts? It's nearly eight o'clock."

"Four. We'd better hurry."

* * * * *

They did the next two interviews quickly. Then it was Sharon's turn.

"I'm Sharon Price," she said to Vivian as she strolled into the room. "Hi, Herb. Eva told me you were here. What can I tell you?"

"How about telling us who killed him?" Vivian said.

Sharon looked startled for a minute, then realized she was being teased. "I wish I could. Several of us would have liked to—me included. He was very offensive."

"Most of the people we've talked to so far seemed to have had some kind of altercation with Tom," Vivian said. "Did you?"

"Just the usual unpleasantness at the bridge table. Eva and I got more than our share of good results from him—which wasn't easy. He was one tough player. But no matter how many times we did well against him, he would sneer and make some remark about beginner's luck or terrible bids that turned out right. He was never gracious about our good scores. And sometimes we *did* make fantastic plays against him. When we play above our abilities against other pros, they compliment us. But not Tom. He couldn't stand to lose to anyone he thought was an inferior player—which in his mind was everyone else."

"Tell us how you spent your time after the game last night," Vivian said.

"Gary Alexander asked me to have a drink with him while we were waiting for the scores. We went to the bar off the lobby. A little later, Eva and Jonathan came in and told us that we had qualified. Then they left, and we ordered another drink."

"How long did you stay there?" Vivian asked.

"We were there till around one-thirty, discussing how to play different card combinations," Sharon said.

"And then?"

"Then Gary asked me to come to his room. He wanted to improve my trick-taking ability."

Vivian waved her out of the room.

Herb laughed. "You didn't even ask her if she saw anything unusual when they left the bar, or if she noticed anything in the parking lot."

Vivian shrugged. "What was the use? She had other things on her mind. Besides, you know Eva and Sharon better than I do. Do you think either one is a killer?"

"Under the right circumstances, either one could probably kill. They're both strong, determined women. But as far as I can tell, neither of them had a motive."

Vivian nodded. "Even if they had some secret reason to murder him, the evidence—if there were any—would probably be well hidden in their homes. I doubt if we'll find anything in their rooms here."

"Doesn't that go for all the suspects?" Herb asked. "Why would anyone leave any damaging information in their hotel rooms? And the motive for the murder could have originated six months or six years ago, with *no* clues available now."

"You'd be amazed at some of the clues that criminals leave around. Often little objects like a paper clip or a birthday candle will be enough to break a case open. If we're lucky, our technical team will have found something to help us. I'll call headquarters as soon as we finish and see if they found anything near the dumpster. We just have Lou Turner left. Let's get this over with."

Chapter Thirteen

* * * * *

Lou barreled into the room. "I didn't kill him," he said without any preliminaries. "Although I wanted to last night."

"He was killed last night, Mr. Turner," Vivian said quietly.

"You know what I meant. He made me furious at the bridge table. I think the man was an out-and-out cheat."

"From what I understand, you can be barred from playing bridge for making unsubstantiated accusations like that," Herb said.

"So? What's he going to do about it? He's dead."

"Why were you so angry at him?" Vivian asked.

"I play a lot on the pro circuit, and I've never enjoyed playing against him. I've always felt there was something unethical about him, but no one has ever been able to prove anything. Then last night, he failed to open a hand that even a beginner would open. I think that somehow he found out that the hand wouldn't make game. By making his original pass, he made sure that he and Cliff wouldn't get to game on a hand that wouldn't make."

"How could he have gotten that information?" Vivian asked.

"There are lots of ways to find out about a hand, if you're really determined. He could have overheard someone at the next table complain about all the trumps being stacked in one hand. Or he could have seen a score before it was turned in. There was no way he would have passed that hand without some unauthorized information."

"What did you do about it?" Vivian asked.

"I called Jennifer to the table. She looked at his cards and agreed with me that it was the kind of hand that Tom would ordinarily open. But there wasn't much she could do. Then he had the nerve to brag about his result. I was really steamed."

"Enough to kill him?"

134

"Probably, for about twenty seconds. After I calmed down, I decided to make a report about it to the District Recorder. They take these complaints seriously and would have kept an eye on him. A lot of people have been wondering if he cheats. Jennifer would certainly have backed me up on my complaint. She wasn't pleased, either."

"What did you do after the game?" Vivian asked.

"I left right away. I didn't need to see our score. I've played in enough games to know that I'd be playing in the consolation today. I went to my room and thought about how I could placate May, my new wife. She wasn't happy that I stayed to play in the money game. She's going to be even more unhappy when she finds out I didn't make the cut for the finals. If I could have come home with lots of money, it might have helped. Now the best I can do is win the consolation."

"Did you see or hear anything else before the fire alarm went off?"

"No. I took a shower and then fell asleep with the television on. The next thing I knew, the fire alarm was ringing. I was lucky I heard it over the TV."

"It's just about game time," Vivian said, glancing at her watch. "Maybe you can win the Consolation and worm your way back into May's good graces."

"I'm afraid it's going to take more than a bridge win," Lou said, and then trudged out.

* * * * *

"He's *still* enraged about a dead man," Officer Rollins observed.

"But was he angry enough to kill him?" Vivian asked.

"Who knows?"

CHAPTER 14

It was almost 8:30. Most of the contestants were in their seats, ready for the evening session. The noise and commotion contrasted sharply from the quiet of the afternoon session. There were heated discussions about the afternoon scores and about the murder.

"We still have a chance," Eva said to Sharon. "Even though we were only fourth this afternoon, our score isn't *that* low."

"I know," Sharon said. "I wish I had made four spades on Board Three. I didn't take the right line of play. How could I have been so stupid?"

"Forget about it. It's over. And you're not stupid. You played well on the other hands. Just think about that. Even experts make more than one mistake each session."

"Yes, but then they usually don't win the event," Sharon said. "It's simple. The winners make the fewest mistakes. At least I did make some good plays. What I liked best was endplaying Jeffrey on that three no-trump hand."

"Yeah. Did you see the look he gave you? He thought he could relax when he saw that we were his opponents. I'll bet he'll have some respect for our game the next time he plays against us. Now, tell me how your interview went."

"Well, I think I told them more about Gary and me than I had to," Sharon said, blushing. "It's just that when I have a good time, it's hard for me not to let the world know."

"The crime they want to solve is murder," Eva said. "It's no crime to be happy. I wonder how much Gary told them about last night."

"I doubt if he told them anything personal about us. He's very discreet."

"Nobody ever accused *you* of that."

"According to Gary, I have other qualities."

Eva groaned.

"Did you remember to go to the checkout desk to look at our bills?" Sharon asked.

They had learned to look at their statements the night before checking out. In the past, charges they hadn't made had been added to their bills. Last year, in Cincinnati, they were billed for seven days of parking even though they didn't have a car there. They tried to tell that to the desk clerk, but she didn't believe them. Exasperated, Eva finally said, "Okay. If you can bring our car around, we'll pay for the parking."

After that experience, they began to check their statements ahead of time. Then they could straighten out any errors and leave in the morning without any hassles.

"I went to the desk right after I finished my dinner," Eva said. "I asked to see printouts for both of our rooms. The clerk was busy flirting with the manager and wasn't paying much attention. She gave me my bill, but she pulled up Cliff Bryce's bill instead of yours. I guess she thought I said Bryce instead of Price. Just be glad you don't have to pay his. It was over four hundred dollars more than yours. I couldn't resist looking to see why it was so high. There were several long distance phone calls charged to his room."

"He probably used his computer to call his company," Sharon said. "I don't know how he can keep up with his business. I'd expect a CEO of any company I'd invested in to be around more often than he is. How about our statements? Did you see any mistakes?"

"Of course. They tried to charge us for dinner the night we ate at Salvatore's. Luckily, I still had the receipt from Salvatore's in my purse."

"I wish they'd examine people's room keys or identities when they let them sign for dinner. I'll bet we bought dinner for a lot of strangers before we started checking."

"It's too late to worry about that," Eva told her. "What we need to do now is concentrate on bridge. We're going to have to rack up a gigantic score tonight if we hope to win any of the major prize money."

Sharon yawned.

* * * * *

Jeffrey's game hadn't been as sharp as usual that afternoon. He and Ralph had lost their lead. Instead of concentrating on the game, Jeffrey had been trying to figure out where Ralph had gone last night. He sat down at the bridge table for the evening session without making any effort to speak to Ralph.

Ralph didn't want to blow their chances of winning, but he was determined not to tell Jeffrey where he'd been. He hated the dilemma.

"We're only a little bit below average," he tried tentatively. "We won that Open Pairs at the Chicago Regional last summer, and we had an even worse afternoon session there than we did today."

Jeffrey stared at him. "Spare me the pep talk. This isn't an ordinary field of players. No one's going to give anything away tonight. With all that money within everyone's reach, there'll be a fight for every matchpoint."

"We can be as tough as any of them," Ralph said. Jeffrey ignored him. "How did your interview go?" he finally asked.

"I didn't have anything special to tell them," Jeffrey said primly. "I said that we did well and that after I saw the scores, I went to the room and went to sleep." Unable to help himself, he asked Ralph, "What did you tell them?"

"Nothing."

"Nothing? Didn't they ask where you were?"

"Yes, but I didn't tell them."

Jeffrey looked at him in amazement. "I thought you had to tell them everything in a murder investigation. What did they do when you refused?"

"What *could* they do? They don't have any evidence that would make me the killer. And I had no motive—other than the same dislike for Tom that everyone else had. They could hardly arrest me for that."

"What would you have done if they'd stopped you from playing tonight because you were withholding information?" Jeffrey asked angrily. "When you refused to tell them where you were last night, you could have screwed up our chances of winning this event."

"I'm here, aren't I?"

* * * * *

"Looks like we have a chance to win this," Jonathan said.

"Yes, but don't get overconfident," Gary replied. "Two other pairs have scores close to ours. And even though Ralph and Jeffrey didn't have a good game this afternoon, I wouldn't count them out. They're tough players."

"That's true, and I guess there's always a wild card," Jonathan said. Then he grinned and added, "Even Sharon and Eva could win."

Gary just laughed. "Don't be smug. They're decent players. I wouldn't count them out, even though they'd have to have an extraordinary game tonight. Their afternoon score was only about a board above average. Still, they are capable of having a super game."

"Since when are you scared of two 'little old ladies'?"

"If *they're* typical 'LOLs,' the term's been misdefined."

* * * * *

Kathy sat down at her table and watched while Linda nervously ripped an old score card into tiny pieces. She'd never seen her partner so tense.

"What's the matter with you?" she asked. "I don't understand why you're so jittery. One of the strongest competitors has been eliminated—in every way—and we were second in the section this afternoon, and neither of us is a murderer. If you want a shot at placing in this event, you'd better relax."

"Sorry," Linda said. "I guess the murder and all those questions have really gotten to me."

"Why should the questioning bother you?" Kathy asked. "You weren't even here after the game, so what could you possibly tell them?"

Linda was surprised that Kathy hadn't heard that she had come back to the hotel. She decided not to tell her. She'd had enough questions from the detective without having Kathy bugging her.

"I just don't like having people snooping into my life," Linda said.

"Why? Do you have something to hide?"

"Doesn't everybody?"

Kathy, thinking about her affair with Tom, didn't say another word.

* * * * *

Cliff Bryce could hardly stand it. Perhaps Dr. Arthur Kingsley knew his way around a surgical amphitheater, but the good doctor simply couldn't score the ace of trump. Cliff wanted to kick himself for picking Kingsley instead of one of the others. He couldn't imagine that any of the other volunteers would have been worse. He didn't know how he was going to survive another session with Kingsley.

"I'm sorry about the three notrump and six heart hands that I didn't make this afternoon," Kingsley said when he sat down across from Cliff. "I guess I was so overawed playing with you that I played worse than I usually do. I'll try to do better tonight."

"I'm sure you will," Cliff said. It would be useless telling Arthur that he played like an idiot. He just wanted to get this awful day over with, get on a plane, and go back to Rochester.

* * * * *

In the consolation game, the commotion was similar to that on the other side of the room. Everyone was a little crazy from the combination of the murder and the last chance to win money.

"If you'll try harder tonight and really concentrate, we'll have a chance to win the consolation," Alan Nestor said to Sybil.

"Don't start," she warned. "The only reason we won our section this afternoon was that you were too unnerved about the murder to criticize my game. See how well I play when you leave me alone?"

"We could've had an even higher score if you'd made three notrump," Alan persisted.

"You really don't want to win this, do you?" Sybil yelled. "You're already badgering me, and the game hasn't even started yet. You must *want* to lose."

"Okay, okay, I'll try to keep quiet. But don't forget to count your winners."

* * * * *

Lou Turner wished he could withdraw from the consolation, but that wouldn't be fair to Jake. Of course, continuing to play wouldn't help much, either. They didn't have a chance to win any of the prizes now. He had never had so many awful sessions in a row. Tom's jibes about how bad a player he was were beginning to ring true. It was embarrassing.

* * * * *

Charles Canning wandered around the ballroom in a stupor. The news media had picked up the murder story and given it national coverage. Orin Staples had called him from Century about an hour ago to find out what was happening. Charles told him what little he knew, and tried to convince him that Century's image wouldn't be harmed. His reassurances sounded hollow, even to himself. In sympathy, Staples ended up comforting Canning . . . which made Canning feel even more helpless. He yearned for the simpler years of playing professional basketball.

CHAPTER 15

"Everyone should be seated by now," Jennifer said. "The hand records are coming out." Ruth and David passed the hand records to each table, and the contestants once again duplicated the boards. Then Jennifer said, "Before we begin tonight's session, Vivian Greene has an announcement."

Vivian walked over to the directors' table, where everyone could see her. "I'm sorry to interrupt," she said, "but since so many of you hope to leave tomorrow, we need to move ahead as quickly as possible. I'm going to give those of you who are staying at this hotel a paper to sign that will give the police department permission to search your rooms. You aren't obligated to sign, but if we wait to get search warrants," she bluffed, "the process could be extended by several days. Officer Rollins and I will pass out the permission slips now."

As they put the slips on each table, they heard plenty of muttering, but no one objected. Vivian wondered if anyone would refuse to sign.

Eva picked up her authorization slip and read:

I, _____, DO HEREBY GIVE THE POLICE OF THE CITY OF VIRGINIA BEACH PERMISSION TO SEARCH MY HOTEL ROOM, NO. _____.

DATE: _____   SIGNATURE: _____

"Oh dear," Eva murmured as she contemplated the form. "I wonder what she'll think when she finds the condoms in my underwear drawer."

"Don't you keep them in your pocketbook?" Sharon whispered.

"Well, since I didn't have any reason to put them there at this tournament, I never took them out of my drawer," Eva replied. "Where are yours?"

"I don't have any left."

* * * * *

Gary Alexander looked at the slip and signed it quickly. Jonathan studied it for a while.

"Aren't you going to sign?" Gary asked.

"Yes, but I resent having someone go through my things. Not that I have anything to hide," he added, "but there's something offensive about having people search your room." He frowned, then picked up his pen and signed.

* * * * *

"I'm tempted not to sign this," Ralph said.

"Why? Do you have something hidden that you don't want them to find?" Jeffrey asked.

Ralph hesitated for a fraction of a second. "No." He signed, then turned the paper over.

Jeffrey wondered about the hesitation. He had shared the room with Ralph all week, but he'd never noticed anything that could possibly incriminate either one of them. Maybe his curiosity over Ralph's disappearance was making him overly suspicious. Still, he wished he could be in the room when Vivian and Herb made their search. He signed his own slip and put it on the table with the others.

* * * * *

"Aren't you glad we're not staying here?" Kathy asked. "I wouldn't want strangers poking through my belongings."

"If they don't find anything incriminating here, they may search our homes next," Linda said glumly.

* * * * *

Cliff Bryce barely looked at the piece of paper. He signed it with a flourish. Then he folded it up and made a halfhearted attempt to discuss notrump bidding sequences with Kingsley.

* * * * *

Lou Turner didn't bother to read the slip. He just signed his name in the blank space. He didn't care if they searched his room. Things couldn't get worse than they already were.

* * * * *

The Nestors carefully discussed whether or not they wanted someone going through their room.

"I don't see any reason for this," Sybil said. "We didn't kill Tom, and I dislike having somebody pawing through all my clothes."

"Do you want to refuse?" Alan asked.

"What'll happen if we do?"

"If they think we have something to hide, they could try to keep us here until they get a search warrant. Legally, I doubt they can do anything, but if we object, we'll instantly become prime suspects. We might not be able to leave tomorrow like we planned."

"But we have to be back home by Thursday for that seminar in family sensitivity."

"Then I guess we'd better sign."

"All right, but it offends me," Sybil said. "I'll sign for both of us." She made an indecipherable scrawl on the signature line.

* * * * *

When everyone had finished, Jennifer said, "Detective Greene will come around now and collect your permission slips. I know that it's been a difficult day, but please try to treat your opponents and partners courteously. And remember, Ms. Greene expects to interview many of you again after the game. Just before the last round, we'll let you know who needs to remain. If everyone is ready, we'll begin the game. North players, please pass your boards to the next lower table. Good luck to all of you."

CHAPTER 16

Vivian and Officer Rollins took the permission slips back to Room 111, where they had agreed to meet Herb. When they looked through the documents, they found that all of the contestants had signed.

"I guess they were afraid not to let us search," Vivian said. "It would look too suspicious."

"It was a good idea springing it on them like you did," Herb said. "I wonder how many of them wished they'd had time to go back to their rooms to hide something."

"I'm glad you'll be helping me," Vivian said. "You're the only one who knows these people personally. We'll be less likely to overlook any clues if we do the rooms together." She turned to Rollins. "While Herb and I work here, I want you to select a team and make inquiries about the local bridge players who're involved in the money game. You won't have much time, but interview as many neighbors, friends, and people they work with as you can. Besides Jennifer and Herb, your list should include Eva, Sharon, Linda, Kathy, and Dr. Kingsley."

Rollins gave her an incredulous look. "That gives us about three hours to investigate seven people. That's impossible."

"I know. But do the best you can."

"I have a suggestion," Herb said. "You'd be wise to send someone over to Jennifer's bridge studio to talk to some of the other bridge players who live here. If there are any secrets or rumors concerning the people on your list, they'd be the most likely to know about them. There's a game going on there tonight, so you'll have many of the people you'd need to talk to all in one place."

"Good idea, Bob ." Vivian said. "You do that, and let the other members of your team do the other interviews."

"Right. I'm off."

"Do you want to do this in any special order?" Herb asked after Rollins left.

"Let's start with the rooms on the highest floors and work our way down. That seems most efficient to me. Ron Albright gave me a passkey, so we won't have to ask for a key to every room. He also gave me a list of all the contestants' room numbers. This is going to be a grubby job. Besides everything else, we'll have at least ten days' worth of dirty laundry to wade through."

"I've searched through a lot worse," Herb said.

Vivian handed the list to him. "Here, you take care of this."

"Okay. Gary Alexander is on the concierge floor. I have a key to get up there, so let's start with him."

* * * * *

They let themselves into Gary's room and went right to work.

"This man is *very* organized," Vivian observed, looking through his dresser drawers. "He even folded his dirty laundry neatly—and according to colors. He'll be able to dump it in the washing machine without even sorting it when he gets home."

"Do you suppose Sharon would be impressed?" Herb asked.

"I don't know. We'll have to see what her room looks like. If hers is a mess, we won't tell him. I'd hate to break up a romance over laundry."

Herb inspected the closet, examining the pockets in the suits, pants, and sports jackets. He bent down and ran his fingers through the toes of a pair of sneakers. "Nothing so far," he reported.

"There's a portable computer on the desk," Vivian said. "I wonder what he uses it for."

"According to Jennifer, a lot of the bridge players travel with computers. They use them if they need to access their businesses or their home computers while they're traveling. Some of the bridge pros keep extensive notes on their bridge systems and consult them when they need to. Jonathan probably uses his to store information for his bridge articles. That reminds me. I wonder if Cliff ever checked his statistical charts to settle his argument with Tom."

"We can ask him tonight," Vivian said. "Let's turn this computer on and see what kind of information Gary stored in it."

"Okay, but we'd better make sure we don't erase anything by mistake."

"Don't worry," Vivian said. "I used to teach a computer class at the community college one night a week. I can handle that part, but you'll have to explain the bridge to me."

"I'll try," Herb said. "I'm only a beginner, though. If there's anything subtle in here, it'll be over my head."

They turned the computer on and did a quick survey of the programs that were available. The screen showed:

WORDPERFECT
DOS SHELL PROGRAM
COMMUNICATIONS PROGRAM (CROSSTALK)

Under WORDPERFECT, Vivian found the "Bridge" subdirectory and retrieved the files. Using the preview feature, she paged through "Leads" and "Percentage Plays" for a couple of minutes, but realized that without any idea of how to play the game, she wouldn't recognize even an obvious clue. Herb, who looked at the screen over her shoulder, didn't see anything that looked suspicious to him. When Vivian looked up with a questioning expression, he shrugged.

She tried the communications program and found several subfiles concerned with the stock market, but nothing there appeared to relate to the murder.

"This is hopeless," Vivian said. "The answer could be right in front of us, and I wouldn't have any idea."

"There's probably a simpler explanation of the murder than anything stored in these files," Herb said. Vivian nodded and turned off the computer.

"So far, the only motive we can find for Gary is that he believes that Tom cheated to win the Vanderbilt. Do you know what Gary would have gained if his team had won?"

"You mean besides prestige and a chance to become internationally famous? To a non-bridge player, that may not sound like motive enough for murder, but according to Jennifer, bridge players would kill for those rewards. Uh, let me rephrase that. I think we need to consider that a bridge player might commit murder for a chance to become an international champion. But that doesn't mean that Gary would."

"Has he ever won any events on as high a level as the Vanderbilt?"

"I don't know, but I can find out. I think we'd better move on. We have lots of rooms to go through tonight."

"Who's next?" Vivian asked.

"Jennifer."

"It would be unprofessional to skip her room just because you're helping me."

"Absolutely," Herb said. "I assume you realize that I'm staying there too. If you'd like, you can inspect it alone. I'll wait in room one-eleven."

"No. You come with me, but I'll make the search."

* * * * *

"I'm impressed," Vivian remarked as she looked around the suite. "Century Bridge Supplies really knows how to treat its employees. No wonder Jennifer wanted to direct this game."

"Yeah, but I'll bet she's wishing now that she hadn't agreed to," Herb said. He pointed to the bar. "It's stocked with everything imaginable. Would you like a drink?"

She let down her defenses for a minute. "Would I ever! But I'm on duty. Fix something for yourself, if you'd like."

"No, thanks. I want to stay alert, too. It's hard enough for me to understand bridge with a clear head. How about a soft drink?"

"Please. Any diet cola will be fine."

Herb fixed them each a drink and handed one to Vivian. "The bedroom is in there," he said, pointing to the right. "There are two bathrooms in the suite. One is off this room over by the bookcase, and the other is across from the closet in the bedroom."

Vivian nodded and made a perfunctory search through the suite. She was puzzled to see some of the papers for Herb's current investigation lying crumpled on the desk. Herb offered no explanation.

"Any observations or comments?" he asked.

"Only that I was told that Jennifer appeared slightly disheveled when she arrived in the parking lot last night. But anyone can put her bathrobe on inside out at that hour. I can't find any reason to believe she committed the murder—unless you and she are in this together and are covering up for each other."

"I was hoping you wouldn't notice. Are you going to arrest me?"

"Not yet. Who's next?"

Herb consulted his notes. "Cliff Bryce, Tom's partner. His room is down the hall."

* * * * *

Cliff's room was immaculate. They took turns going through his possessions, but found nothing incriminating. Cliff's portable computer was on one of the closet shelves.

"You'd think they would give their computers to the front desk for safekeeping while they're out of the room," Herb said.

"Too much trouble to go get them every time they want to use them," Vivian said. "Besides, they're probably insured for theft. Let's turn Cliff's on and see what we can find."

"Is it the same kind as Gary Alexander's?" Herb asked.

"No. His was a different make, and it was two or three years old. This is Compaq's latest toy, and it feels like it weighs less than five pounds. I guess when you're the CEO of a computer company, you can afford the newest ones on the market. This one's a beauty." She turned it on.

Printed on the screen were:

WORDPERFECT 6.1 FOR WINDOWS
LOTUS NOTES
PROCOMM PLUS FOR WINDOWS 95
NORTON UTILITIES 2.0 FOR WINDOWS 95

Vivian looked at the files in the WORDPERFECT directory and found the bridge subdirectory. When she tried to retrieve it, the computer responded with:

ENTER PASSWORD

"Well, that's interesting!" she said. "He encrypted his bridge file. We need to know his password to get into it. We didn't have any problem getting into Gary's bridge file. Why do you think Cliff's protecting his?"

"He might be working on something new and doesn't want anyone to see it. Or maybe he's afraid that someone would maliciously destroy the bridge information he's collected over the years. From what we've heard about Tom, I wouldn't put it past him to pull a stunt like that."

"On his own partner?"

"Well ... maybe that is a little far-fetched. Instead of wasting our time trying to get into an encrypted file, let's ask Cliff about it when we interview him later."

Vivian played with the computer for a few more minutes and had no trouble retrieving any of the other files.

"That's strange," she said. "You'd think Cliff would have encrypted all the information about his computer company that he's stored in here. But he didn't. I wonder why just the bridge files are protected."

"Even if it has something to do with the murder, he's had all night to come up with an explanation ... or to erase anything that he didn't want seen," Herb said. "Let's ask him to retrieve the bridge file when we talk to him later."

"Cliff puzzles me," Vivian said. "He stood to lose the most when Tom died, so he should be on the bottom of the list of suspects. But somehow, I get the feeling he's more relieved than upset at Tom's death."

"Yes, I noticed that too, but I can't figure out how killing Tom would be to his advantage. Now he'll need a new partner when he competes with his Vanderbilt team. It isn't easy to play on that level with a new partner. It takes years to develop partnerships, but now Cliff will only have a short time to get something workable going. You can't afford too many misunderstandings and still hope to win. That's reason enough to want to keep Tom alive."

"We still have no idea where Cliff was after the game," Vivian said. "He says he went to his room and didn't leave until the fire alarm rang, but we have no proof of that. I realize he had a lot to lose by Tom's death. Besides having to find a new partner, he and Tom might easily have won the money tournament. Is he rich enough to casually throw that away by murdering his partner?"

"I don't know. He might be. He's the CEO of a successful computer company. At least I *think* it's successful. With the slowdown in the economy and the competition from so many new companies, it's possible that his company isn't doing that well. But that would give him even more reason to keep Tom alive. He'd need his fifty thousand dollar share of the prize."

"If we can't find the murderer tonight, we're going to have to investigate the solvency of Bryce's company,"

Vivian said. "Why can't there just be a jealous wife who murdered Tom instead of all these complications?"

"If all murders were that easy to solve, you'd be doing something else," Herb said. "You love the challenge."

"Caught me. Who's next?" she said quickly. She was uneasy about starting a personal conversation with Herb. He was beginning to look a little too attractive to her. She was barely over Blake's defection, and here she was considering a flirtation with Herb—even though she knew he was involved with Jennifer. God, she felt shallow.

"Eva and Sharon are the only other bridge players who wangled rooms on the concierge level," Herb said, unaware of the feelings he'd stirred up in Vivian. "They were on one of the lower floors last week, but I'm not at all surprised to see that they ended up here."

When they let themselves into the sisters' rooms, they were pleased to see that the connecting door was open.

"Shall we each take one room to save time?" Herb asked.

"No. It'll be just as fast this way. Besides, you might catch something that I would miss, since you know them."

"Okay." Herb began going through Eva's closet. "This is just as I'd imagined it would be. Eva always wears suits and tailored clothes, and this closet is *full* of them. Everything here is very neat. She even placed the matching shoes underneath the clothes they go with."

"Never mind the fashion show patter," Vivian said, all business. "Go through the pockets and see if you can find anything."

"Yes, ma'am!" Herb mocked her. "You're pretty efficient. Maybe I ought to hire you away from the police department to help me in *my* investigative work." When she ignored his comment, he turned back to his chores. "There's something in one of her pockets, but it won't help us much."

"What is it?"

"A piece of paper with a bridge hand written on it," he said. "There are slashes through each of the numbers. Jennifer taught me to do the same thing when I can't mentally picture what's happening in a hand. It's easier to figure out how to play or defend when you write out the whole hand and then cross off each card as you play it out mentally."

"I don't understand a word you're talking about," Vivian said. She returned to her inspection of Eva's dresser drawers. Then she suddenly laughed.

"What's so funny?"

She held up a couple of packages of condoms.

"Good for her," Herb said.

"It would be better for her if they were gone by now."

When they finished examining all the clothes, they went to the closet and pulled the suitcases down.

"This is amazing," Vivian said. "There are four suitcases here, even though the sisters live in town! Why couldn't either of them go home if they forgot something?"

"Jennifer says they always travel like that. They each take enough clothes and shoes for two people. They want to be sure they have enough with them for any kind of weather. And they're probably smart. A lot of hotel ballrooms and convention centers are either overheated or too cold, and it can vary day by day or even from one session to the next. I think it depends on the complaint of the last person to speak to the custodial staff. *These* women go prepared."

After finding nothing in any of the suitcases, Herb noticed Eva's large makeup case on the bathroom shelf. "Do we have to go through all of that?"

Vivian shook her head. "Let's just open the zippered cases inside the makeup case and make sure there's no gun hidden there." They performed the task quickly, finding nothing.

"All we have left in here is the cooler over there by the window," Vivian said. "I'm surprised they could get all this stuff in one car."

"Jennifer says it's amazing to watch them when they have to keep track of all their belongings while they're busy changing rooms in hotels," Herb said. "She's seen all their luggage make three round trips to the registration desk. They not only monopolize the desk clerk, but also the bellhop. They aggravate a lot of people who would simply like to check in."

"What's wrong with the rejected rooms?" Vivian asked.

"There are *lots* of things that don't suit them. Sometimes a faucet in the bathroom leaks or the air conditioner freezes them or the heater rattles too much. If the rooms smell funny, they leave. They also need lots of drawer and closet space—as you can see. And connecting rooms. The list goes on and on. One thing, though . . . if the hotel is filled and they can't get their choice of rooms, you can bet that by the time they leave, everything in the rooms they *do* occupy will be perfect. Jennifer says she likes to go to hotels and find the room where the sisters stayed the last time they were there. Everything works."

Vivian laughed. "The stories about them sound absurd, but I admire them for insisting that everything be right. After all, their hotel rooms are their homes when they go to tournaments. Why shouldn't they be comfortable?" She bent to open the cooler. "There's nothing here but juice and fruit. She's going to need some ice soon. If we had more time, I'd go get it for her. Do you think she was more involved with Tom than she admits?"

"I doubt it. I believe her when she said she only hired him once. Knowing Eva, she would never put up with his insolence. She would get rid of him and hire a professional she enjoyed playing with. Besides, since Sharon's husband died, Eva's done most of her traveling with Sharon."

"Well, for the moment, I can't find any reason for Eva to have killed Tom. But I'm not ready to eliminate anyone yet. Let's see what we can find in Sharon's room."

* * * * *

Sharon's room looked like a teenager's hang-out. A sweater and several pairs of slacks were thrown over a chair. Books and newspapers were tossed in a heap on the desk; several partially filled drinking glasses were scattered on her nightstand. Two suitcases, one not completely closed, leaned against opposite walls.

"Sharon's closet sure isn't like Eva's," Herb observed as he went through the jumble of clothes. "You'd never guess that they were sisters from the looks of their closets."

"It'd be a lot easier to do this investigation if everyone were as neat as Eva," Vivian said, sorting through the dresser drawers. "Sharon does seem to have some organization here, actually. One drawer has only dirty laundry in it. She uses the other ones separately for her clean nightgowns, underwear, and sweaters." Then she laughed. "Listen to me! I sound like a real fusspot. This search must be getting to me, or else I'm getting tired. We need to get something to eat soon, so I can revive my energy . . . and my sanity. Let's do the bathroom and the suitcases and get out of here."

"My God," Herb said when he walked into the bathroom. The sink was covered with lipsticks, makeup, cotton balls, jars, used towels, and several plastic containers. "Are you sure Sharon and Eva are sisters?" All of Eva's cosmetics had been packed neatly in zippered bags.

"At least you don't have to look through a bunch of containers to find anything hidden," Vivian said from the bedroom. "Everything is right in front of you." She reached up to the closet shelf and pulled the suitcases down. "Do you know if Sharon ever hired Tom or had any arguments with him?"

"I don't know. Like Eva, I suspect she wouldn't have let Tom rile her. From what we've seen, Tom was more apt to pick on people who were weak or didn't know how to fight back." He inspected Sharon's ice chest while he talked. It was larger than Eva's, containing yogurt and bagels as well as fresh juice and fruit. "Find anything interesting in the suitcases?"

"Only the fact that she brought one more than Eva did."

"All right," Vivian said. "Who's next?"

"Charles Canning. He's down on the tenth floor."

"I hope he's not sitting in his room when we get there," Vivian said.

"I don't think he will be. I suspect he's worried enough by now to spend his time at the bridge game. He'll have a hard enough time explaining to his company why he wasn't there all day yesterday."

"If he's lucky, they'll never realize that he wasn't."

* * * * *

When they entered Canning's room, they burst out laughing. Lined up on his desk were all his basketball trophies. And he had mounted two pictures on the wall—one showing him at a victory dinner with the governor of his state, and the other with the vice president.

"Talk about insecure!" Vivian said. "I wonder who he thinks he's going to impress with these. I'll bet he hasn't even asked anyone up to his room."

"It's really kind of sad," Herb mused. "Imagine having to travel with your trophies to prop up your ego. He must be a very lonely man. Jennifer told me that he was engaged once, but the woman broke it off."

"Maybe he plans to award one of his trophies to the person who performs best in his room this week."

"Looks like he may get to keep them all."

Vivian grinned at Herb and said, "Search." She wished she didn't find him so amusing.

They found samples of products sold by Century stacked on the closet shelf, and some correspondence from the company in the desk. Vivian glanced through a few of the letters. They contained updated lists of available supplies and company news. Nothing even slightly related to the murder.

"Well, this is interesting," Herb said. He held up a piece of paper that he'd pulled from a jacket pocket.

"What is it?"

"It's a note from Tom wondering if Century Bridge Supplies knows anything about some basketball games that were fixed when Canning was a star at Syracuse University years ago. Then it mentions how pleased he'd be if he won something in the money game. It's written cleverly enough to dodge a blackmail charge, but I'm sure Canning knew exactly what he meant."

"What a joke on Tom!" Vivian said. "Canning sure kept the fact that he can't play bridge a secret. This note must have scared the hell out of him. That poor sucker couldn't fix a game even if he wanted to. He wasn't even smart enough to destroy the note."

"Are you going to confront Canning with it?"

"I suppose so." Vivian sighed. "I hope he doesn't have a heart attack when he sees that we have it. The poor man just doesn't know how to cope."

"So if Canning interpreted this as blackmail, he does have a motive after all," Herb observed. "At this rate, we're going to end up with too many suspects. Maybe they all did it ... like the Orient Express."

"It's beginning to look that way. Who's next?"

"Ralph Dunbar and Jeffrey Howard," Herb said. "Maybe we can find something in their room that'll give us a clue about what Ralph was up to last night."

"I doubt that he'd leave anything lying around that Jeffrey could see."

"Just wishful thinking."

CHAPTER 17

When they let themselves into Ralph and Jeffrey's room, the first thing they noticed was the twin beds.

"That's a surprise," Vivian said.

"Yeah. Maybe they need their rest for the tournament."

Vivian searched through the drawers while Herb tackled the closet. "This must be Ralph's side. The shirts are larger," Vivian commented. She wrinkled her nose as she moved over to Jeffrey's side. "What a slob Jeffrey is. I wonder how he can tell what's clean."

"Maybe nothing is," Herb said. "They've been here a long time."

After a futile search in the bathroom, Vivian pulled the suitcases down from the closet shelf and opened the one with Jeffrey's name on it. "This suitcase looks like Jeffrey's owned it all his life. It's as scruffy as his laundry."

"He probably has owned it all his life," Herb sympathized. "New luggage is seldom a priority on a teacher's salary." Searching through Ralph's pockets, he found a business card with two telephone numbers on it. "Look at this," he said to Vivian. "It's Arthur Kingsley's card."

"The doctor who filled in for Tom?"

"Yes. Why would Ralph have Kingsley's card?"

"Kingsley is a plastic surgeon. Maybe Ralph wanted to consult him about having his face done."

"I'll bet it was Kingsley he was talking to in the downstairs bar," Herb said. "No wonder he didn't want

Jeffrey to know where he was. There's no reason to tell Jeffrey about this, is there?"

"None that I can think of. My business is acquiring information, not passing it out. At least, Ralph was seen in the bar downstairs with someone. We need to get the downstairs bartender to identify Ralph and Dr. Kingsley and verify the time line. And we also need to find out how long they stayed at the bar. It's possible Ralph could have made his arrangements with Dr. Kingsley and then killed Tom later."

"How soon do you think we can find out the time of death?"

"Let's go back to Room 111 before we continue," Vivian said. "I want to call headquarters and find out what the investigators have come up with."

They left Ralph and Jeffrey's room and headed toward the elevators.

"We need to find out where Tom was killed ... although I don't know what good that will do," Vivian said. "The suspects seem to have been everywhere but in bed. I've never seen so many people wide awake and running around so late at night."

"That's typical of bridge players," Herb said with a chuckle. "They don't seem to need much sleep. Some of them play in a midnight game 'til two or three in the morning, get up to play in another game at nine in the morning, and then play again at one and seven-thirty."

"I wish I had their stamina," Vivian said, enviously. "After they spend all those hours playing late at night and early in the morning, how can they be fresh enough to compete the rest of the day?"

"I haven't the slightest idea."

"Their whole way of life is incomprehensible to me," Vivian said, shaking her head, "but the odd thing is, they all seem to enjoy it. It's an amazing subculture."

When the elevator arrived, Vivian punched the button for the first floor. As soon as they stepped out, they were besieged by television and newspaper reporters. Vivian put them off as politely as she could, then grabbed Herb's hand and pulled him into the conference room.

"I wonder why so many reporters are waiting around," she said. "Don't they have anything better to do? After all, this isn't Desert Storm or a presidential election."

"A bridge game with such a large payoff is unique. With the murder added, you have a plot for a TV story of the week -- like the disease-of-the-week stories they love to do. The public feels virtuous reading this kind of juicy article in their local paper instead of the *National Enquirer*—and the reporters know it. Don't worry. Something else will surface by tomorrow that'll capture their interest."

"I hope you're right," Vivian said. "I find it awkward having them around when I have nothing to say. It makes me feel stupid and inept."

"You're clearly neither. No one expects you to solve a murder in one day. Not even reporters with deadlines."

"Well, if we don't solve it tonight, it's going to get sticky. We can't keep the suspects here forever. While I call headquarters, why don't you go find Ralph and see if you can find out what's going on between him and Kingsley. Maybe you can catch him between rounds." She sat down at her desk and briskly dialed police headquarters.

When Herb returned a few minutes later, Vivian had some new information. "From the bloodstains and other evidence they found outside, the investigators concluded that Tom was shot in the hotel parking lot."

"That's a relief. At least they won't have to look for bloodstains in all the hotel rooms. How did they reach that conclusion?"

"They started with a thorough examination of his room. When they didn't find any evidence of a struggle or any blood there, they studied the area where he was found. They discovered traces of blood on the hotel grounds next to the grocery store lot. The killer must have shot Tom in the parking lot and dragged him over to the grocery store."

"Why do you think the killer bothered to move him?" Herb asked. "Why not leave him where he fell?"

"The hotel parking lot is brightly lit. Maybe the murderer was afraid that someone would spot Tom if he were left sprawled on the ground. The lights over by the dumpster are much dimmer. Since we assume that the killer is someone familiar with the strange hours that bridge players keep, he—or she—would know that there might be traffic in the parking lot at any hour. Besides, who knows what motivates bridge players? I feel like I've entered a twilight zone."

"Don't be too hard on bridge players," Herb said. "They have a certain quirkiness that's appealing. Most of them are well-educated people with quick minds. There are lots of lawyers, doctors, brokers, teachers, and accountants playing the game. You should take it up. The different personalities would fascinate you."

"I think I'll skip that, thanks."

"Maybe you'll change your mind when this is over," Herb said.

"I doubt it." Vivian wondered if Herb was just being polite . . . or if he were really interested in her becoming part of the bridge world. She kind of hoped the latter, but this wasn't the time to pursue the subject. "Did you find out anything from Ralph?"

"I sure did. After I told him we had found Dr. Kingsley's telephone number, he pulled a letter from Kingsley out of his wallet and gave it to me." They read the letter together:

Dear Mr. Dunbar,

Thank you for your inquiry about plastic surgery. I was pleased to learn that my colleague in Boston recommended me. I understand your concern about the fee, but I have a suggestion which might benefit both of us.

I play a fair amount of duplicate bridge, and have seen your name mentioned in *The Bridge Bulletin* several times when you've won tournaments. I don't play anywhere near your level, but perhaps we could trade some of my expertise for yours. If you would like to play professionally with me an agreed number of times, I would waive my fee.

We can discuss this when you come to Virginia Beach for the Spring Championships. If possible, I'll try to kibitz you sometime during the week. If you are interested in this arrangement, we can talk about it after one of the sessions. Enclosed is my card with my home and office numbers.

Sincerely yours,
Arthur Kingsley

"I wonder if Ralph will accept Kingsley's proposal," Vivian said.

"I expect he's delighted with the offer. He'll be able to play bridge *and* have his surgery. Although, if Kingsley is a lousy bridge player, Ralph may wish he'd found a way to pay him cash instead of playing with him. It's going to take a lot of pro dates to make up for the thousands of dollars the surgery would cost, even if Kingsley fails to tell the IRS about his barter income."

"Maybe he ought to ask Cliff how the game went today before he makes his decision," Vivian said. "Do you have any idea how they did?"

"When I talked to Jennifer while you were collecting the permission-to-search slips, she said they'd had a terrible game. Cliff was *not* pleased."

"I can imagine. What a letdown. You can't help but feel sorry for Cliff. He's lost his partner and his chance to win the hundred thousand dollar prize—or any of the other prizes."

"If I had a chance to win all that money, I'd at least wait until after the game was over before bumping off my partner."

"I hope Kingsley isn't as bad a player as Cliff seems to think he is. Maybe playing with Cliff scares him and makes him play worse than usual."

"Getting a chance to play with a pro like Cliff sounds great, but it would terrify me," Herb said. "Kingsley has a tough job. He's playing with one expert, and he's expected to take the place of another expert. That's a lot of pressure for anyone to be under, let alone a mediocre player."

"It can't be easy," Vivian agreed.

"What else did they tell you at homicide? Did they find anything in Tom's room?"

"Yes. They said there was a photograph we'd be interested in seeing. They left one of the copies in the top drawer of the desk for us to look at. Let's go find out what they're talking about."

Herb barely caught the door as Vivian strode out ahead of him.

CHAPTER 18

They took the elevator to Tom's floor and let themselves into his room with the passkey.

"Whew," Herb said, wrinkling his nose. "It smells strange in here."

"That's from the luminol they used to test the carpet and the bathroom floor for blood," Vivian told him. "I've smelled it so often, I don't even notice it anymore. Let's see what they think is so important in the desk."

Vivian pulled out the drawer and began sorting through the papers. Underneath several sheets of notes on which bridge hands and comments were scrawled, she found a photograph.

"This must be what they meant...and it is interesting!" She held the photo up for Herb to see. "If this picture isn't a fake, Ralph and Jeffrey may have had a motive after all."

Herb took the photograph from Vivian and stared at a picture of Ralph and Jeffrey kissing on the beach. "I wonder when Tom took this. I'll bet he followed them around with his camera last week and snapped it."

"It's odd that there was no hint of the photo when we interviewed Ralph and Jeffrey this afternoon. Everyone here seems to know everyone else's business. I'm surprised no one mentioned it."

"Maybe Tom didn't have a chance to show it to Ralph and Jeffrey before he was murdered."

"I think you're wrong. Tom didn't seem the type to wait when he thought he could blackmail someone. He seems to have struck when he had the chance. We'll show the picture to Ralph and Jeffrey tonight and see what they have to say about it. I don't know what Tom thought he'd get from them. Neither one of them makes that much money."

"I doubt if it was about money," Herb said. "I'd almost guarantee that Tom expected to use the photo to take advantage of them at the bridge table. I wouldn't be surprised if he threatened to send a copy to their school. The parents and faculty may have overlooked their living together as long as they were discreet, but something as blatant as this picture would be hard to ignore. They could both lose their jobs."

"The more I find out about Tom, the less I like him," Vivian said. "What a sleazebag."

"He seems to have had something on everybody." Herb added. "They're probably all glad he's dead. I'm surprised we're getting any cooperation."

"That's because none of them wants to be blamed—and they all want to get out of here. It's in their best interest to help. Let's search the rest of the room. The investigative team went over it pretty thoroughly, but we'd better take a look, too. You might find something connected to bridge that they wouldn't have understood."

"I'll check the papers in the desk, and you look in the closet," Herb said. He glanced through all of Tom's notes, but couldn't find anything of obvious importance. "We can take these notes to Jennifer or to someone who knows more about bridge than I do," he told Vivian, "but I doubt if there're any clues here. All I see are bridge hands with some comments in the margins." He handed the papers to Vivian.

"I'll give these to Jennifer when we go back down," Vivian said. "Maybe she can give them a quick look while she's directing. I didn't find anything in the closet. Let's look in his suitcases and then do the Nestors' room. They're next door."

* * * * *

They smiled at the wholesome atmosphere in Alan and Sybil's room. Framed family pictures of Nestor children and grandchildren were displayed on the top of the dresser.

"What a difference from Canning's room," Herb commented.

They quickly went through their routine, but found nothing connected with the murder.

"Unless they killed Tom because he insulted them at dinner—which seems preposterous—I can't find any other reason for them to have murdered him," Vivian said. "I wish Sybil had overheard some words or distinguished the voices she heard when she woke up."

"I wonder if she could tell us if she heard a woman's voice or a man's voice talking to Tom."

"Good thought. I'll put that on my list of questions. Who's next?"

"Linda Mason's next on our list, but she doesn't have a room here."

"Linda is a big question," Vivian said. "She wasn't staying here, yet she was at the hotel during the time Tom was murdered. She admits she was looking for him, but she won't say why. What do you know about her?"

"Very little. I met her after I started playing bridge. I know she's worked in one of the local banks for several years. She and Kathy play together often, and they have a decent partnership. Still, I was surprised to see them playing in this game. Linda's always seemed very conservative—not the gambling type. And I was surprised that she was strong enough to convince Kathy to part with the money to play in this game. I agree. There is something odd here. Remember, Jennifer said she saw Tom and Linda talking last night before the evening session started, and Linda looked upset."

"Yes, but what could Tom possibly have known about Linda to blackmail her with?" Vivian asked. "They live in different cities, and I doubt if they even play in the same events very often. There doesn't seem to be any connection.

Did they even know each other before this game, or did she ever hire him?"

"I don't know if she could afford his fees. But Jennifer said that Linda sure looked spooked when Tom was talking to her last night."

"Even if he had something on her, what could he expect from her?" Vivian wondered aloud. "Surely she doesn't have a lot of money. It doesn't make sense. We're going to have to insist that she tell us why she was here last night."

"It'll be a shame if she has to confess to some unrelated crime to save herself from being arrested for Tom's murder."

"Yes and no," Vivian said. "If she did something illegal, she'll have to pay for it whether or not it was connected to Tom's murder. It's unlucky for her if his death unearths an unrelated crime. If she doesn't tell us tonight what's going on, we may have to get a search warrant for her house."

"I hope it doesn't come to that," Herb said. "I like Linda. Talk about being in the wrong place at the wrong time! Well, it's useless to keep speculating about her. Let's get on with it. Jonathan Meltzer's room is on this floor. We'll do his room next."

* * * * *

Vivian entered Jonathan's room and quickly began searching through the dresser drawers. "Do you know what Jonathan does when he's not playing bridge?" she asked.

"He writes bridge books. He wrote one on bidding and defense that's become a beginner's bible. I read it through twice before I dared to play in my first duplicate game. I tried learning bridge by reading books by other authors, but they totally confused me. Jonathan explains bridge better than anyone."

"I wish I'd read his book before I started this investigation," Vivian grumbled. "Maybe I would understand a little about the game. Here's his computer on his desk. Let's see what's in it." She pushed the catch to open it, but nothing happened. "Damn! It's locked."

"I'm not surprised," Herb said. "Why take a chance? Some of his articles and books contain original bridge ideas or variations of existing systems. I'm sure he doesn't want anyone to see his work before he can get it published. If you'd like, I'll go to the ballroom and ask him for the key."

"It's getting late," Vivian said. "We'll take his computer to Room 111 with the others. He can open it up for us later."

They found several bridge manuals and legal pads full of bridge hands in the desk drawers.

"Jonathan must have jotted these down during the week, but he probably didn't have time to enter them in his computer," Herb said.

"How do we know if we're missing any clues in one of these hands?" Vivian asked. "Maybe one of them has to do with the cheating in the Vanderbilt, or is connected with today's game."

"He'd be crazy to leave anything like that sitting around. It would be locked in that computer. Besides, his team wasn't accused of cheating. Why should he hide the hands?"

"I guess he wouldn't. He did have a motive for the murder, though. He was bitter about the Vanderbilt, and Tom ridiculed him when he failed to bid a game yesterday. But those hardly sound like strong enough reasons for murder. One of the difficulties for me in this case is understanding the bridge mentality. Apparently, something that would just tick you or me off might drive one of these people to murder. It's hard to imagine the overwhelming passion for the game that some of them seem to have. The motivations for murder that I understand are hard to untangle when they get mixed up with bridge."

Herb disagreed. "I think the motives we're working with are universal. Wanting desperately to win, or resenting being cheated out of a victory, or being blackmailed—any of these could be motives in other situations. Top sports players or politicians running for office could easily find themselves with the same reasons to murder somebody."

"That's true," Vivian said, "but I still find that bridge complicates the issues."

"You'll have to pretend that bridge players are like other people, if you expect to come up with an answer."

They couldn't find anything else in Jonathan's room. After a quick look at Ruth's and David's rooms on the third floor, they went to Lou's.

When Vivian pulled out the top desk drawer in Lou's room, she unexpectedly found three letters from May.

"I'm glad to see that people still write letters. I feel like a peeping Tom going through these, but I don't see how we can avoid it."

They looked at the postmark dates, and then read them in order. The first one was a typical letter from a new bride:

Honey,

You've only been gone a few hours and I miss you terribly. When I dropped you off at the airport, I was sorry I hadn't come with you like you asked. But I felt guilty about leaving my job for two weeks. It was too soon after our honeymoon to be away again. I sure miss you.

I knew when we married that you would be leaving to play in tournaments, but I didn't realize how hard it would be for me. Anyway, do well and think about me.

Can't wait to see you,

All My Love,
May

"Nice," Herb said. "Let's see what's in the next one." Its tone was a little different.

Dear Lou,

When you called and told me last night that you were thinking of staying and playing in the money tournament, I was really upset. And the more I thought about it, the madder I got. You must have known that you would play in that event since you had to register for it ahead of time. What kind of marriage can we have if we don't trust each other?   Right now, I have very little faith in your word. I think that since you were so underhanded about it, you should let someone else buy out your entry and that you should come home. We need to talk about this.

May

"Uh oh," Herb said. "Looks like this marriage is in trouble already. I'm afraid to even look at the third letter."

"We don't have any choice." Vivian took the last letter out of the envelope. Together they read:

Lou,

Your explanation won't do. Saying you're playing in the tournament to win money for us is not a good enough reason. I don't want the money. I want you. Or at least I did. You seem to care more for the bridge and the money than you do for me. I won't be in the apartment when you come back. I need to think about whether I want to continue this marriage. I'll leave you a note telling you where I am, but don't try to contact me. I'll call you when I'm ready. I'm so disappointed.

May

"Whew! No wonder Lou was so explosive during his interview this afternoon," Herb said.

Vivian demurred. "He could have been only so upset about May. After all, he didn't go home."

"You're right."

"The only other person on our list is Kathy Jensen, and she doesn't have a room here," Vivian said.

"She says she hasn't had anything to do with Tom lately."

"That's what makes this whole thing so exasperating," Vivian complained. "Kathy could have gone to any city and had an argument with Tom without anyone knowing. It's impossible to know what goes on with these people. Whenever they decide to pick up and go to a tournament, off they go."

"Somehow, I think that if Kathy had an argument with Tom in a hotel, it would be overheard by the whole world. Especially if it were about money. Well, that wraps up the room search. We have just enough time to go get a sandwich."

"Great," Vivian agreed instantly. "I'm starved."

CHAPTER 19

By the second round, Jennifer had already been summoned to three different tables to make rulings. The contestants' focus on winning one of the prizes in either the final or the consolation overshadowed the murder; uneasiness about the killing merely increased their edginess. They called the director on each other for any real or imagined infraction.

* * * * *

Despite all the commotion, Sharon and Eva were playing well. When they sat down for the third round, they knew that three of the four boards they'd played so far were above average.

"It scares me when we start out like this," Eva fretted. "I'm always afraid I'll get too careless after I get good results. Or that one of the opponents will fix me on the next board."

"Don't let yourself get jinxed. You're playing well. Just keep doing what you've been doing, and we'll place somewhere."

When Sharon picked up her new hand, she wished she hadn't sounded so smug. It was a wildly distributional hand, and she was unsure how to bid it. After studying her cards carefully, she made her bid—and then, every time it was her turn, kept on bidding. When she reached the five level, her opponents, thinking they had pushed her too high, doubled. Her judgment turned out right; she made her contract.

"That was an interesting bidding sequence," Eva said when they left the table. "I hope you were the only one in the room who found that imaginative series of calls."

"I doubt it. I can't imagine anyone else selling out with seven cards in one suit and six in another. But they had a good sacrifice at the six level, so we'll certainly be above average."

"It's a good thing you didn't do that against poor Lou. He would never recover."

"Our opponents may not, either."

"Good. Then that's one more pair out of the running."

* * * * *

"Director!"

The shrill call came from the Nestors' table in the consolation game. Jennifer wearily picked up her rule book and went over to their table.

Marla Stevens, the woman sitting in the East seat, was furious. "They can't do that," she yelled when Jennifer arrived.

"What's the problem?" Jennifer inquired with all the patience she could muster.

"Alan failed to alert a bid, and I want an adjustment," Marla said indignantly. After describing the situation to Jennifer, she demanded justice. "We were damaged by their failure to alert, and I want something done about it. With all the stuff they have marked on their convention card, they ought to know what they're doing."

"Do you have a special understanding on that bidding sequence?" Jennifer asked the Nestors.

They looked at each other, and finally Alan nodded. "Yes, we do. I failed to alert when Sybil made her bid."

"In that case, I'm going to adjust the score. I can't decide how things would have gone had you alerted, so your opponents will get an average plus on this board, and you'll get an average minus."

As soon as Jennifer left the table, Sybil and Alan began to argue. "You know you need to alert that bid," Sybil said angrily. "We had a lot of top scores this afternoon, and we had a chance to win the consolation until this penalty. If we don't win, it'll be *your* fault. I don't want to hear one word about how I cost us first place."

Alan, who was not used to being wrong at the bridge table—at least in his eyes—shouted back at her. "What do you mean, my fault? How about the last hand where you failed to take the setting trick? You've made a mistake on every hand we've played tonight, and I haven't said a word. I refuse to take the blame for one small error."

"We'll see how that 'one small error' affects our final score. I bet it'll be more costly than anything I do tonight. Despite what you say, I've been playing well. And I would've taken the setting trick on that last hand if you had given me the correct count. Besides, it won't be a zero. Everyone will make that hand, and some will make overtricks. She just gave us a chance to set it, but it's *always* makeable."

"Well, you never want to take advantage of the opponents' mistakes," Alan shot back. "We had a chance for a top, and you blew it."

"Oh, shut up," Sybil screamed at him. Once again, she stood up and strode angrily away from the table.

* * * * *

When Jennifer went back to the directors' table, she discussed the tension with Ruth and David. "I'm afraid this is just the beginning. Even some of the people who are usually nice are being obnoxious tonight. I hope nobody gets violent. One murder is enough. Whenever you're called to make a ruling, do whatever you can to calm everyone down."

"We're trying," Ruth said. "I had to straighten out a bidding problem in the finals while you were over with the Nestors. Any other time it would have been a simple ruling, but tonight both sides argued with me. I've never seen bridge players behave so hatefully."

"It's a nightmare," Jennifer agreed. "The murderer is scared about getting caught. Everyone else is worried either about winning or about blowing a large amount of money because they took a finesse the wrong way. And they all must feel uneasy thinking they're playing with or against a killer."

"Some of them are also wondering if they'll be able to leave town tomorrow," David added. "Most of them have jobs to get back to or have plans for the rest of the week."

"We'll just have to do what we can to keep the unpleasantness to a minimum," Jennifer said with a sigh. She wished she'd followed her instincts and rejected the job.

* * * * *

As the game progressed, Cliff became more and more upset with Arthur Kingsley's bidding and playing. On the fourth round, Arthur pushed the opponents into a slam that they wouldn't have bid without his pointless interference.

Cliff couldn't stand it. Before the opponents had a chance to play the hand, he stood up and flung his cards across the table. "They never would've reached that slam if you'd just passed like a human being," he spat out.

"Director!" the opponents shouted in unison as soon as the cards hit the table.

Jennifer went to the table and grimaced when she saw Cliff's cards scattered all over. "What happened here?" she asked superfluously.

Arthur Kingsley stared at Jennifer in horror, unable to speak. He had remembered reading an article that recommended disrupting the opponents' bidding whenever possible, and that's what he had done. It obviously wasn't right this time, but how was he to know?

Cliff, chagrined at his tantrum, quickly apologized. "Sorry, Jennifer. I'm afraid I got carried away. My partner pushed our opponents into a slam which they were never going to bid without our help. I lost my temper and threw my cards. I apologize to my partner and to the opponents."

"Even Tom wouldn't have thrown his cards," Jennifer said angrily. "This is going to be an expensive outburst. Since your cards are exposed, declarer can ask for them to be played in the order of his choosing. He also can ask for or forbid an opening lead in any suit, and declarer has various options throughout the play if your partner gains the lead. In other words, you are probably headed for a well-deserved zero."

"We were getting a zero anyway, since we pushed them to slam," Cliff said crossly.

"You have no way of knowing how anyone else bid or will bid these cards," Jennifer told him. "What you *do* know is that what you did isn't fair to the rest of the field. Any of the others who were lucky or skillful enough to bid and make the slam are deprived of their fair share of the matchpoints. And the unsportsmanlike disruption requires me to write a disciplinary report to be sent to your home unit for appropriate action."

"You're quite right, Jennifer," Cliff said contritely. "I would be furious if someone else did that. I'm very sorry."

"If you don't control your temper for the rest of the session, you'll be out of this game," Jennifer told him. "I'm not going to put up with any more nonsense like this tonight."

Looking at Cliff's opponents, she said, "Let's get this hand played. I'll tell you your options as you go along."

After declarer duly took all thirteen tricks, Jennifer left the table.

Dr. Kingsley was mortified. His opportunity to play with one of the world's best players had turned into a fiasco. He wondered if he ought to go through with his deal with Ralph. He didn't want to miss the opportunity to play with him, but he couldn't stand the thought of being humiliated like this again. Maybe he should stick to playing in the local club games. He was used to respect, not contempt.

* * * * *

Sharon and Eva finished their round early and decided to go to the ladies' room. On the way, Sharon said, "I received my driver's license renewal form in the mail last week. I hope they don't make me parallel park. I'll never pass."

"I don't think they do that for a renewal," Eva told her. "You usually just have to take the eye test and get a new picture taken. But if they ask you to parallel park, tell them what I did when we moved here. I told the examiner that I never parallel park. If I need to go somewhere and the only parking spaces available are for parallel parking, I go somewhere else."

"What happened when you told him that?" Sharon asked, astonished.

"He said, 'Nice try, lady, but you still have to show me that you can parallel park.' When I didn't respond, he looked over at me. Something in my expression made him realize I was telling the truth. He shrugged and said, 'I don't know why, but I believe you. You obviously know how to drive, even if you can't parallel park. Since that doesn't seem to be a necessity for you, you can drive back to the station and pick up your license. You passed.'"

"How did you have the nerve?"

"What do you mean, nerve? It's true. If I want to go somewhere and there are only parallel parking spots available, I leave. I go back there later and look for a parking spot that suits me."

"Don't you waste a lot of time?"

"Sure, but it's better than hitting the cars on either side while I'm trying to maneuver into an impossible space."

Sharon shook her head. "Use that same *chutzpa* the rest of the session. You're bound to discombobulate someone."

A few minutes later, Sharon and Eva sat down at Jonathan and Gary's table and exchanged friendly hellos with them. Then everyone picked up their new hands and studied them.

Jonathan and Gary found their way to an iffy 6♣ slam. Jonathan, sitting South, was apprehensive when he saw the dummy, but prospects looked more favorable after Eva's lead of a small club.

```
              ♠A3
              ♡AK5
              ◇9743
              ♣9765

                 N
              W     E
                 S

              ♠8
              ♡QJ97
              ◇KQJ
              ♣AK1083
```

He played ♣5 from the board, and when Sharon played the ♣J, he won with the ♣K. Crossing to dummy with ♡A, he called for the ♣6. When Sharon played the deuce, he inserted the ♣10 with some confidence. This was the whole layout:

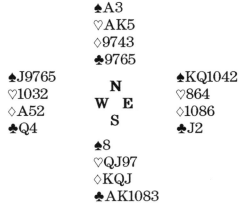

```
              ♠A3
              ♡AK5
              ◇9743
              ♣9765

   ♠J9765         N         ♠KQ1042
   ♡1032       W     E      ♡864
   ◇A52           S         ◇1086
   ♣Q4                       ♣J2

              ♠8
              ♡QJ97
              ◇KQJ
              ♣AK1083
```

Jonathan was crestfallen when Eva took her ♣Q and cashed the ◇A. "Where did you find that lead?" Jonathan asked suspiciously after he went down one trick.

"From your last book," Eva answered disingenuously.

Gary laughed and said with good humor, "I told him the economics of writing books was all wrong. He probably made a dollar on the book you bought, and it just cost him about ten thousand times that amount."

"It's bad enough they just did me in, Gary," Jonathan chided. "Do you have to rub it in?"

"Don't be grumpy, Jonathan. Aren't you pleased that your teaching works so well? Besides, wouldn't you like them to play at this level at all the other tables and knock out our competitors—especially Jeffrey and Ralph?"

"I would like that," Jonathan conceded. He was silent for a moment, and then, his sense of humor restored, offered, "I didn't mean to be grouchy. I just don't like to get bad results. And I have to admit, it pleases me to see my suggestions work—even if you did give us a zero. Reminds me of the Johnny Crawford story—someone gave Johnny a problem on a slip of paper. Crawford wanted to know something about the quality of the other players. 'Three more Johnny Crawfords,' he was told. Johnny crumpled the piece of paper and walked away, muttering 'Game's too tough. I'd never play!'"

Eva, pleased to share the camaraderie, managed to make a good lead on the second board, too. Although it wouldn't be a top score, it would be above average.

"I knew you played well, but I didn't realize how well," Gary said to them when the round was over. "Do the same to the rest of the North-South pairs. Some of them won't expect such flawless defense."

"We'll do our best," Sharon promised.

"Chauvinist," Eva muttered to herself.

* * * * *

"That was a great lead, Eva," Sharon said after they left the table. "I doubt if anyone else here finds it. At least the murder hasn't ruined our concentration tonight. I wonder what's happening with the investigation. I didn't have too much to tell Herb and Vivian about Tom. He annoyed me like he did everybody, but I didn't have any fascinating stories about him. What about you? Did anything interesting happen when you hired him as a pro?"

"No, not then," Eva said. "I told Herb and Vivian that I only hired Tom one time and didn't enjoy playing with him at all. Something amazing *did* happen a couple of years later, though. Remember when you and I won that Open Pairs regional?"

"The one in Toronto or in Daytona Beach?"

"Toronto. Daytona Beach was the Women's Pairs. Anyway, I was playing in a regional in Chicago a few months after the Toronto win. That was the week your children were visiting, and you couldn't go with me. Tom walked over and asked me in his condescending way if I'd won anything lately. I told him that you and I had won the Open Pairs in Toronto. He gave me a funny look and didn't say anything."

"I'm sure he didn't believe you," Sharon said.

"That's an understatement! He came up to me the next day and said, 'You really did win that event. I checked it out in *The Bridge Bulletin.'*"

"You mean he had the nerve to look it up and then *tell* you about it? He might as well have told you he thought you were a liar."

"I know. It really irritated me at the time. But then I thought about it. I'll bet there are plenty of players who claim they won an event when they didn't. I suspect not too many people bother to go check it out in *The Bulletin.*"

"Maybe. Still, I'd have been angry that he didn't believe me. Did you mention that little episode to Herb and Vivian?"

"No. It really had nothing to do with Tom's murder. It was just an obnoxious thing that Tom did a long time ago. They're ready for us at the next table. Let's get them."

* * * * *

"Director!"

Jennifer, following the sound of the latest call, found herself at Linda and Kathy's table.

"What's the problem?" she asked.

"It was my turn to bid, but the opponent on my left pulled out the 1♣ card from the bid box before I could make a call," Kathy told her.

"Do you wish to accept the bid out of turn?" Jennifer asked Kathy. "If you do, the bidding will proceed normally. If not, there'll be some penalties and, if you declare, you may have some options during the play of the hand."

"No, I don't want to accept the bid," Kathy said.

Jennifer turned to the offender. "Since you bid out of turn, you've barred your partner from bidding. You can bid anything you want when it's your proper turn to bid, but your partner must pass every time it's his turn to bid."

Kathy pulled the "pass" card from the bid box. The person who made the bid out of turn was in a quandary. Now that it was her turn to bid, there was no way to tell if her partner had a good hand or not, since he couldn't respond. She finally decided she'd better make a bold bid. She pulled the three notrump card confidently from her bid box and placed it on the table.

Linda glanced at the bid, looked at the twenty points in her hand, and placed her "double" card on the table. Everyone passed. When the dummy came down, declarer realized she'd made the wrong guess. She tried valiantly to take as many tricks as she could, but the situation was hopeless from the outset. Declarer went down five tricks for a certain zero.

"For heaven's sake," her partner exploded when the hand was over. "You act like you've never played this game before. You know that you have to look at the boards to see whose turn it is to bid first. I was warned not to play with a woman in a money game, but I thought my friends were being antifeminists. Now I wonder if they were right."

"None of your male friends would have defended the hand any better than these two women just did," she retorted. "And I've seen plenty of men bid out of turn, so don't give me any of your chauvinistic garbage. How come when a woman makes a mistake, she's attacked because she's a woman, but when a man makes a mistake, gender is never mentioned?"

Her partner, who ordinarily respected woman players, realized how he'd sounded. "I'm sorry," he said. "This game is more nerve-wracking than I ever expected it to be, and I acted like a jerk. Please forgive me."

Seeing that the tempers at the table had cooled down, Jennifer went back to the directors' table. She hoped there wouldn't be too many more outbursts before the game ended. If she had known there'd be a murder, she would *never* have accepted this job. The tension of a high stakes money bridge game is high enough without adding a homicide. Someone would have to do a lot of convincing to persuade her to ever direct another money game.

* * * * *

Jeffrey and Ralph were playing extremely well, but Jeffrey felt sick. He hadn't eaten much for dinner, and now he had stomach cramps. Ralph had gone to the coffee shop and picked up tuna fish sandwiches for them while they waited for their interviews. That was all they'd had to eat all evening. He wondered why Ralph wasn't showing signs of discomfort.

As soon as he found a couple of extra minutes between rounds, Jeffrey ran out to the hotel pharmacy and bought a package of antacid tablets.

Ralph became concerned when he saw Jeffrey pop two more tablets into his mouth at the end of the next round. "What's the matter? Are you okay?"

"Just some indigestion," Jeffrey answered. "I'll be fine when these tablets start to work."

"Those sandwiches we had for dinner were pretty innocuous. Nothing in them should make you feel so bad. I hope you aren't going to be sick. I'd hate to lose this game over indigestion."

"I'm fine," Jeffrey said curtly. "I don't want to hear any more about it."

"Sharon and Eva are coming to our table now," Ralph announced, unaware that Jeffrey suspected him of doctoring the food. "Let's not give anything away to them."

"Hello. How's your game tonight?" Eva asked as the two sisters approached.

"It has possibilities," Ralph said. "We're still in the running. How's yours?"

"We need some tops," Eva said. "What's the matter, Jeffrey? You look pale."

"Just a little indigestion."

"I hope nobody's trying to poison you," Sharon commented. She pulled out the 1♡ card and placed it on the table.

As the bidding proceeded, Jeffrey looked more and more uncomfortable. Sharon's offhand comment had spooked him. He wondered again why Ralph wasn't feeling any discomfort. After all, they *had* eaten the same kind of sandwiches for dinner ... and Ralph had disappeared last night and wouldn't tell him where he'd been.

Jeffrey tried to dismiss these thoughts. Maybe Ralph had a new lover, but he would never try to poison Jeffrey to get rid of him. But, damn it, *where* had he been?

He looked up and realized that everyone at the table was waiting for him to make a bid. He knew he had to focus on bridge, not on how he felt or on his suspicions. With great effort, he brought his mind back to the game and made his bid.

When the hand was over, Jeffrey was sorry he hadn't bid one more time. His final pass allowed Sharon and Eva to play in a four-heart contract, while his side had a good sacrifice in four spades. If he hadn't been thinking about his cramps and worrying about Ralph, he would have made the right bid automatically. What was wrong with him? Maybe Ralph had good reason to look elsewhere.

Although he concentrated on the next hand, the results were only average. Messing up the bidding on that first hand would be costly. He and Ralph would need almost all tops for the rest of the event to win. His stomach felt worse.

* * * * *

Vivian and Herb finished their sandwiches and then Vivian went back to Room 111 to call police headquarters. Herb was on his third cup of coffee when Vivian finally returned to the dining room.

"That took a long time," he said. "What did you find out?"

"We aren't much further ahead with motives or killers," Vivian said unhappily. "And we don't know much more about the physical aspects of the murder. The coroner says the lividity is consistent with the position in which we found the body, but the other evidence seems to me to point the other way."

"I haven't worked with corpses much recently," Herb said. "Can you be more specific."

"Lividity refers to the reddish-brown discolorations on a body that show where the blood settled after death. Stanhope was propped against the wall on his right side when he was found, and lividity does appear on his right buttocks, side, and thighs, as expected."

"Why is this a problem?"

"Lividity is not instantaneous. It takes an hour or more to appear, so if the body was moved shortly after death, without being left in some other position, this evidence tells us nothing about the way death was inflicted. And if Stanhope was killed where we found him, we need to consider a much larger group of suspects. Bridge players would have no reason to go to the grocery store to talk to or kill Tom Stanhope, and he would have no apparent motivation to go there to meet a bridge player. The hotel is the logical place for any such meeting."

"So where does that leave us?"

"On our own. Everything I've learned about our victim tells me he was a drinker, not a drug user, so there's no good reason for him to go across the parking lot. Everything he might want or need is right here in the hotel—alcohol, cigarettes, food, and bridge players. Everyone with a possible motive to kill him is affiliated in some way with this bridge tournament, so I am tentatively going to proceed on the theory Stanhope was killed somewhere in or around the hotel and moved to the grocery store lot immediately afterwards."

"What about the gun? Any news there?"

"None," Vivian said glumly.

"How come the fire alarm went off? Do you think the killer meant for the body to be found last night? Or do you think that was an accident?"

"I wish I knew."

"In past cases, after you've discovered who the murderer is, have you been able to find explanations for all the seemingly unanswerable questions?"

"It's odd how some cases go. I've found that many details fall into place easily after we catch the guilty party. Often, when faced with the evidence against them, criminals furnish the missing elements voluntarily. Many of them like to brag about their cleverness."

Herb laughed. "Let's hope it's a bridge player, then. Many of them are terrific at that. What about the interviews tonight? Do you know how you're going to run it? The game won't be over 'til after midnight. We'll never get out of here if you have to interview each one separately again."

"I've been thinking about that," Vivian replied. "I've decided to call just the prime suspects and have them all meet with us at the same time. When we review the clues and motives, I hope someone will spot something we've overlooked. Often people observe something but don't realize it. Then they make the connections later, when they hear others talk."

"I don't think it'll be difficult getting them to talk," Herb said. "They'll all be wired after the game. The list of the winners won't be ready for a while, and that'll add to the tension. Keeping some of them quiet while others speak may be harder than getting them to talk."

"It'll be good to have them all a little edgy. They're more likely to say something they'd rather keep hidden. While we're trying to solve the murder, David and Ruth will have to figure out who won. We'll need Jennifer with us."

"That should be okay," Herb told her. "One of them can score the finals while the other does the consolation. The directors enter all the scores on computers as soon as they're turned in after each round, so it shouldn't take too long to determine the winners. Are you going to let Ruth and David come in to announce the results as soon as they know who won, or wait until after we finish?"

"Since we may not even find the murderer tonight, I think we'd better let them announce the winners as soon as they know. Maybe the reactions of the winners or losers will furnish some clue."

"If we're down to that," Herb observed, "we're really getting desperate."

CHAPTER 20

Lou and Jake knew they wouldn't be able to win even if they scored tops on all the rest of the boards. Weary and dejected, they sat down to play against the Nestors, who were glaring at each other. A good sign.

"Nice game you had this afternoon," Lou said as he pulled his cards out of the board. "Are you keeping up the good work tonight?"

"We would be if certain people would remember to alert conventional bids," Sybil said.

"I don't want to hear another word about it," Alan snapped. "If you'd pay attention to the game instead of trying to humiliate me, we'd still have a chance to win the consolation."

"Don't be silly, darling. No one would intentionally humiliate a spouse in a bridge game," Sybil said sweetly. She looked at her cards and then pulled the "pass" card out of the bid box.

Lou, influenced by the Nestors' bickering, decided to open a very weak hand. His mistake. Jake had a strong hand and kept making forcing bids every time Lou tried to end the bidding. Before Lou could slow him down, Jake had bid a slam. When he saw the dummy, Jake was disgusted. There wasn't even a remote possibility of making a slam. He played the hand out quickly, going down two tricks.

"Why on earth did you open that mess?" he asked Lou angrily. "I don't understand what you're doing. If you didn't want to play in this event, you should've told me before we signed up. It's too expensive and too time-consuming for me to be here when you bid and play like you've done for the past two days."

"Sorry, Jake," Lou apologized. "I really meant—and needed—to do well. I'm afraid losing this event will cost me more than money and time."

"I'm sorry about your problems with May," Jake said, "but that's not my concern. When I entered this game, I expected to win at least one of the prizes. But that's impossible now. You aren't even making reasonable opening bids."

Lou mumbled another apology, and then unintentionally gave the Nestors a top on the next board. Jake stalked out of the room.

"Now, if you'll just play like that for the rest of the night," Alan said to his wife when Lou left the table, "we'll have a chance."

"Don't be a fool," Sybil retorted. "They gave us those good boards. How we played had nothing to do with it."

"You always have an answer."

"You always have an inane comment."

They sat there scowling at each other until the next round began.

* * * * *

Vivian and Herb returned to room 111 after finishing their coffee. Officer Rollins arrived a few minutes later.

"We have just enough time before the game ends to compare notes," Vivian said. "What did you find out?"

"I talked to several people at Jennifer's bridge studio. One of the men—a slimy, lecherous type—told me, with many winks and raisings of his eyebrows, that Linda had made some major improvements lately. According to him, she used to look quite dowdy, but now she plays bridge in fancy clothes and drives an expensive foreign car."

"Where does he think she got the money?"

"He seems to think she found a sugar daddy somewhere."

"Interesting. What else?"

"When word got out among the bridge players that I wanted to know about the people involved with the money game, a woman named Darlene Olsen couldn't wait to tell me about going to target practice with Kathy. She acted like she hated Kathy and would love to see her in trouble."

"Good. Angry people often talk too much. What did she tell you?"

"About a year ago, according to this Darlene, she and Kathy both bought twenty-two caliber guns to carry in their purses. They go home alone late at night after the bridge games, and were concerned about being mugged. They didn't know how to use the guns, though, so the two of them went together to learn how to shoot."

"Have they ever had to use them?"

"I know Darlene hasn't. She told me that she felt more scared *with* her gun than without it. She was afraid that a mugger would take it from her and shoot her with it, so she put hers away months ago. She doesn't know whether Kathy still carries hers or not."

"Anything else?"

"Just that Eva, Linda, and Kathy had all hired Tom to play—which we already knew. And there were a lot of sly references about Jennifer's affair with Herb, but no one knew of a connection between them and Tom."

"Well, *that's* a relief," Herb said.

Vivian ignored him. "Did you have a chance to talk to the other investigators?"

"Just for a few minutes. They didn't have time to talk to a lot of people. There was one interesting item. One of Dr. Kingsley's rivals in plastic surgery told Sergeant Hendricks he heard that Kingsley's being sued for botching a face lift. I don't know how true it is or if that has any connection with the murder."

"I'll bet Ralph doesn't know that," Vivian said. "I wonder if we ought to tell him." Seeing Rollins' puzzled expression, she quickly told him about the letter Dr. Kingsley had sent to Ralph.

"That's interesting. I don't think it's our business to tell Ralph, though. It's not up to the police department to spread rumors."

* * * * *

Kathy and Linda were playing erratically. They hadn't had a break since their opponents bid out of turn earlier. Linda, who'd been fidgety when the game began, became even more jittery as it progressed.

"What's wrong with you?" Kathy asked after they finished the sixth round. "You must have crossed and uncrossed your legs fifteen times during the last round. And now you're biting your fingernails. I've never seen you do that before. What's making you so nervous?"

"I really wanted to win one of the prizes, but now I'm afraid we don't have a chance," Linda said.

"I don't think we should give up yet," Kathy said. "That last hand we played ought to be above average. Besides, I don't understand why it's so important to you. It's not as if you needed the money. You've got your job, a place to live, and a new car. It's not as if you're about to starve or become homeless. What's your problem?"

"You are the most unsympathetic person I know," Linda blurted out. "You don't know how awful life can be for anyone who has to count every cent. You have all the money you'll ever want or need. You'd feel differently if you had to go to work at the same old job every day instead of sitting in your house waiting for tax-free checks to arrive in the mail."

"Wait a minute! It's not *my* fault that you aren't rich," Kathy told her. "Maybe you should have gone to some of those seminars that your bank gives and learned how to invest what you earned. Then you'd have the nest egg you seem to want, and you wouldn't be so cranky."

"Don't be a fool, Kathy. How could I invest money when I never had any extra? It takes nearly everything I earn just to live."

"Look, Linda, I'm sorry if you're having money problems, but I can't help you. I don't believe in loaning money to friends. If you're so broke, why were you so desperate to play in this game? You'd at least have the money you spent on the entry fee."

"I never asked you to loan me money, and I never would," Linda said, infuriated. "And we're not friends. Friends don't treat each other like you've treated me over the years."

"What do you mean?" Kathy asked, surprised. "I always thought I treated you well."

"I'll tell you exactly what I mean. In all the years that we've supposedly been 'friends,' you've only asked me to join you socially twice. The first time was a couple of years ago when you asked me to have lunch with you at your club. I got there at noon—just like you asked me to. You breezed in forty-five minutes late, waved your hands in the air, and mumbled something about your manicurist being late. But you never bothered to call the club to let me know. I had to sit there all alone for almost an hour, with all your friends staring at me. It was humiliating.

"And the next time, you told me you had an extra ticket for the symphony, and you asked me to join you. I went out and bought a new dress. I was getting ready to leave for the concert when you called. You told me that a friend of yours had come into town unexpectedly that afternoon and you were taking her instead. You hoped I'd understand. I understood, all right! What I understood was that you are not my friend and never will be. Now stop picking on me for crossing my legs or for whatever it is that's upsetting you. We could still win something if you'd concentrate on your own bidding and playing instead of on what I'm doing."

For once, Kathy was nonplussed. Finally she said primly, "I don't like your attitude. Don't expect to play with me anymore after this game."

"I expect I won't be playing much bridge at all after this," Linda said.

"Well, that's your choice."

"I wish that it were," Linda muttered.

* * * * *

Vivian and Herb entered the ballroom as the players began their last round.

"How's it going?" Herb asked Jennifer when they arrived at the directors' table.

Jennifer looked exhausted. "I'll *never* agree to direct a money game again. These people are animals tonight."

"I'm sure the murder has a lot to do with it," Herb said.

"I'm not so sure," Jennifer answered. "Right now, they're all so intent on winning one of the prizes—preferably first—that they're behaving abominably to one another. They're either picking fights with their partners or with their opponents. I don't know why playing in a high-level game brings out the worst in some people."

"At least a few of them will go home richer and happier," Vivian said.

"Yeah, but that won't help me now," Jennifer said wearily. "What's the plan for tonight? Are we ever going to get out of here?"

"I have a list of the people we want to question after the game," Vivian told her. "We'll meet with all of them at the same time. We're hoping that the group interaction will bring out something we've overlooked."

"I don't know how alert they'll be by the end of the session," Jennifer said. "They've had two gruelling days."

"I know they're tired, but they're also anxious to be done with this and go home. It'll be in their own self interest to pay attention to what I have to say. When the game's over, I'll read the list of people who have to stay. It's important to have you at the meeting too, so Ruth and David will have to do the scoring. They can bring the names of the winners to Room 111 as soon as they have them."

"I wish this whole nightmare were over," Jennifer said. "I hope I can find the energy to finish the last round. If anyone calls me for a ruling, there may be another murder here."

"At least we'll know who did this one," Herb said. He bent down and gave her a kiss on the cheek.

CHAPTER 21

The late start of the evening session pushed the playing time past midnight. Finally, when the game ended at 12:15, Jennifer said, "Please give me your attention. Vivian will read the names of the people she wants to question. If your name is on the list, please go to Room 111. Ruth and David will come in there to announce the winners of the games just as soon as they have them."

There were several groans from the tired players, but no one objected. When everyone was quiet again, Vivian read her list. "I'd like to see the following people after the game: Gary Alexander, Jennifer Brandon, Cliff Bryce, Charles Canning, Ralph Dunbar, Jeffrey Howard, Kathy Jensen, Eva Kaplan, Linda Mason, Jonathan Meltzer, Alan and Sybil Nestor, Sharon Price, and Lou Turner. You can take a few minutes to go to the rest rooms or get something to drink, if you wish. I'll expect you to be there in ten minutes."

"No surprises on that list," Sharon said to Eva. "Looks like Vivian and Herb had no trouble zeroing in on the ones who hated Tom the most or who had the strongest motives to kill him."

"Which category do you suppose we fit?" Eva asked.

* * * * *

During the next ten minutes, the contestants slowly filed into Room 111. It was clear from their lack of enthusiasm that they'd rather be anywhere else.

"They sure are a tired and bedraggled looking bunch," Vivian commented quietly to Herb.

"It's no wonder," Herb said. "They've been playing for twelve days now, with very little sleep and lots of stress. It's probably a good time to question them since they're not at their sharpest. They're more apt to make a mistake when they talk to us."

"I hope we're still sharp enough to catch their mistakes. I'm beginning to feel as tired as they look."

The hotel staff had placed several chairs in a semicircle around the desk. After everyone found a place to sit, Vivian started.

"I know most of you are exhausted and would rather be in your rooms packing or on your way home, so I'll try to get this over with as quickly as possible. Tonight, Herb and I will tell you what we've learned. There may be some discrepancies with what you know and what we know. We hope that if you hear something inaccurate, you'll point it out to us. If we don't arrive at the truth tonight, you'll have to stay over."

Several loud objections hit her at once. Luckily for Vivian, however, no one called her bluff on a legal basis.

"It's not possible for us to stay any longer," Jeffrey said vehemently. "We've already taken two more days than we're allowed."

"We *have* to get back," Ralph emphasized. "We can't afford to lose our jobs over this."

"I know, and I'm sympathetic," Vivian said, "but we have a murder to solve. I realize you didn't anticipate a murder when you decided to play in the money game. Nevertheless, one of your colleagues was killed. We'll do everything we can to get all of you out of here by tomorrow, but I can't guarantee it."

"I can't stay longer, either," Cliff interrupted. "I have a board meeting Friday, and I have to get home to prepare for it."

"We have to be back for a seminar," Alan Nestor said at the same time Kathy tried to object.

"Whoa!" Vivian said. "I'm aware that all of you have overwhelming reasons to leave, and I appreciate that. I suggest that instead of trying to convince me that you need to leave, you listen to what I have to say. The sooner we solve this, the quicker you can go."

There was a hostile silence in the room, but the group grudgingly gave Vivian its attention.

"Okay. This is what we've put together from what you've told us. Immediately after the game, Lou, Cliff, and the Nestors went to their rooms. Gary and Sharon went to the bar for a drink, while Jonathan and Eva waited for the scores in the ballroom. As soon as the scores were posted, Jonathan and Eva went to the bar to tell Gary and Sharon that they'd all qualified. Then Jonathan and Eva left for their respective rooms.

"Jeffrey and Ralph left after the game, but Ralph disappeared when Jeffrey stopped to talk to Kathy and Linda. Jeffrey looked around for Ralph, but couldn't find him. He claims he didn't see Ralph again until the fire alarm rang.

"Jennifer saw Sharon and Gary going up on the elevator around one-thirty. Sybil Nestor woke up around two o'clock and heard voices in Tom's room, which is next to hers.

"Linda Mason, who's not staying at the hotel, came back because she wanted to talk to Tom about an undisclosed matter. She called Tom's room, but he wouldn't talk to her. While she wandered around the hotel trying to figure out what to do, she saw Ralph in the downstairs bar with someone. She went up to Tom's room around two o'clock and knocked on the door. She thought she heard voices when she approached the room, but no one answered. After waiting a few minutes, she left and went back to the lobby. Around two-thirty, she saw Ralph come into the lobby and take an elevator up. The fire alarm rang soon after.

"All of you, except Kathy—who's not staying here —appeared in the parking lot during the fire drill. Linda was seen leaving the parking lot by several people." She looked up from her notes. "Does anyone have anything to add?"

"Linda was *here* during the fire alarm?" Kathy asked in amazement. Nothing else in Vivian's synopsis had registered.

"That's correct," Vivian answered.

"Well, what was she *doing* here?" Kathy wanted to know. "I thought she went home. After all, she's not staying here."

"I'm afraid you're going to have to answer that question now," Herb said to Linda gently.

"No ... I'm not going to do that," Linda said, clamping her mouth shut.

"In that case," Vivian said, "I have to warn you that we're going to contact your bank tomorrow. From what we've pieced together, a look at your recent financial activities seems to be in order. If there's anything you ought to tell us, it might be better for you to tell us tonight."

"I have nothing to say," Linda said.

Kathy stood up and shouted, "I knew there was something wrong. Linda was awful to me today. When she attacked me, I thought she was just being obnoxious, but now I see there was something behind it. I definitely think you ought to go over all her accounts and see what she's been up to." She sat down and crossed her arms, looking extremely righteous.

Vivian was appalled. Whatever Linda had done, she didn't want to add to her misery by letting Kathy lord it over her. She waited until she could speak calmly, then said, "I'm sure whoever investigates Linda's activities will do a thorough job. Now, I'm going to question each person individually as we did before. Only this time, everyone will be able to hear your answers. I suggest that you tell the truth and not try to hide anything, as everyone here seems to know what's going on with everyone else. I'll begin with Gary."

"Go ahead, I'm ready," Gary said. "I have no secrets," he added rather primly.

"It's been fairly well established that you went to the bar with Sharon after the game," Vivian began.

"That's right," Gary said, offering nothing more.

"Did Sharon go with you to your room after you finished your drinks?"

While Gary tried to figure out how to protect Sharon but still tell the truth, Sharon settled the matter by speaking up. "Guilty," she said. "So?"

Vivian frowned at Sharon's interference. "Did you hear or see anything unusual after you left the bar and went to the room?"

"Saw," Gary said.

"Heard," Sharon said.

Vivian ignored the snickers and quickly continued. "Okay, Cliff, it's your turn. When we searched your room tonight, we found your computer. We retrieved some of the files, but when we tried to pull up the bridge file, we weren't able to. It requires a password."

"Of course it does," Cliff said. "I play in national and international competition. I don't want anyone to be able to pry into my files."

"Why not?" Vivian asked. "We could get into your company files without a password. I would have thought your business files would be more important to protect than your bridge files."

"I don't travel with any company files that could damage me if someone were to see them," Cliff replied. "My company secrets are in special files that I keep in my safe in Rochester. I connect with my company every day on my computer to see if there's anything I have to take care of, but I don't bring sensitive material with me if I can help it."

"What do you have in your files under bridge that you wouldn't want anyone to see?"

"Some new theories that I'd been working out with Tom," Cliff replied. "We always discussed new bidding methods. When we found some that we wanted to try, I'd put them in the computer. Some worked, some didn't."

"Why would you care if anyone saw them?" Vivian asked.

"If we came up with something special, Tom would write up the new convention and try to get it published," Cliff said. "He earned most of his money playing professional bridge, but he supplemented his income with articles. I kept them in my computer where no one could see them and publish them before he had a chance to commercially exploit his ideas."

"Do you have anything in there now that you wouldn't want anyone here to see?"

"No. I have some hands in there from the Vanderbilt that we were going to discuss. We wondered if there were better ways to bid a few of them. The hands aren't any secret. Several of the people here played them last week."

"If that's all that's in it now, I don't understand why that file was encrypted," Vivian said.

"It's done automatically. That way, if I do put some sensitive material in, I don't have to worry about it," Cliff answered.

"I brought all the computers that I found in the rooms down here," Vivian said. "Since you insist that you have nothing to hide in your bridge file, would you mind retrieving it?"

"I don't see how this will help you solve the murder," Cliff said irritably, "but I must insist on doing it without anyone seeing my password."

"That's fine," Vivian agreed.

Cliff picked up his computer, put it on Vivian's desk, and turned it on. Then he turned his back to the room while he entered his password.

"Okay, here it is," he said, turning around. "Now that you can see it, what do you think you're going to do with it?"

Herb went to the computer and looked through the "bridge" directory. When he came to the VNDBLT entry, Jonathan, who had moved up next to the computer, told him to stop. "Let me look at the date when those Vanderbilt hands were entered," Jonathan said. Everyone looked at the screen. The date for the VNDBLT entries was two days before the hands were played.

"How did you get these hand records into your computer two days early?" Gary asked. "No wonder you made all the right decisions on the slam hands. You cheated after all!"

"That's absurd. There must be some mistake in the dates on my computer," Cliff said. "Everyone knows there's no way to get a copy of the hands ahead of time."

"The dates on your computer can't be wrong," Gary said. "Unless you program in a new date, the dates that you last used a specific file come up automatically when you pull it up again. Surely, the CEO of a computer company should know that."

"I just thought of something," Eva interrupted. "When I went to get a copy of our bills last night, the clerk mistakenly handed me Cliff's bill instead of Sharon's. She thought I said Bryce instead of Price. Cliff's bill had over four hundred dollars in charges on long distance calls. Many of them were to Tennessee—where the bridge headquarters are. That's where the bridge hands are created. You ought to check his bill and see what numbers Cliff called."

"You can save us some time, Cliff, by telling us," Vivian said.

"The answer to that is easy," Cliff responded. "Several of the calls were made to Memphis, but for a reason that has nothing to do with bridge. I've been dating Margery Holcomb, one of the editors of *The Bridge Bulletin*, for the past couple of years. I met her when I went to a regional in Memphis and have been seeing her whenever I get the chance. Since when is it a crime to call your girlfriend?"

"I'll bet she fed him information about the hands," Gary said.

"Absolutely not!" Cliff objected. "Just because I see her from time to time, it's totally unfair to mix her up in this. Besides, the security surrounding the bridge hands is impenetrable. *No one* sees the hands before the games start."

"Then how did you get the hands on your computer two days before the event?" Jonathan asked.

"I told you, it must be a computer glitch," Cliff insisted. "Somehow the date must have been entered wrong. I never saw those hands before I played them in the Vanderbilt."

"Turn off your computer and turn it back on again," Herb told Cliff. After Cliff obliged, Herb asked him to see the date that appeared on the beginning menu. "That's today's date," Herb said. "Obviously your calendar is correct."

"It's correct now, but it may not have been when the Vanderbilt hands were entered. There's no way you can prove otherwise."

"Dates don't get changed arbitrarily on a computer," Jonathan said. "You must have figured out how to tap into the computer at the ACBL and get a copy of the hand records before the Vanderbilt started."

"Is that possible?" Herb asked Vivian.

"We'll find out," Vivian said. "Does anyone here know who prints the hand records after the hands are created? Are they done by the ACBL in Memphis, or does another company print them?"

"I have the number of the CEO of the ACBL," Canning volunteered, taking out a small telephone address book from his briefcase. "We can call her and find out."

"Good," Vivian said. "Let's do this officially."

She called the front desk and asked for a printout of Cliff's bill to be sent to her right away. As soon as it arrived, she reached for Charles's telephone book and dialed police headquarters.

"Hello, Arnie," she said to the sergeant on duty. "I need you to call the Executive Director of the American Contract Bridge League and find out all you can about how and where the tournament hands are created. I also have a couple of Tennessee numbers I want you to trace." She gave the sergeant the information he needed, and hung up. "I hope the Executive Director won't be too upset at being awakened," Vivian mused, "but probably no one else has the clout to get things moving in the middle of the night. While we're waiting for the information from Memphis, I'd like to ask Jennifer some questions."

"I'm ready."

"You told us that when you finished at around 1:30, you saw Sharon and Gary getting on an elevator. While you were waiting for the next elevator, did you notice anything else?"

"As I told you before, something did catch my eye," Jennifer said. "I saw a woman going into the ladies' room off the lobby. She had a dress on with a print like the one Kathy wore yesterday. But I knew that Kathy wasn't staying at the hotel, so it's possible the dress only made me think it was Kathy. I just caught a glimpse of the woman, and really couldn't be sure who it was."

"It couldn't have been me," Kathy said. "I wasn't here then. After Linda and I talked to Jeffrey, we both left. I went straight home and went to bed. I thought Linda did too ... but apparently I was wrong about that," she added with satisfaction.

"Do you have anyone at home who can confirm that's where you went—and stayed?" Vivian asked.

"No. I live alone. But why on earth would I come back here?"

"For the same reason I would," Linda said suddenly. "Because of Tom. He botched up your hopes for a simple divorce settlement. I don't know what you did to him, but I do know he got his revenge. He sent your husband copies of checks that you had endorsed to Tom Stanhope. They were for nice fat sums. After your husband's lawyer saw them, he subpoenaed your bank records to see what else you were hiding."

"You don't know what you're talking about," Kathy said.

"Oh, yes I do. I was the one at the bank who handled the transaction. Since it was you, I was curious. I took a good look at the information when it passed through my hands. You made a mistake, Kathy. You should have paid Tom whatever he asked when you had the chance. Now your lawyer and soon-to-be ex-spouse have enough ammunition to dirty up your simple divorce."

"How dare you look at my private accounts—and then broadcast what you saw?" Kathy said, enraged. "My lawyer is going to hear from me as soon as I get out of here. And, believe me, you won't spend one more day at that bank."

"Your threats don't faze me," Linda said. She was pretty sure she wouldn't have a job to go back to by tomorrow anyway.

"When did you find out Tom had sent copies of the canceled checks to your husband?" Vivian asked.

"Right now," she said angrily, "and I don't appreciate hearing about it in public. Tom told me earlier that he wanted money from me to keep my husband from seeing the checks, but I wouldn't give him a cent. I wrote those checks to him for professional fees. I didn't realize he'd already sent copies to my husband, or that my accounts had been subpoenaed."

Ralph, who had been sitting quietly all this time, looked puzzled. Herb, seeing his look, asked, "What's wrong, Ralph?"

"Something about Kathy's story troubles me, but I can't figure out what," Ralph replied.

"Well, think about it. Maybe it'll come to you," Vivian said. "And since we're talking to you, Ralph, we need to clarify a few things."

Jeffrey, who'd slumped down in his chair and nearly fallen asleep, sat up straight and looked expectantly at Vivian. He was sure he'd find out what Ralph had been up to last night. He thought he was smiling inwardly, but everyone could see his grin.

Vivian fooled him. "I'd like to talk to you privately out in the corridor for a couple of minutes," she told Ralph. As soon as she stood up and started walking toward the door with a relieved Ralph, there were several loud objections from the others.

Chapter Twenty-One

"Why should he get special treatment?" Jeffrey blurted out.

Kathy agreed. "Nobody minded that I was humiliated in front of everyone. What could Ralph be hiding that's worse?" she asked, angry that Ralph had questioned her story. "How can we pick up any of his lies if you question him privately?"

"What I'm going to discuss with Ralph has nothing to do with the murder. If something connected with Tom's death comes out, I assure you that you'll all hear about it." With that, she and Ralph worked their way through the crowded room and stepped into the hall.

"We decided to respect your privacy, since we couldn't find any connection to the murder with the proposed surgery," Vivian said after they closed the door. "It wasn't too hard to figure out that you didn't want Jeffrey to know about it."

"I'm really grateful," Ralph said. "I would've been terribly embarrassed if you'd brought it up in front of Jeffrey or the others."

"What'll you tell Jeffrey if you start playing bridge with Dr. Kingsley?"

"Just that he liked the way I played when he kibitzed me here, and he decided to hire me as a pro," Ralph replied.

"You won't have any extra money to show if you trade your bridge skills for surgery. Won't Jeffrey be suspicious?"

"I'd be playing with Kingsley over a long period of time, so I wouldn't have that much extra cash all at once. Besides," he added bitterly, "who knows how much longer Jeffrey'll be part of my life? The surgery may not make any difference if he's really looking for someone younger."

"Have you ever considered that if it takes surgery to make a difference with Jeffrey, it may not be worth it?"

"It's worth it to me."

Vivian didn't comment. She thought that Ralph would end up hurt no matter what he did, but it was none of her business. "How long did you and Dr. Kingsley stay in the downstairs bar?" she asked.

"We talked until the bar closed, somewhere around two o'clock. Then, when we got up to leave, I felt rather woozy from all those drinks. I'm not used to that much liquor. We kept getting refills while we discussed the surgery-for-bridge plan. We both have busy schedules, so we needed to figure out times we'd both be available. When the bar closed, I took the elevator up to the lobby with Kingsley and walked him out to his car. It was beautiful outdoors—in the sixties—so I decided to take a walk to clear my head. I didn't want to have a hangover for the bridge game."

"What time did you get back to the hotel?"

"I don't know exactly. Somewhere around two-thirty. I was exhausted by then. I noticed Linda in the lobby and vaguely wondered why she was sitting there at that time of night, but it didn't register in my brain that she wasn't staying at the hotel. I went straight to the room, undressed, and fell asleep. Then the fire alarm rang, and I had to get right back up. I was damned annoyed."

"I take it Jeffrey was sleeping when you got to the room?"

"He was. Apparently the fire alarm woke him up immediately. He told me that he yelled at me several times, but he couldn't wake me up. I think I would have slept right through if he hadn't finally come over and shaken me."

"Well, at least he wasn't mad enough at your disappearance to let you burn to death."

Ralph made a face. "That's sick."

"Just realistic," Vivian said. "I've seen a lot. When you arrived in the parking lot, did anything strike you as unusual?"

"Nothing that I didn't tell you before. Jeffrey gave me the third degree about where I was, but I wouldn't tell him. You know the rest."

Vivian shook her head in frustration. "I wish I did. Okay, let's go back in."

When Ralph and Vivian entered the room, they interrupted a bitter tirade from Kathy.

"Looking at my records and then broadcasting what you saw is the most unprofessional behavior I've ever heard of," she yelled at Linda. "Not only will I get you fired from your bank, I'll make damn sure you won't work in any other bank around here."

Linda shrugged. "Do your worst."

Kathy's face was contorted with anger. "What do you mean, do my worst? How can you mean that after you complained so bitterly to me about not having any money? If you're fired, how will you support yourself? Maybe you've saved plenty of money over the years and just got on my case because . . . because . . . " she sputtered. She couldn't imagine why anyone would attack her.

The contestants, who had been concentrating on Kathy's tirade, suddenly realized that David and Ruth had entered the room with the list of winners. Everyone looked at the directors . . . both expectantly and fearfully.

"I know you want to know who the winners are right away, so no speeches," Ruth said. "I'll just announce the top three winners in both events, and then post all the winners' names by the door. The three overall winners in the finals are: First place, Gary Alexander and Jonathan Meltzer; second place, Ralph Dunbar and Jeffrey Howard; third Place, Sharon Price and Eva Kaplan.

"In the consolation, the top three overall winners are: First place, Jan Stolman and Marian Wells; second place, Alan and Sybil Nestor; third place, Danny Penn and Karen Brown."

She barely got the list of winners taped to the wall before the crowd surrounded her. Linda showed more animation than she had all night as she rushed over.

"Let me see that," she said, pushing aside the other contestants. She quickly scanned the list of the winners in the finals, but hers and Kathy's weren't among them. Groaning, she made her way back to her seat.

Kathy, who was right behind her, didn't know whether to be satisfied that Linda was disappointed, or unhappy because she'd lost her entry fee as well as any profit. She settled for both.

Lou didn't bother to look.

There were praises, tinged with jealousy, for the winners. Gary and Jonathan, who knew they'd had a good game, modestly accepted the congratulations of their peers. The $50,000 that they would each receive would at least be some compensation for not winning the Vanderbilt, although Jonathan would rather have won the Vanderbilt. Gary wasn't sure.

Gary went over to Sharon and gave her a hug. "Congratulations! I knew you and Eva would do well," he said, smiling at her.

"And congratulations to you, too," Sharon said, as happy for his first place win as she was for her third place. "I would've been pleased to be anywhere among the winners. Being third is unbelievable."

"I don't think so," Gary replied. "I thought you might even be second."

"Next time, we plan to win."

Eva, sitting next to the Nestors, traded congratulations with them. "I know you must be happy. I'm pleased for you."

"Thank you," Alan said. He turned toward Sybil. "See, it didn't even hurt us when I forgot to alert."

"But it did," Sybil said indignantly. "I checked the scores. We missed first place by half a point. Our average minus on that board cost us ten thousand dollars."

Alan refused to take the blame. "Well, if you had defended that three notrump hand better, we still could have won."

"*That* was an average board. *I* didn't do anything where points were *subtracted* from our score."

"I don't see what you two are arguing about," Lou said bitterly. "You're going away from this with twenty-five thousand dollars. I'd think you would be grateful. A lot of us are walking away with nothing." He hoped that would embarrass them into silence, but they continued as if he hadn't spoken.

"Just think what we *could* have won if you had put a little thought into your bidding," Alan said.

Sybil gave him a caustic look. "At least I didn't forget to alert."

* * * * *

Ralph and Jeffrey were ecstatic. Ralph realized he could afford the surgery without playing with Dr. Kingsley if he chose. He'd have to ask Cliff how Kingsley's game was. It must have been awful. Their names weren't listed anywhere among the winners. He hoped Kingsley wouldn't be too upset with him if he offered cash instead of bridge expertise. He didn't want the doctor who worked on his face to be angry at him!

Maybe it would be wiser to find another doctor in a different city. While he was thinking about this, Jonathan came up to congratulate him and Jeffrey.

"Nice game," Jonathan said. "Gary and I have noticed how well you've done lately. If you're free for the Knockout games at your regional in Boston next month, we'd like to play with you."

"Great," Jeffrey said, enormously flattered with the invitation. "And congratulations to you." Feeling euphoric, Jeffrey momentarily forgot about Ralph's secret life. He slapped his partner on the back when they returned to their seats and grinned. "Did you ever imagine that Gary and Jonathan would ask *us* to play? I can't believe it!"

Ralph gave him a silly grin.

* * * * *

"Before you continue," Charles Canning said to Vivian, "I'd like to get an announcement of the winners to the newspaper and the television reporters, if there are any still around at this late hour. We've been stalling them for a long time, and at least this is some news for them."

"And some positive publicity for Century," Vivian muttered to Herb. She asked Ruth and David to make copies of the list of winners and give them to Charles to distribute.

* * * * *

Kathy was furious. "I knew I shouldn't have entered this event with you," she shouted at Linda. "What a waste of two thousand dollars. Now that I know how you really feel about me, I'm glad I'll never have to play with you again."

"Then it was worth every penny," Linda retorted. She felt dreadful. At least, if Tom hadn't been killed, she might have had time to find another way to cover her theft. But with the murder and her refusal to account for her presence at the hotel last night, she couldn't see how she could avoid being caught.

As bad as that was, what she resented even more was that she'd cheated to give Tom a top board when she deliberately underbid. If she had known someone was going to kill him anyway, she'd never have thrown him a board. And now that bastard had found a way to torment her even though he was dead.

* * * * *

"Did you notice how many of the winners were women?" Sharon asked Eva.

"Yeah! And this time it was for money as well as master- points."

"Did you happen to get the information on the Concorde? I didn't want to jinx us, so I didn't do anything about it."

Eva pulled some brochures from her pocketbook. "Aisle or window?"

CHAPTER 22

The bridge players absorbed the results of the game, exchanged a few more congratulations and sympathies, then slowly brought their attention back to the murder.

Before Vivian could continue her questioning, Kathy began to harangue her. "I resent having to stay here going over the same old stuff," she complained. "I think you should let us leave. We're all tired, and we want to go to bed."

Over loud objections from the others, who wanted to arrive at a solution tonight, Vivian heard the phone ring and picked up the receiver. She waved her free hand to the crowd after she answered it, indicating that she couldn't hear over the din. By now, even the winners were weary. They calmed down quickly. Vivian took notes as she spoke, not giving anything away with her expression. Finally, she finished.

"That was Sergeant Tower, at police headquarters," she said. "Among other things, he found out how hand records are devised and stored. To create them, someone at the ACBL enters a date and an arbitrary code number into a computer program that is specially designed for that purpose. The program, following its instructions, creates a random set of thirty-six bridge hands. Then the ACBL sends an order with the same code number to a service bureau which prints and packages the number of copies needed for a tournament. The packages are sent to the tournament sites, where they remain sealed until the event begins."

"That's what I've been trying to tell you," Cliff interrupted. "You can tell from all those safeguards that there's no way I could have seen the hands ahead of time." He leaned back in his chair, looking smug.

"Apparently there is one way," Vivian said. "The hands can be retrieved from the ACBL computer at any time if the proper code number is entered."

"That may be true, but how could I possibly get the code number? You said yourself that arbitrary numbers are used each time. Even if I could've found out the password to get into the program—which I didn't—I'd have had no way of knowing what number to punch in for a specific set of hands."

"You could find out if you had an accomplice down there—such as Margery Holcomb, the woman you told us you were dating."

"Margery would never do anything like that. Ask anyone who knows her. She's worked there for years, and no one has ever questioned her integrity. You have no right to imply she'd cheat for me or for anyone else."

"Maybe she didn't knowingly get the code numbers for you, but she may have inadvertently given you access to them."

"How would she do that?"

"I don't know yet, but we have people working on the problem right now. If you found a way to hack into their computer, they'll find out how you did it."

"They won't find anything," Cliff said, but he didn't look quite so smug.

"While we're waiting for more information about the hand records," Vivian said, "we'll continue. I have a photograph that I'd like Ralph and Jeffrey to come and look at."

Ralph and Jeffrey glanced at each other, but didn't say anything as they got up from their chairs and walked to her desk. In her hand was the photo of them kissing on the beach.

"Have either or both of you seen this before?" Vivian asked.

"We saw it yesterday," Ralph mumbled.

"I think you should let the rest of us in on the secret," Kathy said. "You keep saying you want our cooperation, and then you're secretive about your evidence. How do you expect us to help if you don't tell us what's going on?"

"It's a picture of Ralph and me kissing," Jeffrey snapped. "Apparently Tom took it some time last week. We didn't know about it until he showed it to us yesterday. He obviously hoped it would upset us enough to keep us from winning."

"Is that all he wanted?" Vivian asked. "Just to keep you from winning?"

"Isn't that a lot? Look at all the money involved. What else could he have wanted?"

"There *are* other things. Did he ask you to give him money to keep anyone else from seeing the photograph?"

Again, Ralph and Jeffrey exchanged looks. Finally Ralph answered. "He said he didn't want any money now, but he'd keep the picture in his files. He was sure that the school authorities and the parents of our students would be very interested in the photo if he chose to show it to them sometime in the future."

"What did you say to that?" Vivian asked.

"We tried to be cool about it," Ralph said. "We laughed at him and told him the school was very liberal and that they knew all about our lifestyle. Jeffrey offered him a stamp to mail it to the school."

"How did he react?"

"He gave us one of his nasty smirks and told us he was sure that picture could hurt our careers."

"Was he right?"

Jeffrey sighed. "Potentially, the photo could be very damaging to us," he admitted. "Our school board members are fairly liberal, as long as one is discreet and doesn't flaunt a lifestyle that's not in the mainstream. But if this picture were passed around, they couldn't ignore it. Some of the parents would certainly object."

"What did Tom do after you refused to take his threat seriously?" Vivian asked.

"He made a big show of carefully putting the photo in his briefcase. He told us we'd talk about it again after we'd had time to think about what would happen if he decided to make the picture public. He said our nonchalant reaction was a good try, but that he knew we were bluffing."

"Did you try to change his mind?" Vivian asked.

"Not right then," Jeffrey said. "It was almost time for the game to start. But I was worried about what he might do, so I went up to his room last night to try to talk to him about it."

"Then you're changing your story," Vivian said. "When we talked to you before, you told us you went to your room after the game and went right to sleep."

"Well, I did go to my room, like I said," Jeffrey replied, "but I had trouble falling asleep." He still didn't tell them that he'd been out earlier looking for Ralph. "I went to Tom's room a little before two o'clock. When I got to the door, I heard voices. I didn't want anyone to know I was there, so I quickly left."

"Can you prove that?"

"No. But why would I even tell you that I was there, if I had something to hide? Obviously no one saw me. And I didn't see anyone else."

"Perhaps it was *you* that other people heard talking to Tom at that hour."

"It was *not* me," Jeffrey said vehemently.

Vivian eyed him for a moment. "Could you distinguish any words or recognize any of the voices?" she finally asked.

"No." Jeffrey visibly relaxed as Vivian backed off. "Once I realized someone else was there, I wanted to get out of there as fast as I could."

"What did you expect to do if he'd let you in? He surely wasn't going to give you the photo or the negative."

"Well, I did think about forcing him to give them to me," Jeffrey admitted. "I know how that sounds now, but it doesn't matter. I never got into the room."

"How do we know that?" Kathy interrupted. "Maybe it was your voice that some of the others heard in Tom's room. Why should we believe you?"

"I never got into that room," Jeffrey shouted at her. "And," he said pointing at the picture still in Vivian's hand, "Tom obviously still had at least one copy of the photo. If I had gone in there and killed him, I never would have left any of these pictures lying around."

"At least we can clear you on that point," Vivian said, "because we know that he wasn't killed in the room." Then she attacked again. "Since you admit to being there around two o'clock, you could have been the one who lured him outside. Then, after you killed him, you could have gone back to search his room for the negatives. When the fire alarm rang, you had to get out of there quickly. You never had a chance to find the negative or the photo."

"That's crazy," Jeffrey said. "Ask Ralph. I was in my bed sleeping when he came in. When the alarm rang later, I woke up first and I was the one who had to wake Ralph up."

"That's true," Ralph said. "He wouldn't have had time to kill Tom out in the parking lot, then get back in bed and fall asleep before the alarm rang."

"But *you* would've had the time," Vivian said, turning to Ralph. "You told us you went for a walk late at night, but instead of being outside on a walk, you could have been the one talking in Tom's room."

"No, he couldn't have," Linda said. "I saw Ralph come into the lobby from outside and take the elevator up. It was after two-thirty."

"Fine. You've just confirmed that Ralph was outside the hotel around the time the murder was committed," Vivian said. "How do you know what he was doing outside? He could have been taking a walk like he said—or he could have been murdering Tom."

Linda looked at Ralph. "Well, I guess that's true. I don't know what he was doing."

"This is absurd," Ralph protested. "I've already told you where I was and what I was doing. I never went near Tom's room. All I did was go outside to take a walk and clear my head. I can't help it if Tom was killed while I was taking my walk."

"I can't believe all this is happening," Charles Canning moaned. He had found a reporter and given her a list of the winners, and then had rejoined the group. "This was supposed to be a game to bring the products of Century Bridge Supplies to the attention of the public. What kind of publicity will they get from all these revelations? It seems like everyone here has some tawdry little secret, and Tom Stanhope managed to ferret them all out. Now the whole world's going to think of scandals and murder whenever they hear our company mentioned."

"Speaking of scandals, Charles," Vivian said, "this may be a good time for you to tell us about a note from Tom that we found in your room."

"Oh, my God!" Charles leaped out of his chair and looked around frantically. "Didn't I throw that away?"

"Take it easy," Vivian said. "Even if Tom threatened you, it doesn't mean you killed him. Why don't you sit back down and tell us what that note was all about?"

Charles collapsed in his seat. After a few minutes, his color came back, but he sat there in a stupor.

"Well," Vivian coaxed. "Let's hear your story."

"It goes back to the time when I was playing basketball at Syracuse University," he began. "During my senior year, there was a question about points being shaved from some of the games. The newspapers listed the names of all the players on the team, and we were all suspended during an investigation. It turned out that two players on the team really had shaved points. They were brought to trial and convicted of the charges. Eventually, they were fined and expelled from school."

"Then what's the problem?" Vivian asked. "If you weren't involved, Tom had nothing on you."

"I know. But he showed me the article that listed all our names as suspects. I was the star player at the time, and my name was on the top of the list. I hadn't scored my usual number of points in the last few games, and people were suspicious. Even though there was no evidence against me, people still wondered."

"Were you ever brought to trial?"

"No! There was no evidence against the rest of us, because we didn't do anything wrong."

"Then I don't see how the article Tom had could've hurt you."

"He threatened to show it to the board of directors at Century. Even though I didn't do anything wrong, they might not want someone who'd been associated with a scandal to represent them. They would probably fire me, and in this economy, it's not easy to get a job like mine. I don't want to lose it."

"What did Tom expect you to do?"

"He cleverly didn't spell out his demands in the note. He just wanted to get my attention and make sure I'd worry about what he was up to. He told me later that he wanted me to fix the game so he'd be assured of winning at least some of the money. It was ridiculous to expect me to do that. I told him so."

"What did he say to that?"

"He told me he was sure I'd find a way."

"Did you try?" Vivian asked.

"Of course not. I have no idea how to fix a bridge game. I suppose he realized that, but it didn't matter to him. He was sick. He enjoyed making people sweat."

"It seems he went to a lot of trouble to dredge up a story that old. How did he even know about it?"

"I'm sure he'd been aware of the scandal for years. He's from Rochester, and this took place in Syracuse. It was in all the upstate papers when it happened. He probably remembered it and looked for the articles when he found out I'd be representing Century."

"He certainly went to a lot of trouble to find everyone's weaknesses," Vivian said.

"He was a horrible person," Charles said bitterly. "But even though he tried to blackmail me, I didn't kill him. I don't know who did, but it wasn't me." He looked around the room defiantly.

No one challenged him. They were all too busy thinking about his revelations and how they could tell their own stories without saying more than they wanted the others to hear.

"We'll move on to you now, Jonathan," Vivian said. "We found your computer when we searched your room, but it was locked."

"I always keep it locked when I travel," Jonathan replied. "Other than playing professionally, I make my living from writing books and articles. I can't afford to have anyone steal my ideas. I know you want to see if I've locked any secrets in there—as Cliff seems to have done—and the truth is, I have. But they're not the kind of secrets you're looking for. They're just things I'm working on for my next book. I really object to having anyone see what I'm working on before it gets published . . . especially a room full of bridge players."

"I understand that, but we can't make any exceptions in a murder case," Vivian replied. "Look at how important it was to look at Cliff's bridge files. If what you spotted there is correct, and Cliff did see the Vanderbilt hands ahead of time, his team will have to forfeit their win. For all we know, there may be something equally incriminating in your computer."

Jonathan scowled. "There's nothing in my computer like that," he insisted. When Vivian didn't back down, he reluctantly handed over his key.

While Vivian turned on the computer and began paging through Jonathan's bridge files, Sharon whispered to Eva,

Chapter Twenty-Two

"Did you know that Jonathan once wrote a novel about bridge and sex?"

"No. What did he call it?"

"*Humping and Trumping.*"

Sharon looked at her sister. "C'mon."

"I'm not kidding."

"I don't remember any book named that."

"The publishers made him change the title."

"To what?"

"He came up with *The Art of the Deal.*"

"But—"

"I know. His third title was *Let's Make a Deal.* It had four doors on the cover. Each door had either a spade, heart, diamond, or club on it. The murderer was supposed to be behind one of the doors. Apparently, there was some argument about the odds of guessing the right door after one of the doors was eliminated. You know how bridge players are always trying to figure out the best percentages. There were so many arguments, the publishers finally decided to eliminate that title too."

"Did the book ever get published under *any* title?"

"Yes. He finally called it *Bridge Over Doubled Squawkers.* Hardly anyone knows about it."

"How do you know about it?"

"I bought one of the copies. It was so bad, I couldn't finish reading it. The ... pace ... was ... too ... slow."

By that time, Vivian had gotten into Jonathan's computer.

"How come you don't encrypt your files?" she asked.

"It isn't necessary to do that when I keep the computer locked. If you tell me what you're looking for, maybe I can speed things up. I hate seeing all my unpublished work flashing by on the screen."

"I'd like to make it easier for you, but I'm not sure what we're looking for."

Cliff interrupted. "As long as everyone looked through my files, I'd like the same opportunity to look at Jonathan's. I certainly know enough about bridge to see if he's hiding anything." He strode over to the desk, pushed Vivian aside, and began paging through the documents. Since Vivian didn't know what to look for, she didn't try to stop him.

"He just wants to see what I'm going to publish," Jonathan objected. "I'd better not see any of my work under his name."

"Don't worry. I have better things to do with my time than steal your work," Cliff said. "I just want to be sure you don't have anything here that shouldn't be."

While he spent the next several minutes going through Jonathan's bridge notes, Vivian quietly talked to Herb.

"I'm glad Cliff insisted on doing this," she said. "If there's anything there, he'll find it a lot faster than we will."

"Yeah, but there's something unsavory about the way he's going about it. Look at the expression on his face. He's getting a kick out of making Jonathan miserable. And he knows that if he finds *anything*, it'll take some of the pressure off him."

Cliff scrutinized several more pages of bridge hands and theories, but finally gave up. All he could find to say to Jonathan was, "That's not a true triple squeeze. You'd better rethink it."

"What are you trying to do?" Jonathan asked angrily. "Now that Tom's dead, you seem to be doing your best to take his place. You're becoming as offensive as he was."

"Jonathan, how can you say that? I'm just trying to save you some embarrassment if you publish that article."

Jonathan glared at Cliff, but then thought maybe he *was* being oversensitive. "Well, if that's all you meant, thanks for the tip," he mumbled.

CHAPTER 23

Everyone jumped when the telephone rang. At first the bridge players tried to eavesdrop, but as the conversation lengthened, they gradually began to whisper among themselves.

"It looks like you've got a lot of explaining to do," Vivian said to Cliff when she finished her phone call. "George Nelson, one of the computer experts at the ACBL headquarters in Memphis, has been trying to figure out how you could have intercepted the bridge programs stored in their mainframe computer. He began by talking to Margery to see if she could help him."

"There's nothing Margery could have told him," Cliff said confidently. "The file that's used to create bridge hands is encrypted for protection, and Margery never gave me the password for it. You don't have to be a computer expert to know there's no way I could have retrieved the file without knowing the password. Even if I could've somehow gotten the file, I could never have found the code number assigned to any specific hand records."

"Nevertheless, you *did* find a way," Vivian said. "When George talked to Margery, at first she was angry at the implication that she would betray the ACBL. She told him that she would never give you or anyone else the password. After George finally calmed her down, he tried another tactic. He asked what she knew about your computer company."

"My company? I don't see the connection," Cliff said, puzzled. "She knows very little about my company—and the company has nothing to do with the ACBL."

"Apparently while you were trying to quiz her about the ACBL computer system, you gave her more information than you meant to. Margery remembered how fascinated you were when you learned that the firm that prints and packages the duplicate hand records for the ACBL is the same one that handles your payroll system."

"So what?" Cliff asked. "It's a service bureau. They perform services for companies throughout the country."

"Yes, but when you found out that it serviced both the ACBL and your computer company, you realized it gave you a way to intercept programs from the mainframe computer at ACBL headquarters. Right now, there are experts working on the programs in Memphis and at the service company, trying to figure out how you managed to get the password and retrieve the bridge hands. It's only a matter of time until they come up with the answer."

Cliff looked stunned. Not wanting to admit anything, he weighed his options, realizing that anyone knowledgeable about computers would sooner or later figure out his Vanderbilt scheme. Better to admit to cheating and computer fraud, he decided after a moment's reflection, than to be fingered for a murder he didn't commit.

Finally he spoke. "Since they're concentrating on the break-in, it shouldn't take them too long to find out what I did. Before they figure it out, I'd like to tell my story to my bridge colleagues. Someday, when they get over their anger, they may at least intellectually appreciate what I managed to do."

"If you want to tell us, you may. But first I'm going to read you your rights." Vivian pulled a slip of paper from her pocketbook and read Cliff the *Miranda* rights. "Now that you know that you may remain silent, you may choose to talk to us if you wish. Before you do, I have two more questions to ask you, and I'll need you to sign a waiver."

"Ask away."

"Do you understand these rights that I have explained to you? Having these rights in mind, do you wish to talk to us now?"

"I understand my rights perfectly," Cliff replied. He took the waiver from Vivian, then signed and dated it. Herb signed as a witness.

There was total silence in the room; everyone stared at Cliff. Instead of speaking with his usual confidence, he sounded quite vulnerable.

"I needed that win," he said in an almost pleading voice. "Tom was an excellent partner, but I knew I couldn't stand playing with him much longer. I realized that if we didn't win the Vanderbilt this time, I would have to find a new partner just to keep my sanity. The problem was that I had very little chance to reach the same high level with a new partner. At least not quickly. That's when I decided to do whatever I needed to do to win."

Even though he knew that he was condemning himself, Cliff became more and more animated as he told his story.

"I decided to assure our win by finding a way to see the Vanderbilt hands ahead of time. If I could find the password to get into the program, I knew I could find a way to retrieve the hand records.

"Actually, it was fairly easy. I made several trips to Memphis and took Margery Holcomb out to dinner each time. During the evening, I would casually bring our conversations around to hand records and computers. She told me that the ACBL had taken extra precautions to make sure that no one could gain access to the hand records. The password that was needed to construct and retrieve them consisted of two nonsense words made out of numerous consonants and numbers. She admitted that the configuration was so complicated that she had to look it up every time she needed to access the files.

"That's all she told me, but it was enough. When I went to pick her up for dinner the next day, I arrived at ACBL headquarters early, knowing that she had a meeting to go to. Since she knows that I'm the CEO of a computer company, she didn't think anything of it when I asked her if I could play with her computer while she was at the meeting. She had no idea I'd try to find the password to get to the hand records."

"Wasn't it pretty naive of her to let you use her computer?" Vivian asked.

"Not really. Everyone knows that computer people are always interested in fiddling with other computers. And she had never told me anything I shouldn't know—at least she didn't realize she had. There was no reason for her to be suspicious."

"How did you find the password?"

"I knew that she had to have the information close by. I looked through her desk—without much hope. Then I decided that she might have put the password into the computer where she could retrieve it when she needed it. I went back to the WORDPERFECT screen and scanned the entries. The word 'cnfig' caught my eye. I remembered that she described the password as a complicated configuration. I retrieved the 'cnfig' data, and sure enough, there were two nonsense words. I didn't want to write them down, so I sat for a few seconds and memorized them. Then I tried them out in the computer. That's all it took. I could construct or retrieve any hands I wanted."

"Can you show us on your portable computer?"

Cliff turned on his computer, and at the C:> prompt, typed:

C:> t24r89pnc64j

After a few seconds, the bridge program appeared:

WELCOME TO THE WORLD'S BEST PROGRAM FOR CREATING DUPLICATE BRIDGE HANDS. PLEASE ANSWER THE FOLLOWING SERIES OF QUESTIONS:

NUMBER OF HANDS TO CREATE> 36

RANDOM NUMBER FOR GENERATING HANDS> XXYZZ543

PLEASE WAIT ...

THE HANDS HAVE BEEN CREATED. WOULD YOU LIKE TO PRINT THE GENERATED DUPLICATE HANDS (YES OR NO)?

Chapter Twenty-Three

> NO

WOULD YOU LIKE TO SAVE THE GENERATED DUPLICATE HANDS?

> YES

FILE FOR THE HANDS TO GO INTO:

> TOURN.NAC

WOULD YOU LIKE TO LEAVE PROGRAM (YES OR NO)?

> YES

Cliff turned off the computer and looked rather proudly at Vivian and Herb. Although he realized he was in trouble, he was still pleased with his achievement.

"Okay, you found out how to get into their program," Vivian acknowledged. "But I assume the Vanderbilt hands hadn't even been created at that time."

"That's right, but it didn't matter. I had a stealth shell program on a diskette in my pocket to add to their own operating system. I just had to find a way to be able to break into their security area whenever and from wherever I wanted. I knew that after the ACBL generates the hands, they send an order with the code number to the service bureau that prints and packages them. As you found out, I knew from Margery that the company they sent the order to was the same one that does the payroll for my company."

"I still don't understand how you could get to see a set of hands that would be created in the future," Vivian said. "And how did you keep the computer people at the ACBL from realizing what you were doing?"

"My stealth program was camouflaged. If accessed by one of the League's computer techs, it would show up as 'clock.sys', which looks like an operating system file. That way, no computer jock at the ACBL would become suspicious and delete it. With the password, the stealth program could intercept the files of generated deals and add an instruction to search for a link on my company's payroll files. Then it would duplicate the deal files within the payroll files. All I had to do was call up 'clock.sys' from the payroll file to access those files of deals."

"Ingenious," Vivian said, genuinely impressed. "But how did you know which ones would be used for the Vanderbilt?"

"I brought my portable computer here and kept running the program until the date on the hand records corresponded to the date of the Vanderbilt. It showed up a few days before the game. Then I used their code number that was listed right there on their program and retrieved the hands."

"My God!" Gary said. "With that setup, you could've seen the hands for every single event."

"That's true, I could have. But I wasn't interested. I didn't need—or care about—an advantage for any of the other events. I figured I could win any of them on my own. It was the Vanderbilt that I wanted to win."

"I can't believe it," Jonathan said, amazed. "All this time, we thought it was Tom who cheated us out of the Vanderbilt win. I'll bet he found out what you did, and that's why you murdered him. You couldn't risk having him let people know you were a cheater. You were afraid you'd lose your cushy CEO job."

"You're right about one thing. He did find out about it . . . and I still haven't figured out how. But I didn't kill him. I knew there wasn't much he could do about the information. If he accused me of cheating, he'd lose the Vanderbilt too. Knowing Tom, I'm sure he would've tried to blackmail me later, but he had too much to lose to do anything like that until after the International Team Trials and possibly the world championships."

"And that's why you killed him now," Gary accused. "You couldn't stand for it to come out later."

"Just think for a minute! This would be the *worst* time possible for me to kill him. We've just won the Vanderbilt, and we had a good chance of winning the money game. I'd be crazy to risk all that. If it was important enough to me to cheat so that I could have a chance to represent the United States in international competition, why would I kill the partner I'd just won with? Tom wanted to play internationally just as much as I did. He definitely wouldn't have done anything to ruin his chances now. You'll have to look somewhere else for his killer."

"That's a pretty glib answer," Gary said. "How can we believe anyone who stands up here and smoothly brags about how he cheated to win the Vanderbilt? If you could figure out something so complicated with computers, you could easily figure out a way to lure Tom to the parking lot and murder him."

"I probably could have, but I didn't."

"Now I understand what all your long distance charges were that I saw on your bill," Eva said. "They weren't calls to Margery. They were charges for accessing the service company when you searched for the Vanderbilt hand records. But how come the calls were to Memphis? Your company is in Rochester."

"The data processing division of my company is in Tennessee," Cliff explained. "I called them several times each day last week until the hands showed up on my payroll file. That's why the phone bills were so high. And except for inadvertently helping me find the password, Margery had nothing to do with my breaking into the computer. I'm confessing to the cheating, but that's *all* I did. *I* didn't murder Tom."

CHAPTER 24

Before Cliff could return to his seat, Ralph suddenly blurted out, "I just figured out what was bothering me about Kathy's story. She *was* here last night. I saw her."

"That's impossible," Kathy objected. "I went home right after the game."

"Maybe you did, but you came back. I knew something was bothering me when Jennifer said she thought she saw you going into the ladies' room around one-thirty and you denied it."

"Of course I denied it. I had gone home by then. Jennifer must have mistaken someone else for me."

"I don't think so," Ralph said, shaking his head. "I'll bet it was you she saw, because I saw you later. When I was out on my walk, I saw a white Mercedes speed by. I glanced in the car and recognized the flowered dress that you wore yesterday."

"That's preposterous," Kathy said. "Lots of women have flowered dresses. How could you possibly tell one from another—especially in the dark? Besides, I was nowhere near here at that hour. I was home in bed."

"What kind of car do you drive?" Vivian asked.

"I drive a white Mercedes. So what? It's not the only one in Virginia Beach."

"I doubt if there were many of them cruising around at that hour of the morning—especially with drivers wearing flowered dresses," Vivian said. "Did you get the license number?" she asked Ralph.

"No. There was no reason to. All I know is it was the same kind of car Kathy drives, and the person driving it looked like Kathy to me."

"Come to think of it, I never saw you leave the hotel after the game," Linda said to Kathy. "When I left, I thought you were right behind me. But when I got to the parking lot, you had disappeared. And your car was still in the lot, parked near mine. Where were you?"

"*That's* when I went to the ladies' room," Kathy said. "Jennifer must have been mistaken about the time."

"I couldn't possibly have seen you right after the game," Jennifer said. "I was still in the ballroom finishing up the scoring."

"Well, I can't help it, that's when I went to the ladies' room," Kathy snapped. "Then I went straight home."

"I don't think so," Linda persisted. "Before I came back to the hotel, I called your house, and there was no answer. I wanted to talk about one of the hands we played, but all I got was your answering machine. I waited a few minutes before I came back to the hotel, but you never returned my call."

"My answering machine is in the den, and I didn't go in there to check it for messages. It was late when I got home, and I certainly didn't want to return calls at that hour. As soon as I walked into my bedroom, I turned the phone off. I didn't want to be disturbed in case it rang early in the morning. So if you called *after* I got home, I wouldn't have heard the phone ring."

"Whenever I've called you after one of our local games, you've always answered, no matter how late it was."

"I know what you're trying to do, Linda. You're trying to deflect people's suspicions away from yourself and on to me, but it won't work. You think you can keep me from getting you fired by pinning this murder on me, but you're wrong. Even if they charged me with the murder, I'd never let you off the hook."

"You lied about something else," Linda said, ignoring Kathy's threats. "You *knew* that Tom had sent copies of the canceled checks to your husband before I mentioned it here tonight."

"You don't know what you're talking about," Kathy cried, enraged. "I just found out about those checks when you told the whole room about them."

"I've been thinking about your story, and it doesn't make sense," Linda said. "You *must* have known that your husband had copies of the canceled checks. His lawyer had to have them in order to give a judge sufficient reason to subpoena your records. And you must have received the subpoena. That's routine. So how can you tell us that you didn't know anything about it?"

"Because I didn't!"

Linda was enjoying herself. "You must have been furious," she said. "Those canceled checks gave your husband's lawyer enough ammunition to get the subpoena and see what else you were hiding. You knew he was on a fishing expedition, but you were stuck. No matter how much you deny it, you knew that Tom had sent the copies. So you had as much motive as anyone had to kill him."

"We seem to have conflicting stories here, Kathy," Vivian said. "You say you went home right after the game, but Jennifer and Ralph both say they saw you here later. And if what Linda just told us is true, you knew that Tom had sent copies of the checks to your husband. It's time to tell us the truth. But before you say anything, I'm going to read the Miranda warning to you."

She proceeded to reread the rights to Kathy and to give her the same option of signing the waiver that she had given Cliff.

"I'll sign the waiver and tell you my story because, unlike Cliff, I have nothing to hide," Kathy said. She took the waiver from Vivian and signed her name. "I did go home, like I said, but I turned around and came right back. You don't have any idea what it was like being blackmailed by Tom. It looked like he was going to cost me a lot in my divorce settlement. It's true. I did know about the canceled checks. I needed to convince him to tell the truth about the checks before he left town."

"If he'd already sent copies of the checks to your husband, wasn't it too late?" Vivian asked.

"No. There's still lots of negotiating to do with my husband before the divorce is final. I wanted Tom to tell the truth—that the checks were payment for professional bridge services, and nothing else. I didn't want my husband to have any ammunition that would let him get his hands on my estate."

"What time did you get back here?" Vivian asked.

"Around one-thirty. Jennifer was right. I saw her just as she was coming out of the ballroom, and I ducked into the ladies' room, hoping she wouldn't recognize me. I didn't want anyone to know I was going to see Tom. I was so upset with him, I didn't think about being seen until I got back here. I waited in there a little while, then went up to Tom's room a little before two o'clock."

"We must have just missed seeing each other," Jeffrey broke in. "It's beginning to sound like a Mack Sennett farce with all of us sneaking around the corridors, just missing each other."

"How did you get Tom to let you in his room?" Vivian quickly asked, miffed at Jeffrey for interrupting. She didn't want Kathy to lose her momentum.

"I used the house phone near the ladies' room and called him. When he answered, I told him that I was in the hotel. I said that I'd been thinking about those checks and that I had come up with a proposition that would help both of us. Tom was always interested in making money, so he gave me his room number and told me to come right up.

"I got on the elevator and went to his room, grateful that no one I knew saw me. Tom let me in and told me it had better be a good offer. He knew he had a chance to win the money game, and he wanted to get a good night's sleep."

"And was your offer good enough to convince him to tell the truth?"

"I thought so. I told him that if he told my husband and his lawyer that those checks were for professional fees only, I'd give him five thousand dollars in cash. He just laughed at me."

"What did you do?"

"We started shouting at each other."

"That must be what woke me up," Sybil broke in. "I told you I heard voices next door."

"And then?" Vivian asked.

"A few minutes later, someone knocked on the door. We stopped talking and waited for whoever it was to go away."

"That must have been me," Linda said. "Remember, I told you that I went to Tom's room and knocked. I thought I heard voices, but no one answered. And just think, you were in there all along, Kathy . . . and not home in bed like you said."

"Don't you dare criticize me. You aren't any better, skulking around hotel corridors in the middle of the night. And what did *you* go to his room for? If everyone else has to tell the truth, how come we haven't heard why you came back?"

"We'll get to that later," Vivian said. "Go on with your story, Kathy."

"I was furious, but I decided that I'd better give Tom some money to keep him quiet. I had too much to lose if he decided to lie about me to my husband's lawyer. I told him that I would *never* write another check with his name on it, but if he'd go with me to the ATM machine on the next block, I would draw out some cash. I told him I would give him more as soon as I could discreetly get enough out of my other accounts. Tom got dressed, and we took the service elevator to avoid being seen. We went out the side door off the lobby.

"When we arrived in the parking lot, I tried again to negotiate with him. I asked what it would take to get him to admit that my checks were payments for bridge fees, and nothing else. He smirked and told me that he wanted a share of what he would be saving me."

"Did you agree?"

"I did not! I told him ten thousand was the highest I would go. If he wanted any more, then I'd take my chances with the judge. I wasn't about to offer him another cent.

"Tom said I was being foolish," Kathy continued. "My husband could potentially take me for half my estate. He'd be willing to settle for fifty thousand. Otherwise, he would be glad to testify that the money was for sexual favors. I told him that I thought he was going to be reasonable in the amount he wanted, but if he felt that way, I wasn't going to give him a cent. I turned around and left."

Vivian stared at her for a full thirty seconds. Then she quietly said, "Can I see your gun, Kathy?"

Unnerved by the question, Kathy tried to stall. "How did you know that I own a gun?"

"Officer Rollins cross-checked the registration records against the list of competitors this afternoon."

"Well, I used to keep it with me all the time, but I stopped carrying it a few weeks ago."

"Where is it now?"

"I can't find it."

"That's not true," Linda interrupted. "I saw it yesterday when you took your check out of your pocketbook to pay your entry fee."

"I'm going to call police headquarters right now to request a search warrant for your house," Vivian said. "You'll be detained until we get it. You've lied about everything. You did come back here, you did have your gun with you yesterday, and it's clear that you had a motive to kill Tom."

"Stop badgering me!" Kathy shouted. "I didn't have any choice. Tom was blackmailing me. That bastard was going to help my husband get half of my money. I was never going to let that happen."

"Wait!" Vivian said. "I want to warn you about your rights again. You may choose to tell us your story voluntarily, but you may stop any time and call your lawyer."

"My lawyer won't be able to do much once you get the search warrant," Kathy said resignedly. "You might as well know how it happened. When Tom demanded fifty thousand, I told him I would kill him before I'd give him that much money. He just laughed at me—until I pulled the gun out of my purse. He looked scared for a minute, but then he started to make fun of me ... said the little gun looked like it was for a girl scout and that I'd never have the nerve to shoot him. His smugness was so overwhelming, I lost control and shot him. Just before he crumpled to the ground, he stared unbelievingly at me. The look of astonishment on his face was almost worth what this will cost me. He wouldn't have been more surprised if I'd won the Vanderbilt."

"Only a bridge player would come up with that comparison," Herb muttered.

Kathy didn't seem aware that Herb had spoken. "When I suddenly realized what I had done, I panicked," she continued. "I didn't know what to do next. When I saw how bright it was under the lights in the parking lot, I decided to move the body. I grabbed Tom and pulled him over to the grocery store wall where it was darker. Then I got in my car and left. I wanted to be home in bed by the time someone discovered him."

"Where's the gun now?"

"It's in my safe. I just tossed it in there when I got home. I planned to get rid of it tomorrow."

"Good Lord!" Linda said suddenly. "You'll be spending the next several years in prison."

Kathy found just enough strength to answer her. "After all your hysterical accusations today, I'd think you'd be delighted."

"Any other time, I would be. Sometimes punishments really are unfair."

"Well, I'm glad to hear you're at least sympathetic," Kathy said, totally misunderstanding.

CHAPTER 25

"Kathy Jensen," Vivian said, "I'm placing you under arrest for the murder of Tom Stanhope. You may call your lawyer, if you'd like. You can use the telephone here or wait until we take you to police headquarters. The rest of you—except for Cliff—are free to go. Congratulations to all the winners, and my sympathies to the losers."

Officer Rollins took charge of Kathy. It was one of Linda's most pleasurable moments when she sat back in her chair and watched him put the handcuffs on Kathy.

"Wait a minute!" Cliff said. "Why are you detaining me? I didn't kill anyone. It's true I admitted breaking into the computer, but that's not a federal offense. And the ACBL is a non-profit organization. What difference does it make to you if I cheat in a bridge game or break into a private organization's computer?"

"The cheating part is a matter for the ACBL to take care of. We have no jurisdiction over that. But breaking into a computer is something else. You used interstate wire communication facilities when you infiltrated the ACBL programs with your computer. That *is* a federal offense. You also invaded the computer system of the company that prints the hand records. Non-profit status has nothing to do with it. I'm going to turn the case over to the FBI in the morning. They'll have to untangle the precise charges. In the meantime, Cliff, you're under arrest. The *Miranda* warnings are still in effect for you. When Kathy's done with the phone, you may call your attorney, if you wish."

Jonathan watched as Rollins put handcuffs on Cliff. "I'm going to call the ACBL in the morning and tell them that you admitted that you cheated to win the Vanderbilt," Jonathan told him. "I'd appreciate it if you'd tell them what's happened."

"It's going to be hard to have that conversation from my jail cell," Cliff replied bitterly. "You'll just have to wait until I get around to it."

"I'll be glad to call the ACBL president tomorrow and tell her what Cliff told us," Vivian said. "I can make copies of the Vanderbilt hands that he had in his computer, and let her know about the dates on that file. I think I'd better hang onto the computer, though. I'm sure the FBI will want to go over it thoroughly to see if Cliff was up to any other mischief."

"Thanks," Jonathan said. "That'll be a big help."

* * * * *

"I almost feel sorry for Cliff," Gary said to Jonathan as they left Room 111. "He's lost his reputation, his partner, the Vanderbilt ... everything he's ever worked for. He's certain to be barred from playing for a *long* time. And who knows what'll happen because of the computer break-in. He might very well end up in prison."

"How can you feel sorry for him?" Jonathan asked. "We lost the Vanderbilt because of his cheating."

"You'll have to admit," Gary said, "it was a very subtle way for Cliff to cheat. It would've been difficult for an observer to discern a pattern, since Cliff only cheated on slam hands—and not even on all of those. And Tom didn't have any knowledge of Cliff's scheme at the time, so he couldn't give it away. Tom's denial of cheating must have been very convincing to the committee since, from his point of view, it was true."

"But, at some point, Tom did find out," Jonathan said. "We'll probably never know how." Then he snapped his fingers. "Hey! We are going to be named the Vanderbilt winners! It just sank in!"

"I was wondering when you'd realize it," Gary said with a grin.

"No wonder you felt sorry for Cliff," Jonathan said. "I suddenly do too." Uncharacteristically, he danced the rest of the way to the elevator.

* * * * *

Vivian turned toward Herb and smiled. "I can't thank you enough. You were extraordinarily helpful. I think I would have lost my mind when we searched the rooms if it hadn't been for your humor and support."

Herb smiled back. "I enjoyed every minute of it. Even though I'm an investigator, I was certainly surprised to find myself investigating a case involving bridge."

"You think you were surprised!" They both laughed.

They were still smiling at each other when Jennifer joined them at the desk. Herb got up, walked around the desk, and put his arm around her. "We were just laughing about the absurdity of our working on a case involving bridge," he told her.

"You both did a great job," Jennifer said, hiding her uneasiness. She hoped she didn't look as exhausted as she felt. She was glad to see that Vivian looked drained.

When she couldn't stifle a yawn any longer, Herb grabbed her hand, waved goodnight to Vivian, and led her out of the room.

Vivian watched them go, feeling more than a little envy.

* * * * *

Sharon unlocked her door, and Eva followed her into the room. "What time is it?" Sharon asked.

"Almost two-thirty."

"Want to go home?"

"Tonight?"

"Why not?" Sharon said. "We're both still wide awake. Let's pack up and check out. Then we'll be in our own beds when we wake up in the morning. I might even throw in a load of laundry when I get home."

"What about Gary? Don't you want to say good-bye to each other in the morning?"

"We already did that. He's leaving on an early plane. I told him I wouldn't be up."

"Have you made any plans to see each other?"

"He asked me to play in the Mixed Pairs with him at the Summer National Championships."

"A new love, a pro for a partner, and a third-place money win. Three terrific accomplishments. And all managed in a couple of days. Not bad."

"You're jealous."

"Yeah."

"Want my share of the money?"

"I'd rather have the other two."

A few minutes later, while Eva was arranging her shoes neatly into shoe bags, she heard someone knocking lightly on her door.

She frowned. "Who is it?"

"What? Did you say something?" Sharon shouted back from her room.

"Someone's at the door."

"Don't open it till you find out who it is."

Eva went to the door, stood up on her toes, and peered through the peephole. Linda was standing there, getting ready to knock again.

Eva opened the door before Linda could make any more noise. "Why on earth are you still here at the hotel?" Eva asked. "We're so anxious to get home, we're packing up and checking out tonight. I'd have thought you'd be home in bed by now."

"I know it's late, but I'm in trouble. I need to talk to you and Sharon tonight. Right now, in fact." And she burst into tears.

"Sharon," Eva called, "come into my room for a minute. Linda's here, and she needs to talk to us."

"At this hour?" Sharon groaned. "Can't we do this tomorrow? I just want to finish packing and go home." She went through the connecting doors to plead with Linda to wait until they'd all had some sleep. But as soon as she saw her friend crying, she moved over to the bed where Linda sat, and put her arm around her. "What's the matter, Linda? This isn't like you."

"I'm in a mess, and I don't have anyone else that I can ask to help me." Before the sisters even had a chance to see if they wanted to be involved in Linda's problems, she launched into her story of gambling and embezzlement.

When she finished, the sisters looked at each other and then back at Linda. Sharon nodded her head slowly up and down.

"You're right about one thing. You are in trouble. You're going to need a lot of help. I know a couple of good lawyers that I could recommend."

"I'm afraid even a good lawyer won't be able to keep me out of prison. I'd hoped to win some money in the tournament and put back what I took before the theft was discovered. But I didn't win anything. I need to find a way to replace the funds as fast as possible. The auditors were due next week, but Vivian said that she was going to send someone to the bank tomorrow to see if Tom had any reason to blackmail me. And Kathy's furious at me. Right now, she's too busy trying to stay out of prison to put me in, but she's going to be after me the first minute she gets. That woman is hell on grudges."

"What would you like us to do?" Eva asked.

"You won nearly seventy thousand dollars between you in the money game," Linda said. "I was hoping you would loan me what I need so I can pay back what I took before the auditors get to the books."

"If we help you, how do we know that you won't just take the money and disappear with it at the blackjack tables or the slot machines in Atlantic City?" Eva asked.

Linda thought for a moment. "How about this? While you finish packing, I'll write out a confession saying exactly what I did. I'll make payments of two hundred dollars each month, which is all I can afford, until you're repaid. I promise not to gamble 'til everything's paid back. If I miss any payments, you can turn in my confession."

"I don't know if we want to get involved with this," Eva told her. "We'll go into Sharon's room and discuss your plan. You start writing."

* * * * *

They returned a few minutes later. Linda looked up anxiously and raised her eyebrows. "What've you decided?"

"We don't think it's right to help you break the law," Sharon said. "Accessories after the fact, or whatever the legal term is. And we don't want to end up in prison. But we'd hate to see you spend the rest of your life there. Besides, it would be cruel and unusual punishment if you ended up with Kathy for a cellmate. We'll help you, but if you miss even one payment, we'll use the confession."

"I don't know what to say." Tears welled up in Linda's eyes. "I'm so grateful. I really didn't think I'd find any way to get out of this mess. As long as you've agreed to help me, I need another favor. Will one of you meet me at the bank early tomorrow morning so I can replace the funds immediately? I'm afraid Kathy may ask her lawyer to start an investigation as soon as she has time to think about it. She's really ticked at me. Vivian will probably be too busy or too tired to get an auditor there before noon."

"We have to go to the bank tomorrow to deposit our winnings," Sharon said. "We'll meet you there at nine o'clock. One other thing. When we get to the bank, we want you to sign your statement in front of a witness and have it notarized."

"But they'll see what I wrote."

"No, they won't. We'll cover up the confession part. All they have to do is witness the signature."

Chapter Twenty-Five

"Okay, I'll do that. You don't know how relieved I am. I'll see you tomorrow."

After Linda left, Eva said, "Is any of this legal?"

"I doubt it, but so what?" Sharon replied. "We're not hurting anybody. And we can't let Linda go to prison, if we can help it."

"If they catch us, we'll be right there with her."

"But look at the caliber of bridge we'd have," Sharon said with a grin. "What a daunting prison foursome—you, me, Cliff, and Linda."

"What about Kathy?"

"Absolutely not. We have standards. No murderers allowed."

"What if they imprison Cliff in Rochester? Then there'll only be three of us."

"If that happens, we'll lower our standards."

CHAPTER 26

As soon as Eva and Sharon boarded the Concorde and found their seats, the cabin crew passed out magazines and toiletry kits, then hot towels, aperitifs, and champagne.

"What's in the goody bag?" Sharon asked Eva, too lazy to open hers.

"Let me see." Eva opened up her travel kit and rooted around inside. She pulled out a pair of slippers, a toothbrush, toothpaste, and some other toiletries. At the bottom of the kit, she found a sleep mask.

"I think I'll save mine and give it to Gary to put on the first time I put down a dummy," Sharon said.

"There must be something better that you can do with a mask with him," Eva said.

* * * * *

The sisters dined in grand style on lobster salad, rack of lamb with truffles, and chocolate silk cake. Choosing a wine from the extensive list was challenging, but they were up to it. Eva smiled contentedly when she finished her after dinner drink. "This is perfect," she said. "Now all I have to do is find someone like Gary."

"You've got your chance right now," Sharon said. "I looked up the statistics on the Concorde before we left. Eighty-five percent of the passengers are male."

"Really? That needs checking out. I think I'll take a walk down the aisle."

Sharon grinned. "I like the sound of that phrase."